Adirondack Mysteries

And Other Mountain Tales

Volume 3

Adirondack Mysteries

And Other Mountain Tales

Volume 3

Compiled and Edited by Dennis Webster

John H. Briant • Tico Brown • Cheryl Ann Costa
Marie Hannan-Mandel • G. Miki Hayden
Jordan Elizabeth Mierek • Jenny Milchman • W.K. Pomeroy
Woody Sins • Gigi Vernon • Dennis Webster • Larry Weill

North Country Books, Inc.
Utica, New York

Adirondack Mysteries
And Other Mountain Tales
Volume 3

Design by Zach Steffen & Rob Igoe, Jr.
Cover photograph by Carl Heilman II

ISBN-10 1-59531-055-X
ISBN-13 978-1-59531-055-2

Library of Congress Cataloging-in-Publication Data

Adirondack mysteries, and other mountain tales / compiled and edited by Dennis Webster.
p. cm.
ISBN 978-1-59531-032-3 (alk. paper)
1. Detective and mystery stories, American--New York (State)--Adirondack Mountains Region. 2. American fiction--New York (State)--Adirondack Mountains Region. 3. Adirondack Mountains Region (N.Y.)--Fiction. I. Webster, Dennis, 1966-
PS648.D4A28 2009
813'.0872083587475--dc22
2009034547

North Country Books, Inc.
220 Lafayette Street
Utica, New York 13502
www.northcountrybooks.com

Dedicated to a good friend and fellow author John Briant -DW

Contents

Ghosts of Santa Clara

by John H. Briant

For years, stories of ghostly sightings have been written involving the Adirondack Park. A group of us from central and northern New York have been snowmobiling in the Santa Clara region of these mountains for a number of years. We favor a lodging known as the Santa Clara Hotel, where there have been reports of mysterious lights and sounds, but none of us have actually witnessed any of these alleged occurrences until this year. I will endeavor to do justice to the story of what happened; I can tell you it sent shivers up our spines.

The snowmobile season was nearing an end, and it was to be our last get-together at the Santa Clara, our final chance to enjoy the pristine beauty of this region of the Adirondack Park. During the month of March it is hard to predict what the weather might be, but we were blessed this March. There was plenty of snow in the woods and on the trails.

It was Friday, and our hotel keeper was preparing fresh salmon for supper. Fannie Mullins was well known for her culinary artistic ability. Just five foot tall, slender, and in her eighties, she had the stamina of a forty-year-old. We had just finished sledding for the day, and several of our group went to St Regis Falls to purchase some supplies. I stayed at the hotel and wandered into the large Adirondack kitchen to see if Fannie needed any assistance.

"Fannie, can I give you a hand with peeling potatoes or help you with the coleslaw?"

"Jason Black, you just sit down and I'll pour you a cup of coffee. I know you like a little cream with it."

"There's nothing like a good cup of your coffee, Fannie. I don't know how you accomplish so much working all alone."

"I'm used to it. You know, years ago when the logging was plentiful here in the Santa Clara area this place was buzzing. Back then, I had a helper in the kitchen and a bartender. We kept those lumberjacks full, and with all the beer they drank, they sure didn't have a thirst problem. Once in a while one of those fellers would get a little rowdy and I'd have to shut them off from drinking, but over the years they caught on to my rules. Gee whiz, I sure miss some of those woodsmen. They were honest, hardworking men, some with families they sent money home to. Many times they'd ask me to put cash in my safe to hold it for them. Yep, they were a hardy group; no one messed with them."

"How did you handle those one or two trouble makers if they drank too much?"

"I'd simply tell them to knock it off or I'd call the state troopers. Oh! I had to contact the troopers a couple of times over the years. But if those loggers knew that Trooper Oscar Swenson was on duty they would settle right down, for they had seen Oscar in action. He was from a family of hearty woodsmen and talked their jargon. Back then he was in his forties and stood about six foot five. There was a man for you. He could whip about four of those loggers all by himself, and the majority of them knew and respected him."

"I never knew Oscar Swenson. He was around before my time on the job, but I have heard some mighty interesting tales of his exploits from several older troopers. One story comes to mind from back at the end of the horse era. I don't know the horse's name, but apparently that foolhardy creature was making it difficult for Oscar to place his saddle in position. Now, those story tellers revealed that Oscar had a little temper when stressed. The story goes on to say that Oscar was so upset with his horse that he went around to its head and staggered the unruly creature with a slap. That solved that problem! Yes, Fannie, from what I have heard, he was one of New York State's finest, a dedicated trooper serving the citizens of this great state."

"I believe I heard that story, Jason, but it has been so many years I've forgotten all the details. I know that Oscar sure loved my vittles, and he'd eat all the fried salt pork that I could cook. You remind me of him in that way, Jason"

"By the way, I want you to know how much I appreciated the work you did when my bowl and pitcher were stolen by those two fishermen from Maine. That set was priceless to me."

"I'm glad I was able to help you, Fannie. Those fellows sure were surprised that day in Warrensburg when I arrested them."

"I bet they were. Nowadays I keep that pitcher and bowl locked up in a special place."

"That's a good idea. I know you had it displayed proudly for your customers to see, but you can't be too cautious these days. Our society has changed a lot."

"Thank goodness for people like you and your great group of friends, Jason. All of them are so polite, and each morning they leave their rooms in wonderful order. It makes my job easier."

"Yes, they are a good group. I just hope we're not making too much noise at night before we go to sleep."

"You are no problem at all. In fact, I hope you all return next winter with your sleds. And in the meantime I think I'll update my menu to give everyone a good choice of meals."

"Fannie, that sounds great. We've always enjoyed your meals, and we sure do appreciate all your efforts. Now let me change the subject. Can you tell me what you know about the ghost rumors?"

"I will, Jason, but would you mind if I waited till after dinner when the whole group is here? Then I will share everything I know about those stories."

"I think that would be a good idea. I'll wait until after dinner," I agreed.

A short time later the rest of our group returned from St. Regis Falls, some with purchases and others empty-handed. All in all they had enjoyed their visit to that community, and some had taken pictures of the area.

While the rest of the group went to their rooms to prepare for dinner, I talked with my friend and co-organizer of the sledding trip, Charlie Taylor.

"Charlie, how was your shopping trip?" I asked.

"It was good. St. Regis Falls is a nice, friendly community. I bought a couple pairs of warm work gloves and looked at a .30-06 hunting rifle with a scope. The price tag on it was three hundred dollars. I would have purchased it, but I didn't have that much money with me and didn't want to use a credit card."

"How much do you need, Charlie?" I asked.

"Oh! That's alright, Jason. My wife wouldn't want me to spend that much money anyhow, although it appeared to be a good buy. No, I'm passing on this one and maybe next fall I'll look for another of that caliber. Some of my friends would like me to join them on an elk hunting trip next year and I'd like a heavier caliber rifle than my .30-.30."

"Well, if I can help you out, you know I will. Guess we'd better wash up for dinner. I believe Fannie has everything almost ready for us."

Charlie and I went to our rooms and prepared for dinner. In about five minutes we returned to the dining room and took a seat alongside our friends at the long oak table, which was lined with ten matching chairs. The table was covered by a white tablecloth and the settings were neatly placed. Two large platters of salmon were situated at each end of the table, with the space in between filled with bowls of mashed potatoes, carrots, and cut green beans, and side dishes of white gravy. There was tartar sauce made with chopped boiled eggs and baskets of fresh, hot, homemade rolls. Dishes of pickled beets were placed at each setting.

Before we began our dinner, Charlie said a blessing for the food we were about to eat. After that the dishes were passed and we all dug in.

The usual laughter and animated conversations filled the air, accompanied by countless requests for serving dishes to be passed, as almost everyone had second helpings. Even though Fannie told us to speak up if we needed anything else, she still kept checking on us, refilling the roll baskets and serving dishes as needed. As always, she was a most attentive hostess.

For dessert, there were pies and a chocolate cake with a white frosting and ice cream in the freezer. There was also sharp cheddar cheese for the homemade apple pie. One of the guys helped Fannie serve the desserts.

After the delightful meal, several people offered to assist Fannie in the kitchen with the dishes and pots and pans. The rest of us proceeded to the living room where we set up card tables under the watchful eyes of several mounted, large-racked deer heads. Charlie Taylor and another man played a game of pool.

When the card games were over and the pool cues returned to the rack, we all lounged around the large room and told stories, but when Fannie joined us, the room fell silent. It was time for her to tell us about the ghostly lights she observed at the old, abandoned camp. Everyone leaned in to hear her spooky tale.

Fannie began her story: "It all started with a late summer night's walk I took with my Great Dane, Ralph. It was dark and I had walked Ralph further than I wanted to, but he pulled me along the foot path and I could hardly hold him. He was acting strangely, in a way I had never seen before. I gave him the command to stop, but he ignored me; it was as if he didn't even hear my voice. I'm never out for a walk when it's that dark out, as we've had some aggressive bears in the region and my late husband warned me several times to limit my walking to daylight hours, so I wanted to turn back. I continued trying to get Ralph under control, when all of a sudden he stopped dead in his tracks near an abandoned camp. All of a sudden I heard a swishing sound coming from the direction of the building. I saw a bluish-colored light in the window which went out as soon as I spotted it. I was frozen in my tracks, just like Ralph was. I felt a chill go up my spine.

"Next I heard a moaning sound, and a white light flashed in the window. I have to admit that I was frightened. I managed to get Ralph moving and we hightailed it for the hotel. I've heard many stories about such happenings over the years, but never experienced anything like that myself until that late evening in July. And that's all I can tell you about it. End of story."

There was total silence in the room, and then the group erupted with questions for Fannie about the incident and about the location of the cabin. She told us it was a short ways off the snowmobile trail that passed right by her hotel. We all agreed that we wanted to see that cabin, and we decided to conclude our week at the Santa Clara Hotel by paying it a visit. We were eager to check out the ghostly noises and eerie lights Fannie witnessed that summer evening, so we would make our visit at night. We'd drive in a ways, park our snowmobiles, and walk in to the cabin late in the evening the next day. We all thanked Fannie for her story and her hospitality and decided to call it a night.

"What do you think, Charlie?" I asked as we walked to our rooms. "I doubt very much we'll see anything, but I do believe Fannie's story because she's such an honest person."

"I agree. We'll go as a group and leave our machines as we discussed in an area a distance away from the camp. Whatever happens, it will be a good way to end our vacation. And who knows—maybe we will see something. You and I both know that life is a mystery."

"You're right about that. I think there's a part of all of us that is intrigued about the prospect of ghostly apparitions. But maybe what Fannie observed was just a visit by the former owner of the camp or a member of his or her family."

"Well, try to get a good night's sleep, Jason, and we'll see what develops tomorrow."

I said good night and closed the door to my room. After reading for a while, I turned off the lamp and soon drifted off to sleep thinking about Fannie's story.

When I awoke, I turned over to check my watch on the night table. It was seven in the morning, and I could detect the smell of bacon wafting in the air. My room was over the hotel kitchen, and the smell of anything cooking downstairs would eventually come through the vents. This morning I was going to have some of that great bacon for breakfast along with my favorite scrambled eggs.

I got out of bed and hit the shower. The hot water felt good on my back, sore from riding the trails for several days in a row, and I enjoyed the scent of the soap and the large fluffy towels furnished by the hotel. After my shower, as I shaved and brushed my teeth, my thoughts revisited the ghost story that Fannie related to us the previous night. That would be something if we could make those observations ourselves, but

I have to admit I doubted we would. I knew my friend Charlie felt the same way I did.

I got dressed and went downstairs to the dining room. A few of the guys were already sitting at the oak table drinking coffee and waiting for seven forty-five, when Fannie would start serving our breakfast. We knew she already had our lunches ready for the day's ride, which we would enjoy along the snowmobile trail. This morning we had a choice of juices, French toast, Adirondack flapjacks, ham or bacon, and eggs. Oh…and plenty of homemade biscuits and hot coffee.

The main topic of discussion was the abandoned cabin and the possibility of a ghost sighting. As Fannie brought in trays of food, she told us something she'd forgotten to mention the night before—that years ago someone had taken his or her life in the camp we were going to visit. She didn't know the name or anything else about the victim because she was a young child when it happened. That really sparked our interest, and we listened closely as she repeated the story about her experiences that late July evening. It was all of the unknowns that sparked our interest.

Our breakfast was wonderful and piping hot. Personally, I don't tolerate a cold breakfast very well, but that was something you never needed to worry about at Fannie's.

Some of the group joined Fannie as she cleared the table and helped her with the dish washing. Several hands made the job easier and we've always been grateful to Fannie for unfailingly going that extra mile to make our visits to her hotel the very best possible.

It took a little time after breakfast to put on our snowmobile suits, and it was nine-thirty when we started the first engine. As always, everyone gathered around Charlie before heading out. At the beginning of each trail ride, Charlie would take the time and effort to inform everyone about weather predictions for the day, along with everything we needed to be cognizant about along the particular trail we'd be following. He was a stickler when it came to safety, and we all listened to him.

Charlie was our trail leader, and he always manned the first sled. If we came to a highway, he would watch the crossing of the sleds, one at a time. The Santa Clara region was perfect for trail riding, with numerous beautiful vistas all along our route. We stopped on a prearranged signal to take photographs of spectacular scenes. My own camera was always ready to capture landscapes, cabins, trees, and anything else that caught my eye.

We rode for miles on trails and logging roads, and sometimes we came across deer, foxes, and coyotes. Once in a while we would be lucky enough to see a buck, lying along a hedge row or standing in a grove of trees. We always had our phones or cameras with us; two of our group members even had tripods for still shots. On occasion, the resultant pictures were outstanding.

It was nearing twelve-thirty when we decided to stop for lunch. We wouldn't know what Fannie had prepared for us until we opened our brown bags—and we were eager to find out.

Everyone shut their snowmobiles off and gathered around Charlie, who was already starting a fire. He carried some wood on his machine, and we all gathered dry branches that had fallen from trees. Soon, the fire was roaring and everyone stood in a circle around it for warmth and conversation. Prominent in all of our minds was the adventure that would take place later that evening. It was speculated by a few that we would indeed see something; however, the majority of us were doubtful, and a few thought it was a waste of time. Nevertheless, we all agreed we would be at that abandoned camp in the dark of night.

Fannie's trail lunch never disappointed. The sandwiches were thick, and between the slices of fresh French bread was a chicken salad that was beyond wonderful, accompanied by a crisp leaf or two of lettuce. Yesterday, Fannie surprised us with homemade whole wheat bread piled with tasty ham salad that was right out of this world. Today, along with two hearty sandwiches, we each had a red delicious apple, a plastic bag of almonds, and a large container of chocolate milk. Everyone raved about that lunch.

We warmed our hands over the fire while one of the fellows had to replace a spark plug on his machine. It was almost two o'clock when we started our sleds and continued our trail ride. One could easily imagine the old logging days and the activities that took place in and around

Santa Clara; there was even a school for girls in operation during that period of time.

Fannie had told us how she and her husband had operated a grocery store and in one part of the store was a small U.S. Post Office where Fannie was postmistress. It was not difficult to imagine the lifestyle of the 1920s and the years before that. Life in the Adirondack Mountains must have been really hard back then. Nothing came easy for the worker who was raising a family and trying to exist. The rich, however, came to the Adirondacks and used the mountains as their playground until they started their travels to Europe. Many of the Great Camps of the Adirondacks still exist today, and some of them are visited by tourists from all over the world.

With our late-hour adventure looming before us, we decided to go back to the hotel and rest for a while. The men who assisted Fannie in the morning had learned that we were having roast pork and dressing for dinner. This sounded good to our ears: Fannie bought the finest pork available and cooked it to perfection.

We arrived back at the hotel at about three-fifteen. Fannie met us at the door and told us she would call us when dinner was ready. I think we all agreed it was an adventure in and of itself to observe her running this hotel, taking care of the meals, the rooms, and the bar, and purchasing the supplies. Fannie Mullins was an amazing lady.

I must have fallen off to sleep, because the next thing I knew, Charlie was calling me to dinner.

"Yeah, yeah, Charlie. I hear you. I'll be right down."

I splashed some cold water on my face, combed my hair, and went downstairs to join our group in the dining room. Fannie had already brought in the carved roast of pork and side dishes of dressing, mashed potatoes, and corn. There were also fresh, leafy salads at each of our seats and a selection of homemade dressings. The majority of the people had finished their salads by the time I got there, and they were already passing the serving dishes around the table. I made up my mind that I would eat my salad after the main course.

The dinner was spectacular. There was very little chatter going on at the table as we all enjoyed a fantastic meal. It would be our last dinner here at the hotel until next year. I could tell that Fannie put all her culinary talents to work. She was a wonderful cook and a tremendous person. We all loved her dearly.

Fannie was known for her exceptional pineapple upside-down cake, and tonight she topped it with real whipped cream. It truly gave this dessert a special flavor, and there were seconds for anyone that wanted another helping. I was one of six people who took her up on her offer. I was stuffed.

Just like at previous meals, several people helped Fannie clear the table and wash the dishes. The rest of us went into the sitting room and lounged in the comfortable chairs. While we enjoyed our last evening around the fire, we chatted about our plan for approaching the abandoned camp as quietly as we could.

It was about ten-thirty when we left the hotel, dressed in the darkest clothing we had. We wore sweaters under our heavy jackets because the night was cold, with temperatures dipping to thirteen degrees above zero. Charlie slowly led the way, and we followed in a line, our headlights and flashlights all turned off. Some of us brought phones or cameras—just in case we were lucky enough to need them.

We arrived in the vicinity of the abandoned camp at about eleven o'clock. No one spoke except Charlie, who cautioned in a whisper that we shouldn't even move around, as our boots might make noise in the icy snow. You could hear a pin drop. The camp looked spooky from our observation point, and the sound of a coy dog off in the distance added to the already eerie scene. Two people had night vision binoculars which they quietly passed around so the others could have a closer look at the building. The roof was sagging precariously; if anyone wanted to bring the camp back into a livable condition it would be costly.

The minutes went by and we saw nothing. It was bitter cold—and getting colder. We were all ready to call our ghost-hunting expedition a failure when it happened. A reddish flash of light showed in the window of the camp. My spine tingled with excitement. Then a white light appeared in the same window. It was almost like a flash from fireworks.

Then there were more flashes and what looked like a ghostly figure appeared in the window for a few seconds, followed by a low-pitched moaning sound. Could this actually be happening? Yes, it was, right before our eyes.

At that point we broke our "vows of silence" with utterances such as "unbelievable" and "holy cow" (and others I can't mention). I had never seen anything like this in my entire life. I'd heard it from others—and doubted their grasp of reality—but I do have to believe that, on that night, we saw a ghost—the Ghost of Santa Clara.

Does the ghost have something to do with a previous owner of the camp? Is it the ghost of the person who committed suicide? We'll never know, but one thing is certain—at the end of our week of snowmobiling in one of the greatest places in the world, we all saw a ghost. We will never forget that night.

Beyond the Blue

by Tico Brown

Dedicated to my brother Anthony who is now beyond the blue.

The dream slipped from him. He was awake.

The man rubbed his weary eyes with his hands and then opened them. Before his gaze, his own worn fingers quietly rocked in their joints. Despite their weathered form, his fingertips flexed like the wings of a butterfly, freshly severed from its chrysalis. Like the imago, he sought to soar through those skies that had until now been just beyond his reach. Those endless, cloudless skies.

The urge for a smoke brought his consciousness back to this plane. The celestial dome around him metamorphosed into the walls of a room he didn't recognize. He was in a bed of some kind. The mattress was harder than he'd been used to. Either that or he'd been lying there for long enough to strain his back. He shifted his body to loosen the tension.

Whiplash. Sudden throbbing. Ringing in his ears. The man felt the back of his head, but there was no hair. He felt only thick, matted gauze. What had happened? Where was he? *Who* was he?

His vision blurred for a moment, restoring itself as he blinked his eyes. Once stabilized, they widened, as if nourished by the colors, textures, and sounds of the room itself.

Sunlight floated gently through the small window, illuminating most of the room. The olive-colored walls betrayed a cinder-block pattern and, save for a simple oak desk and chair, the room was empty. The only door stood ajar, allowing the scent of jasmine—or perhaps hyacinth—to straggle in.

It could have been ten minutes or two hours before the door opened further, revealing the form of an older woman in her early seventies or so. She hunched forward due to some sort of spinal deformity and walked with a cane. The woman wore loose clothing covered by a makeshift robe of indigo. Her other hand carried a ceramic bowl filled with water.

"Oh," she said, in a croaking, wheezy voice. "You've awakened."

"Who are you?" asked the man as he inched upwards in bed. "And where am I?"

"I am Miko," she said. "We are descendants of the Abenaki of Missiquoi. We discovered you outside the grounds of our village, so we brought you in and nursed you back to health."

The man sat up and felt his forehead. His memory was not returning.

"Here," the woman said. "Perhaps some water will help."

The man's weathered hands accepted the bowl and raised it to his lips. The water felt refreshing as it streamed down his throat. He wiped two stray droplets from his lips.

"If I might ask, how old are you?" she asked.

"I don't remember who I am," he admitted, "much less my age."

"It's only been an evening since we first found you. Your memories might take some time to return."

The man stretched out his arms to test them. After a few moments, he turned his body so that his legs hung off the side of the bed.

"I seem to be well enough," he said.

"As far as I could tell, you only hurt your head. You're welcome to stay in our village until your memory recovers. My son, Azeban, will help take care of you. He lives with his wife two houses down."

The man wrapped himself in the sheet and slid off the bed, his feet meeting the floor with a low thud.

Walking around the small village provided the amnesiac with no clues to his identity. Azeban had been out, so he toured the area with the old woman, Miko. After spending several hours attempting to figure out who he was, the stranger became hopelessly convinced that no one in the village had ever seen him before, nor did he seem to have any reason to be there.

Miko had been right. It would take some time for his memories to return. What she hadn't told him was that until they did, the anguish of adapting to an entirely new reality would be too immense to describe. His head had throbbed on occasion since he left Miko's house, but the pain diminished quickly. He was getting better.

Although the physical pain had subsided, the emotional pain had become much more unbearable. In his frustration, he turned to Miko. In an attempt to soothe his anguish, she had made an appointment for him to see the village chief, a man named Mateguas. From what the amnesiac could put together, the village was too small to be considered a legal entity, but this man, Mateguas, seems to have served as a de facto mayor.

The amnesiac and Miko sat together in an almost empty hallway, an antechamber to the room that Mateguas used as an office. The walls were plain and painted an eggshell color. The floor was covered in a red rug that had seen far better days. Its color had all but faded, and the edges were fraying. Miko rested her cane against the wall beside her.

While the man was still unconscious, Miko had cleaned the clothes he was found in. He wore them again now, though they were nothing special—just an off-white, button-down shirt and a pair of old, discolored jeans.

"What is this Mottagwos like?" the man asked, mispronouncing the foreign name.

"Mah-tuh-gwoss," Miko corrected him. "Mateguas is a younger man, but he has taken care of us for a number of years now. In many ways, we would be lost without someone like him."

"Wouldn't neighboring settlements be able to help? Don't you fall into the jurisdiction of another city's government?"

"Yes, but our ways are different from theirs. Our struggles are also different. We do our best to live as our own community and settle all of our own affairs internally. That way, we aren't perceived as creating problems for other peoples. Live and let live."

"Interesting," he muttered, unsure what to make of their wish for independence.

Miko didn't respond, so he changed the subject.

"Where is Azeban?"

"Probably at the hospital with Behanem," Miko replied. "She has been ill of late, and their child will come soon."

"Will she be all right?"

"Oh, she'll be fine. And so will the baby."

The man nodded.

"How's your head?" Miko asked suddenly.

The man massaged his temples lightly.

"I think the pain is all gone. It hasn't been that bad since I first woke up."

"Good."

The two were not waiting long before the doors opened and a man entered the hallway. A young man, whose thin frame supported a red polo shirt and khakis.

"The chief will see you now," he said, beckoning them inside.

The amnesiac rose first and then helped Miko to her feet. He reached for her cane and gave it to her. At her age, it took longer for her to rise from a chair, especially when alone. She didn't lack the ability to stand, but she welcomed the stranger's aid. He wasn't a young man himself, but the differences between them were clear.

Once the companions entered the office, Mateguas's aide left, closing the doors behind him. The room was small but functional. It was colored the same way as the hallway, but Mateguas's rug was in slightly better shape. Inside the room were a large but simple wooden desk, a few filing cabinets, and an old touchtone phone.

The man who sat behind the desk was young and well built. He seemed no older than thirty, but he had a frame like an ox. He wore a light sweater and jeans.

"So," Mateguas said, "you have brought the outsider to me."

Miko nodded quietly, turning her head to her companion.

"I, uh…" began the amnesiac. "I don't know where to start. I can't remember who I am, where I was going, or even how I ended up here."

"I understand," the chief responded with a warm and welcoming tone. "In that case, you are welcome to stay in Ojihozo until your memory recovers."

"Ojihozo?" asked the man.

"The name of our village," Miko chimed in. "Chief Mateguas, with your permission, he is more than welcome to stay at my residence. Azeban and his wife are willing to help out."

"Good," said the chief. "Then our business is concluded?"

"I think so," said the amnesiac. "But it'll probably take some time getting used to this place."

"That's all right," Mateguas said. "Ours is a very small village. We will all do our best to help you recover."

"Thank you."

Despite having lost his memory, when the man stood up he knew he should reach for Mateguas's hand. The chief responded and they shook.

"It was a pleasure meeting you."

"I am happy to help."

The man helped Miko to her feet again, but she took the cane herself. She motioned towards the door. As the stranger opened it, Mateguas spoke again.

"Oh, Miko," he said, "I trust your preparations are underway?"

She looked at him and pushed her lips into a very small smile.

"They are. I will leave in the morning."

"In that case, I wish the best of luck to you and your family," Mateguas said, bowing slightly.

The outsider and the old woman shut the door to the office behind them.

The two walked along the street. It would be several minutes before they reached Miko's house. The first two of those minutes were spent in silence as the stranger took in their surroundings.

Ojihozo looked like any average village from a few decades ago. There were brick buildings and paved streets and electricity like a normal village, but the people still drew water from a well, and it seemed like the kind of place where no one would have a cordless phone, much less a cellular device. People still walked from place to place. Some had cars, but there were very few of them around.

The village had a certain embracing feel to it. He may not have remembered where he came from, but the outsider knew that it was not so bad for him to stick around.

Perhaps, he mused, if his memory never returned, he might be able to forge a new life among the people of Ojihozo. Granted, he himself was already advanced somewhat in age—he'd guess forties or fifties—so he couldn't exactly start a *brand* new life. But a new life nonetheless. He could at least make *something* of himself here. Or so he felt.

"You're... going somewhere then?" asked the amnesiac, breaking the silence. "How long will you be gone?"

Miko stopped for a moment, seemingly unsure of how to respond.

The man looked at her aged face. He might not remember anything about his past, but he was no fool. Some secret seemed to be hidden behind her eyes—eyes that betrayed a sense of youthful longing despite their age.

The man sensed her answer before she gave it.

"I... I won't be returning," Miko finally said, continuing to walk. "Azeban has agreed to take care of you in my absence."

The outsider followed her.

"But why?" was all he could muster.

Miko's head sank. Her hunched back created the illusion that she was coiling her upper body into a ball like a caterpillar. She spoke slowly, but devoid of sadness.

"It is a tradition long passed down from our ancestors. Our storytellers speak of a man named Wlôwi who had raised a wonderful family on his own. He had children and grandchildren who loved and cared for him dearly."

The stranger nodded.

"However," Miko continued, "Around the time he reached sixty years, he is said to have had a strange dream. Tradition seems to have lost precisely what Wlôwi dreamt of, but the dream was certainly significant.

After waking, he told his children and grandchildren that he loved them very much, but he would be leaving them. Of course, they begged him to stay, but he told them that as he aged, he would become a burden to them."

The stranger suddenly understood why Miko had asked for his age.

"Wlôwi eventually left them and traveled to a nearby mountain. He ascended it himself and remained there until he passed away naturally."

"So that's what you're doing? Climbing a mountain alone and staying there until you die?"

"No," she responded, without the slightest trace of sadness. "We don't go alone. Our children escort us to the top of the mountain, bid us farewell, and then part ways. We stay on the mountain just as Wlôwi did."

The stranger was overcome with grief. He had just met Miko that morning, and already she would leave his life forever.

"You must understand," she said. "This is our custom, our tradition. This is not something that was thrown onto my shoulders. I knew from an early age that this was to be my destiny. And it's something that I wish for."

A tear escaped the stranger's eye.

"How can you possibly want to leave your son and his wife alone? And what of me?"

Miko shook her head slowly.

"Azeban is old enough to take care of himself. And Behanem, for that matter. And I'm sure that you'll find your way in time, my friend. It's not that I *want* to leave you all alone. But it is my time. And I am ready to pass from this world and discover the secrets of what comes next."

"What do you mean, your time?"

"When we become as old as I, we begin to keep track of our dreams. As village chief, Mateguas helps us to interpret them. Other members of the village council assist in this. The night before I found you, I had a strange dream, so I wrote it down. Mateguas in particular thought it was as meaningful to me as the dream that Wlôwi had before he left his family. Thus, I must do likewise, and follow him up the mountain."

The amnesiac couldn't believe it.

"Don't worry," Miko said as they neared her house. "I'll have Azeban's help to make it to the top of the mountain. You are welcome to come, too, if you like."

The outsider nodded.

The following morning, roughly around ten, the three companions made it to the foot of the mountain on which Miko would be abandoned. Azeban had referred to it simply as Mount Wlôwi. This was of no help to the amnesiac as he tried to figure out precisely where he was.

The formations before them weren't mountains in the strictest sense. They weren't wholly vertical climbs that only a well-equipped professional could attempt. The slopes of these mountains were such that anyone of average health could walk through trails and across the cliff side until reaching the summit. The one that interested Miko didn't seem any more difficult to climb—it was simply a bit taller than the rest.

Miko required some assistance climbing to the peak. While the stranger was younger, he was still old enough for the mountain to seem formidable. Azeban was the closest of the three to being in his prime. He was in his late thirties, and visible muscle tone emerged from his plaid, button-down shirt.

The stranger had never found a moment to ask what Azeban did for a living, but he figured it might be something as old fashioned as cutting lumber or perhaps delivering it. That was the kind of place that Ojihozo was.

Azeban had two canteens of water strapped around his shoulder. While he would be fine with minimal nourishment on the climb, he could not predict the needs of the outsider after the accident that led him to Ojihozo.

The village stood about half a mile behind them. Even at such a short distance, it seemed small from the outside. Although he had only been in the village for a short time, somehow the stranger felt that he belonged there. And he couldn't shake the feeling that Miko still belonged there too.

It has been said that a thousand-mile journey begins with a single step.

It was nearly noon when they caught sight of the peak of the mountain, but not because it had been a rough trek. Initially, Miko walked at a much slower pace than the others, so they shortened their strides. However, as their elevation increased, the climb seemed to become easier for the old woman. The stranger couldn't help but notice that each step Miko took seemed to increase her enthusiasm. Her steps had become surer, steadier, stronger. It was as if some strange sorcery had hastened her approach by slowly whittling away the effects of age upon her grey body. He half expected her to drop her cane before making it to the summit.

The scene was breathtaking. While little grew on the mountaintop, the granite edifice was spotted with explosions of vivid greenery—grasses, weeds, and a few small trees in which birds chirped audibly. The sky was a splendid shade of azure. The intense light of the midday sun pierced through a tiny crack in a patchwork shield of puffy clouds. It smelled as if it were about to rain, and yet it wasn't—the only clouds were as white as winter.

The stranger walked forward to the far edge of the peak. The mountain was not steep enough to end in an actual cliff. But the mountain range had hidden something he had not been able to see from below. These mountains served as a natural barrier; the town of Ojihozo stood on one side, and a vast freshwater lake rippled silently on the other.

"That is the Blue Lake," Azeban said. "It's quite a sight, isn't it?"

The outsider nodded. "I don't think I've ever seen anything quite like it. I wish I could remember, but…" He reached for his forehead.

"Are you all right?" Miko asked.

"Yes," he responded. "I am. I just… I want to take in this view for a while. No more beautiful view of nature exists in my memory, so I'd like to make this one last as much as possible."

"I understand," Azeban said. "How long do you intend to stay?"

"I'm not sure yet. I feel something familiar about this place. How soon do you need to get back?"

"We should go," Azeban said. "Our job was only to bring Ma here. We are discouraged from staying on this mountain before it's our time to do so."

"Then go," the stranger said. "I remember my way."

"You're going to stay?" Miko asked.

"I'm not one of you. I'm not Abenaki. I can at least give you some company while it's still daylight out."

Miko looked at her son, who returned her gaze.

"As you wish," he said.

Azeban walked towards his mother and bent down towards her. Opening his arms, he gave her an impassioned hug. Miko embraced her son.

"I love you," he said. "And we will all miss you dearly."

Azeban's eyes closed as if tears were welling up behind them, but upon opening them, those tears never fell. They ran instead through his heart, and no one else would ever be privy to them. He wanted so badly not to lose his mother. But this was her destiny. He had known that for as long as he could remember. And this was his destiny too. The only element of chance was the stranger who would be the last person his mother ever spoke with.

Azeban handed his mother one of the canteens, then reached into his shirt pocket, pulled out a small packet, and gave it to Miko. Taking it in her small, withered hand, she placed it in a pocket. Though this action was silent, Azeban trembled under the gravity of the situation.

Taking a deep breath, he composed himself and stood upright.

"Here," he said, taking the full canteen from around his shoulder. "Use this for the way down."

"What about you?" asked the amnesiac, taking the canteen.

"No need to worry. I've done this many times without water."

Azeban reached his hand out. The stranger's other hand took it.

"Thank you for helping me bring my mother up here."

The outsider nodded.

"Thanks for taking care of me. I really owe you one."

Azeban nodded back.

"I wish we had met under different circumstances," the burly Abenaki volunteered. "I'll see you soon."

It didn't take Azeban long to disappear down the mountain. Once he had, the stranger began to speak.

"I'm guessing there's nothing I can do to change your mind about this?"

The old woman chuckled and shook her head.

"Why are you doing this? Can't you see you're not meant to die yet? You could easily live for ten or fifteen more years!"

She raised her hand, signaling him to stop.

"Do you think Azeban hasn't asked me to reconsider? I've heard it all. I know what I'm doing. Right now, I want only one thing."

She walked closer to the edge of the summit and pointed her cane towards the clear sky.

"That's what I want. I want to be out there somewhere, with Wlôwi and all of the others. Drifting past the sky into whatever lies beyond it."

Her conviction seemed impenetrable. The old woman really sought to die out here. What would happen? Would she die of hunger or thirst? Or exposure? Would some wild animal find her here? Would she be a willing offering of carrion for insects, birds, and whatever else lived in the crevices between these ancient mountain rocks?

"What about the pain?" the stranger finally asked.

"What pain? The pain of leaving my family?"

"Yes. And the pain of death. I know you're pretty eager to hand over your life, but your options at this point aren't particularly painless."

The stranger suddenly found himself hoping that Miko did not intend for *him* to take her life.

"You are just like my Azeban, you know? Anticipating this moment, he spent months trying to convince me otherwise. He even devised an elaborate plot where he would leave me here, but come back once the darkness fell. He would take me back to the village and hide me from Mateguas in the basement of his house, acting like I was dead, but feeding me and allowing me to live as long as I could. I tell you, he tried everything."

She sighed, withdrawing something from her pocket. It looked like a small piece of paper folded several times.

"He gave me this in case it gets too rough up here. It's a fine powder. If I put it under my tongue, it'll numb the pain and kill me quickly."

"A poison?"

She nodded, sighing again.

"I will miss that boy. But my mind is made up."

She pocketed the drug. The stranger went silent for several minutes.

"What about your granddaughter?" he asked suddenly. "Won't you miss her?"

Miko was caught by surprise.

"She—It's going to be… a girl?"

"I don't know," the amnesiac admitted. "But wouldn't you want to find out? Won't you live for her, if not for yourself? Can't you see there are other people in this world worth living for?"

The old woman closed her eyes in silence.

It would be later that night when Azeban finally returned home, after the hospital closed at nine. Behanem's condition had stabilized, but it was very likely she'd deliver the child within a few days, well or not. With the recent loss of his mother, Azeban refused to allow his wife or his child to perish in birth. Thus, he sought to spend as much time with her as possible. And the outsider understood.

The amnesiac would be waiting for Azeban when he returned. They had met briefly for an early dinner, after which Azeban left to continue his steady vigil over his wife. The Abenaki man had been so concerned for her that he couldn't even recall what he'd eaten for dinner—much less the particulars of what they had talked about.

As he headed home after his visit, he noticed that the stars were particularly beautiful. The lack of clouds made the Big Dipper especially prominent in the evening sky. Beautiful as they were, they thrust the reality of his situation into him like a dagger in the stomach. His mother, Miko, was gone. She was now beyond the endless sky, floating somewhere in that sea of stars.

A tear escaped his eye and slowly slid towards his chin. Before he could wipe it from his face, it beaded and launched itself, spiraling towards the ground. It landed directly atop a blade of crabgrass, sliding down its stem towards the earth it would silently nurture.

Azeban opened the door to his house, revealing the weak flutter of candlelight. It led to his kitchen table, where the amnesiac sat, waiting for him.

"I couldn't do it," the amnesiac said suddenly. "I couldn't leave her."

"What happened?"

"We were talking and talking, and she seemed so… motherly to me. She was the first one to take care of me when I ended up here."

Tears started to well in the stranger's eyes.

"I may not have any idea who I am, but I do know that I owe her more kindness than to let her die alone on a mountaintop. She told me your plan, to hide her in the basement."

"So, once darkness began to fall," Azeban offered, "you brought her back here?"

The outsider nodded.

"She's asleep now, on the spare bed in the basement. I put clean sheets on the bed and left her there."

Azeban shook his head.

It had proven rather easy to keep Miko's existence a secret. No one but Azeban had any reason to go down into his basement. As long as she didn't leave the house, she would be safe. Mateguas seemed to have assumed that Miko's abandonment had occurred as planned, and he never stopped by Azeban's house to check for sure.

However, the days became more and more difficult for her caretaker. Behanem would go into labor soon, and he would have to be beside her, both for emotional support and to help deliver their child. Sometimes, in Azeban's stead, the stranger would go down to the basement to offer Miko food, drink, or simple conversation. Even small things such as the aroma of chicken soup lit up the old woman's eyes.

Miko had changed somewhat from her ordeal. She was no longer intent on scaling the mountain as Wlôwi had. Now she had a renewed raison d'être, as if she herself had been reborn by the experience.

The amnesiac presumed that this was due to his mention of her unborn grandchild. Perhaps the chance to meet a newborn family member tugged at her motherly instincts, pulling her away from death.

How grand, he mused, *that the mere idea of life could bring one from certain death.*

In time came the day Miko had been waiting for—the day her only granddaughter would be allowed to come home from the hospital. Behanem had given birth naturally and, despite her illness, the baby was born healthy. They named her Mamijla—"Butterfly."

Azeban brought her back alone, as the doctors thought it best for Behanem to remain hospitalized for a few more days. The stranger hadn't been told what illness she suffered from. Even if he had, the Abenaki name for it would not help him understand it.

The stranger greeted Azeban with open arms, as if they had been long-time friends. Azeban carried the infant in his arms, wrapped in a bright pink blanket. To the visitor, she seemed tiny, especially in the arms of a solidly built man like Azeban. The baby's eyes were small, but of a bright, vivid green. Her hands were no larger than a half dollar.

"Congratulations!" said the outsider. He noticed first that the baby Mamijla had Azeban's face. Their cheekbones and nose looked very similar. Perhaps the similarities would continue when she grew up.

"Will you take her to see her grandmother?" the stranger asked.

"Yes, I must." Azeban said. "Will you get the door for me?"

The amnesiac opened the basement door and led Azeban down to see his mother. They found Miko lying in the bed, though not asleep. The wooden cane was at her side, propped against the bed. Her eyes were open, as if she knew the newborn Abenaki was coming.

Miko sat up at the sight of her young granddaughter bundled up in the arms of her loving father. She said nothing, but the tears in her eyes spoke volumes.

Azeban brought the young Mamijla to his mother's side. She reached out her arms, and Azeban gave her the child.

"She's in perfect health," he said. "Not a single problem."

As Miko laid the baby in her arms, Mamijla started to coo softly. The stranger smiled at the sight of this. He did not recall his past, but they were his family now.

A sharp knock at the door shattered the silence. Azeban's gaze met the outsider's. No one must know that Miko was there. No one.

Half a minute passed in a heartbeat.

"Hello in there?" called a voice from upstairs.

It was Mateguas. He was letting himself in.

"Take the baby," the stranger whispered. "I'll hold him off."

A few heartbeats later, the outsider reached the top of the basement stairs. Mateguas had made it into the kitchen, but not yet in sight of the basement door.

"Hello, Mateguas," the amnesiac said, pronouncing his name correctly.

Mateguas was alone, but came with a bouquet of carnations. It was a small, inexpensive arrangement of yellows and reds, a thoughtful gesture.

"How do you do, my friend?" the chief answered. "Is Azeban around?"

"He'll be up in a moment. Is there anything I can help you with?" The stranger couldn't think of much to buy time.

"I was hoping to check in on the newest member of our village. I brought her some flowers."

"Here," the stranger said. "I'll get a vase."

He took a vessel from the counter and filled it with water.

"She's such a beautiful little girl," the stranger continued. "My memory hasn't been recovering, but even so, I don't think I've seen such a young baby for some time. Her eyes are the same green as Azeban's, and she seems to be quite healthy."

Mateguas didn't reply.

"Would you like to sit? Can I make you some tea or something?"

The chief began to sit. Then, suddenly, the baby's cry came from behind the stranger. Azeban had emerged from the basement with his daughter in his arms.

"Chief Mateguas," he said, "it's a pleasure to see you."

"The same to you," Mateguas replied, "and to your new child. I brought flowers."

The amnesiac's offer of tea had already been forgotten. It would've made little difference, as he didn't know where Azeban kept his tea.

"Thank you. They look beautiful. Perfect for a young girl."

"So what have you named her?"

"It was Behanem's decision," he said. "With my… my mother's passing… she thought it appropriate to use a hopeful name. So she suggested Mamijla."

"I see," Mateguas said. "Are you doing all right now that Miko has passed?"

"Yes," the stranger said out of turn. "We're doing as well as can be expected."

Azeban's gaze met the outsider's. "That's right," he said. "I miss her… but I will manage."

Mateguas nodded. He knew it was a difficult subject, and he knew not to press.

"Is there anything else I can do for you while I'm here?" asked the chief.

The stranger looked at Azeban.

"I don't believe so," Azeban said. "I think we have everything under control here."

"Then I shall be off. Please give my regards to Behanem. I fear I may be too busy to visit her before she leaves the hospital."

"She should be out in the next couple of days," Azeban said. "If you get a chance, I'm sure it would mean a lot to her."

"I'll do my best. In the meantime, best of luck to you all."

With a quick wave of his hand, Mateguas was gone.

Several minutes passed, and the two men did nothing but breathe. It was almost too close a call.

Mamijla began to fuss, breaking the silence.

Azeban rocked her in his arms.

"What?" he asked the baby rhetorically. "Do you want to see grandma again? OK. We'll go down to see her."

"It should be safe now," the amnesic said. "But if you don't mind, I could use a drink of water."

Azeban chuckled as he headed down to the basement.

"Help yourself."

The stranger walked towards Azeban's kitchen sink and took a clean glass from the dish strainer, filled it with water from the pitcher on the counter, and took a few gulps. After Mateguas's visit, it felt more refreshing than he could have imagined.

A short scream from the basement shocked the man. It was Azeban.

The amnesiac bounded down the stairs as fast as his legs could take him. As soon as he reached the bottom, he discovered what had happened.

Miko had vanished. Her cane lay silently on the floor, but she herself was gone without a trace.

The two men stood speechless in the open basement, knowing there was nowhere she could possibly be. Mamijla began to cry.

Suddenly, the amnesiac gripped his head. A ringing sound flashed through his ears. Searing pain tore at him for the first time since his memory loss. He buckled to his knees, his eyes clenched shut. He couldn't tell if Azeban tried to help him; he could neither see nor hear anything but the ringing; he felt nothing but the pain.

The whole world descended into darkness around the stranger. He screamed out in terror, but found himself unable to hear his own voice over the ringing. Pain. Whiplash. Ringing. Death. All around him, pain and death.

In the flash of an instant, a single image darted into his mind. An image he could never have predicted. As quickly as it had appeared, it vanished again into the black void of death that he experienced now. Pain, loss, depression, death.

More ringing.

The stranger knew that he would die, but he would no longer be alone. The image that had appeared to him was clear as day. Though it lasted only a moment, he experienced each and every detail of it.

He had seen Miko's elderly body, lying atop the summit of Mount Wlôwi, covered in the blue of the afternoon skies. Her eyes and mouth were open in fear, and she was not breathing. In her right hand, she gripped a piece of folded paper. It had contained the poisonous powder that Azeban had given her.

Miko had ingested the poison before the outsider had ever helped her down from the mountain. She had already been dead for eight days.

The dream slipped from me. My eyes pierced through the darkness of the cell. My memories were quickly returning. That's right. I was detained several days ago under suspicion for a string of murders occurring in the Adirondack Mountains. My name… is Mingan.

"That's right," I muttered to myself. "The Great Bear of the mountains."

The longing for a smoke tore at my heart. I did not belong here. I needed release.

I hoisted myself up from my cot and peered through the sole barred window in the cell. I had somehow been beyond that sky, but now the sky was once again my cage. And now, it might always be. I was no longer the butterfly that I had just dreamed myself to be.

But I *had* seen the dream. Somewhere out there, somewhere out beyond the blue.

The Prescott Preserve Affair
A Roxanne Kane Mystery

by Cheryl Ann Costa

Prologue

The body was carefully lowered into the mortared stone freehold.

A gentle hand reached over the fixed and dilated eyes to close the lids. With the eyes closed, the child looked peaceful and simply sleeping.

Attention was given to the hands. As this was intended to be a last resting place, the hands had to be carefully and properly folded on the chest.

Finally, appropriate care was taken to smooth the wrinkles from the clothing. All was done; all was in order.

Old Forge, New York – The offices of the Kane Investigative Service

My name is Ms. Roxanne Kane, and I am a licensed private investigator in the state of New York. I reside in the Adirondack town of Old Forge.

Upon first glance you might wonder why a rustic, little village like Old Forge needs a private detective. The honest answer is it doesn't. The truth is the Internet has made it easier for businesses to promote their services across great distances. In my case, I can live anywhere in New York State and still do a roaring business.

I make a comfortable living providing contract services to out-of-town investigative agencies. So it goes without saying that if the woman in New York City who has a cheating husband hires a city-based detective agency to surveil him in the big city, they might hire me to keep eyes on him were he to take a long weekend "fishing" trip here in Old Forge. Or sometimes an out-of-town agency needs someone to serve papers of various types. I'm easily contracted to do those sorts of chores in the upstate and Adirondack region.

I hesitate to mention my minor sideline, but it's been interesting, not to mention lucrative. A few years ago I was hired by a spirit medium to contact some guy and deliver a message to him from a relative in the great beyond. Except for the obvious strangeness of the assignment, it was as routine as serving divorce papers. Needless to say, that assignment went so well that the medium client told her friends and colleagues and overnight I became the go-to private detective to hire for passing along messages from the afterlife to those in the world of the living. Hey, to me it's just another job, and it helps pay the rent.

Now most people might think that mediums and clairvoyants should deliver their own messages. Judging by the number of times recipients don't like the news they are getting and decide to take a swing at me or chase me down the street yelling profanity, I think the little old ladies are smart to hire a combat veteran like myself.

One of the perks of the job is follow-on work. Sometimes the recipient of the message will hire me to chase down some long-lost relative. That's good work when you can get it.

22 December 2012 – A routine job call

The day began normally enough. It was the day after the highly hyped, no-show Mayan apocalypse, and I was quite happy to be still alive and open for business.

The phone rang, and I answered with my usual, "Kane here."

"Good morning, Roxy," came the reply. I quickly recognized the voice of one my best medium clients, Alice Devonshire. "Roxy, I need you to look into something," she said in a jovial but professional tone.

"What do you have?" I queried.

"Can you come down to Utica? I'd rather not discuss this on the phone."

22 December 2012 – The Celtic Harp Restaurant and Pub, Utica

Alice Devonshire and I met at noon. After a friendly hug, we sat down, ordered our respective lunches, and got down to business.

"Roxy, have you ever seen a ghost?" she asked in a calm, matter-of-fact manner.

I must have looked surprised.

"I take it you haven't?" Alice remarked.

I danced round the answer, finally saying, "Frankly, I don't know if I have or not."

Alice took a sip of her iced tea and smiled before replying, "Don't worry, my dear, most people don't know if they have really seen a ghost or not."

I must have still looked puzzled. Alice continued, "Most apparitions look real, just like any living person, except you might be the only one in the room who is aware of them."

I sat studying the foamy head on my Guinness and considered what she had said for a few moments. "So, if I see a ghost, it might look as normal as you and I?"

"Exactly," she said.

"Please tell me that I'm not delivering one of your messages to a ghost," I said with a grin.

Alice shook her head in the negative and asked "Roxy, when were you born?"

"1980," I replied. "Why?"

"This story started eight years before you were born," she explained, "back in 1972. There was a missing child whose disappearance made rather big headlines in the state. A ten-year-old boy was lost and never found despite a massive search."

"What was the kid's name?" I asked.

"William Wessex III. A year or two after he went missing, his prominent family sold their large Adirondack preserve to the Hudson family."

"I can imagine they wouldn't want a reminder of the tragedy."

"No doubt," Alice replied. Then she clammed up. It was an uncharacteristic silence. Of course, I prodded her.

"Alice," I whispered, "Don't tell me the kid's ghost showed up selling candy bars for the Boy Scouts or something."

She rolled her eyes at the jest, then quipped, "Actually, that's not far off."

I choked on a mouthful of beer. "What? How?" I squeaked, still recovering from my coughing fit.

"The Adirondack preserve I mentioned is a lovely place. The people who own it use it as a summer camp. From the photos I've seen of it, the place looks pretty upscale," she continued.

I just nodded while chewing on some bangers and mash.

"A couple of weeks ago a member of the family that owns the place called me about a young boy who has been seen wandering the grounds."

"Couldn't it have been some neighborhood kid?" I inquired.

"Not possible—the camp is located in an isolated area of the Adirondacks. The closest populated village is nearly twenty miles away."

"What do you mean by 'populated' village?" I asked.

Alice took a sip of her tea before replying, "Oh, there are several mining ghost towns on the fringes of the preserve area."

I wasn't delighted with where she seemed to be going, so I interrupted, "Alice, I'm not a ghost hunter; I'm a private investigator."

She held up her hand to cut me off, saying "Roxy, I don't need a ghost hunter, I need a detective."

I gave her an interested look, and then simply replied, "I'm listening."

"It's been my experience that when the ghosts of the restless dead show up, something or some recent event has disturbed the spirit."

Alice let me ponder what she had said as she dug into a piece of apple pie.

"Okay Alice, I'll help you any way I can, but what is it exactly that you want me to do?"

"I want you to interview the current owner of the camp and document the place or places where the ghost was seen," she replied as she shoveled another piece of pie into her mouth.

I took that opportunity to remind her there would be my usual travel expenses and fees.

"Of course. I'm under contract to the Hudson family to look into the problem, and I'm authorized to secure your services. They want answers."

I nodded my head. “Okay, I’m on board. I guess we can start after the holidays?”

She gave me one of those looks my sergeant used to give me when there was a catch to an assignment.

“Did I mention the clients want you to spend the holidays with them at the camp?” Devonshire said.

“Whoa! Why? Come on, Alice, be square with me.”

Now she gave me a different look, this one the kind the banker gives you just as he or she is telling you the interest rate for your car loan.

“The Hudson family has noted the presence of the spirit for years, almost always during the holidays. Their kids and grandkids have reported seeing a lone little boy sitting near their Christmas tree on and off since they bought the place.”

I was struggling with the idea of spending Christmas with a bunch of strangers. “Wait,” I exclaimed, “I thought you said something recent had happened. Darn it, Alice, this thing sounds like the ghost of Christmas past.”

Alice flagged down the waitress for the check before replying. “Roxy, last week the boy was seen walking the grounds in broad daylight. That is the odd part; something strange is going on.”

The whole thing was strange as far as I was concerned, but a job is a job, so I grudgingly replied, “Okay, give me the details and contact information, and I’ll go spend Christmas with these folks in hopes of getting to the bottom of it all.”

Alice smiled broadly as she reached into her bag and removed a thick manila envelope and said, “I’ve taken the liberty of doing some research for you. Here are a good map to the property and all the phone numbers you should need.”

I just stared at the envelope on the table in front of me before asking, “Anything else?”

“Yes!” she added as she signed the credit card receipt. “The Hudsons are expecting you tomorrow afternoon.”

I’m not exactly sure why, but suddenly I had an overwhelming sense of dread.

23 December 2012 – The Hudson family camp at Prescott Preserve
The trip on upstate highways was straightforward enough. My handy GPS guided my drive pretty much in sync with the written directions provided to me by Mrs. Devonshire. It was the last turn off the state highway onto a private road that gave me fits. The GPS just gave me a blank screen. I half expected a little GPS voice to say, "*Here be dragons*" or some such thing.

Finally, the five-mile-long private road ended at a very impressive-looking front gate, with massive posts made out of igneous rocks. The huge gates themselves were well-maintained wrought iron; one sported a sign stating: Private Property, No Trespassing.

I inched my car up to the intercom and pressed the large yellow button. There was a beep, followed by a young woman's voice asking, "Can I help you?"

"Hello, I'm Roxanne Kane. I am expected."

There was a silence of a few moments before an adult female voice with a more inviting tone said, "Welcome, Ms. Kane." Then there was a loud click and a buzzing sound as the iron gates swung open. After I drove through, the great gates closed behind me with a clank.

I drove perhaps another five hundred yards up a curved road before the trees opened up into a clearing in front of a two-story, stone house. The house was long and bridged over to a five-car garage with a carriage house at the end. All it needed was some turrets and it would have looked like a small castle.

A teenage girl dressed in a parka came out a side door and pointed to a place to park my car. As I pulled in and shut off the engine, a woman with a bright smile, perhaps in her late thirties, exited the house. She wore a parka as well. As I got out of my car, she introduced herself.

"I am Margaret Hudson. Welcome to the Prescott Preserve, Ms. Kane." As we shook hands, I replied, "Please call me Roxy, no need to stand on formality."

She gestured toward the teenager. "Roxy, this is my daughter, Lucy."

The teen smiled, then blurted out, "Are you here to find the ghost?"

Mrs. Hudson gave her daughter a look that told me they'd had this conversation previously. I figured I should nip this ghost-hunter nonsense in the bud, saying, "Actually I'm not a ghost hunter; I'm a private investigator."

The teen's face got excited. "A lady private eye, wow," she blurted out. That was when she glanced down at my left foot and saw my blade prosthetic and got wide eyed and abruptly silent.

I grinned, remarking simply, "I'm a war veteran."

Mrs. Hudson took it in stride, smiled, and offered to help with my bags. Upon entering the house my first impression was simply "old money." The decor was reminiscent of a nobleman's hunting lodge or a ski chalet. We stopped at the door to the huge, airy kitchen, where I was introduced to Mrs. Garcia, the cook.

The kitchen adjoined a grand dining space that housed a large wooden table. The dining room opened into a living or family room that was at least twenty by sixteen feet, with a fireplace similar to one you might see in an English manor house in the movies.

Lucy spoke up, "I suggested that we put you in the carriage house. But Mom wants you in the family wing."

"Anywhere is fine," I commented.

Mrs. Hudson chimed in as she led me down a long hallway. "You're our guest, and I'm not going to put you in that drafty carriage house."

"Really, I can be comfortable anywhere," I reassured her.

"No, no, the family wing, I insist. Lucy just wants you to stay in the carriage house because it's reputed to be haunted," Mrs. Hudson explained as she opened the door into an obvious guest room. "I do hope you'll be comfortable here."

"Mrs. Hudson?" I started.

She interrupted me, "Margaret will be fine."

"Okay; Margaret. How formal are you for meals?"

She laughed and said, "This is a hunting lodge. We're casual and tend to wear a lot of sweaters. Help yourself to any of the ones in the lower drawers. After you're settled I'll get you a parka."

"I've got a winter coat," I explained.

"Sorry, house rules: everyone wears a camp parka outside. I'll explain later after you've gotten settled."

With that she excused herself and left me to unpack. I reached into my purse and removed my cell phone. I checked it for coverage and saw no bars. Drat! I wouldn't be able to call Alice for advice.

After about twenty minutes, I wandered out towards the family room. Margaret was working on a large jigsaw puzzle with Lucy. "All settled?" she asked.

"Yes, I am, and may I say, this place is quite impressive."

"Thank you," Margaret acknowledged. Then she changed the subject. "So Roxy, do you have any preliminary thoughts on our ghost situation?"

I was dreading this sort of direct query from the client, especially given that I really didn't have a firm handle on their expectations. So I decided to go fishing.

"All I know is what Mrs. Devonshire told me—that someone here saw a little boy wandering the grounds. She told me you folks want it looked into."

Margaret seemed amused. "You've certainly got the TV listings synopsis. Let's go for a walk."

She rose from her seat and gestured for me to follow her. She led me to a mud room where a number of identical parkas were hanging. She handed me one and explained, "These are camp parkas equipped with a personal locator beacon and a GPS device for tracking purposes."

I must've looked surprised, because she asked, "You're wondering why?"

"Well, yes."

"The Prescott preserve is over fifteen hundred acres of rugged, mountainous terrain. We have plenty of trails that are mostly well marked, but it's still easy to get lost if you aren't paying attention," she expounded.

She reached over to my parka and pointed to something clamped on the zipper that resembled a laminated, seasonal ski pass; it had a large number 5 on it. She then stepped over to a dry erase board and wrote my name and the number 5. Under her name and Lucy's name there were already coat numbers.

"In an emergency we can determine your position via GPS."

"That's some system," I remarked.

"It's sort of at the heart of why you're here."

"You mean the missing boy?

Margaret responded solemnly, with a simple "Yes."

After a pause, I asked, "You were going to tell me about him."

"Of course." She grabbed a parka and said, "Let's go."

We left the house and walked around behind the residence, past the fenced area surrounding a swimming pool.

"Nice pool," I complimented.

Margaret waved her arm towards the empty, yawning concrete pit and said, "Charles's grandfather and father put it in before I was born."

As we walked behind the fenced-in area there was a clearly evident path leading off into the woods. It got darker as we moved into a forest of tall pine trees.

About one hundred yards in, the trail split three ways, each marked with aged, carved signs. The left one said "Lake," the center one, "Overlook," and the sign on the right said "Fairy Circle."

Margaret announced, "I want to show you something at the lake."

"Before we go may I ask a couple questions?"

"Sure."

"Were these trails part of the original property?"

Margaret nodded, "Yes."

"What about that one?" I asked, pointing to an overgrown, unmarked trail to the far right of the other three.

"It's interesting you should notice it. Most people don't, especially in the summertime when it's lush with growth."

She gazed down the unused pass silently for a moment before answering, "The Wessex boy had a rather nice tree house over there. I suspect it's a ruin by now. Out of respect for him we leave it in peace."

"Any chance you could take me there later?"

"Yes, if you'd like, but I ask that you not mention it in front of Lucy." I nodded in agreement, and we resumed our walk.

The lake trail was flat at first, and then sloped at about a thirty degree grade downward. The end of the trail opened up to a lake and a dock with a dark brown, wooden boathouse that blended into the surrounding landscape. Margaret stopped about one hundred feet from the dock and stood quietly, looking at the ice-covered lake, before starting her story. "Our family was at the camp on Thanksgiving this year, which is unusual as we rarely come here then."

I kept my silence and listened carefully.

She continued, "I was down here with Lucy and two cousins. We all saw a boy perhaps ten or twelve years old. He was dressed in summer shorts and a T-shirt. My first thought as a mom was *It's too cold to be out here in shorts*. It's usually very cold here by late November."

She dropped her eyes and continued, "That's when Lucy and her cousins remarked, 'That's him, the Christmas boy.'"

"So several of you saw him?"

"Yes, there were four of us—Lucy, Julie, Marilyn, and myself."

"So what happened?"

"Julie yelled to him. He looked up and walked down the pier towards us, and then he disappeared right there in front of us." She shivered for a moment, before continuing, "It gives me goose bumps just thinking about it."

After that we carried on small talk about the boathouse and Margaret's summers at the lake over the years. Just as we were about to start walking back, I picked up the previous conversation. "Was this the first time the boy had been seen on the grounds other than at Christmas time?"

"Yes," Margaret replied.

"Were there any other sightings during the Thanksgiving holiday?"

Margaret frowned and replied, "Well, yes." She hesitated before saying, "We were in the midst of a family argument when we saw him in the house."

"And was that the only other time you saw him at Thanksgiving—during the argument?"

She turned and looked at me with a troubled look. "No, later he was seen in the carriage house where the girls were sleeping."

I stood there, quietly thinking about everything she had said, and then decided I had to ask: "What was the argument about?"

"I'd rather not say; it's personal," she replied with a nearly defensive tone, and then she turned and started to walk back towards the split in the trail. As we made our way I decided to make my case.

"I'm not an expert at these ghost things, but I find it interesting and I think it's relevant that your family was arguing when the boy appeared in the house. That argument may have triggered something that brought his ghost out of hiding or disturbed its rest.

She stopped walking up the trail and turned to face me. "Do you really think so?"

"It's a definite possibility," I suggested, hoping to get her to fess up. The look on her face told me she was hedging. I pushed the issue further, saying "I take it that the argument wasn't about a board game or what to watch on satellite television."

Margaret shook her head. I gave her space to think—and it worked. She whispered, "My eldest daughter revealed something to us."

I didn't react to her revelation but I did ask her for more information. "Was it something about drugs, radical politics, an eating disorder, what?"

Margaret's eyes opened wide, "Oh, no, nothing so awful. She simply told us she is gay."

I took the revelation in stride. "Was there a significant pushback from the family, you, or your husband?"

Margaret stared at the sky for a few moments. "It was the initial shock. At first we thought she was just being rebellious. We tried to blow it off."

"So you all argued?"

She began to walk again and gestured for me to follow. "Let me show you the fairy circle," she said in an obvious attempt to change the subject.

I considered it best not to push, so I simply agreed, "Yes, let's."

After about five minutes we entered an opening in the dense trees. There in the forest was a natural clearing of about fifty feet in diameter. In the center was a well-constructed fire pit, and around the pit were about a dozen seats fashioned from sections of tree trunks.

Margaret sat down, so I took a cue from her and found my own stump to sit on.

"We've been going through the typical stuff with teenage rebellion and pushback on parental control," Margaret began.

"So you thought she was just trying to pull your chain?"

"Yes," she grinned, "the heated discussion was less about her being gay and more about discussing the implications."

"Implications?" I queried.

"Stupid stuff really," Margaret glanced at her wristwatch. "We best start back. It will be dark soon and we didn't bring flashlights."

As we stood I felt compelled to ask one last question. "Not to belabor a point, but it might prove helpful for me to know about the 'stupid stuff' you mentioned."

"It was really inconsequential things: What will the neighbors think? How will we break it to Grandmother and the aunts? And what about her debut?"

"I see."

She stopped abruptly and turned to face me and pronounced, "All of it doesn't amount to a hill of beans. We all love our Lucy. We will adapt to her nature and that will be that. Now, we need to get back to the compound before dark, so let's go."

As she started to walk I thought about what she told me and wondered if and how it might have been connected with the ghost situation.

As we left the trail and arrived at the compound, Margaret turned to me with a serious look on her face and asked, "Please, no discussion about this in front of Lucy."

"My lips are sealed," I promised.

I noticed a couple more cars in the parking lot and gestured towards the vehicles. Margaret explained, "Oh, my husband and my cousin Kate and her girls have arrived."

The family dinner was interesting to say the least. At one end of the table was Mr. Charles Hudson, the CEO of Hudson Oil. On his right were Christie and Toni Hodges, the teenage cousins, and their mother, Kate Hodges. Margaret sat at the other end of the table. I sat next to Lucy.

Charles had lots of questions about my exploits as a private investigator. I did my best to downplay my adventures but made sure that the stories I told them were colorful ones.

We were about to have dessert when Toni blurted out, "So Roxy, are you going to sleep in the carriage house with the ghost boy?"

Margaret immediately quashed that idea, insisting that as a guest, I should stay in the family wing. Charles agreed with her.

Then Lucy rolled her eyes, exclaiming, "Well, if Roxy is here to help us find our ghost, she should stay in the carriage house where we've seen him."

I glanced around the table. The adults clammed up, and it was easy to see that they were uncomfortable.

"Okay," I announced, "Mr. Hudson, I was hired to look into this situation. Perhaps it does make sense that I stay in the carriage house."

He gave his wife an inquiring look. Watching her eyes meet his, I knew there was something they weren't saying.

Again I spoke up. "I get the impression there's a big unspoken something," I said. "If I'm to do my job, I need to know what it is." I paused and looked around the table before saying, "Please tell me everything."

Charles spoke first. "Roxy, to be honest with you, contacting that medium was Margaret and Kate's idea. I've never seen this supposed ghost, but just about everybody else has. At least they say so."

The others around the table were nodding their heads in the affirmative.

"All righty, perhaps we need to figure out what everyone in the family knows about this apparition," I remarked.

After receiving a nod of approval from Margaret, Kate asked, "What do you want to know?"

Turning to Charles, I said, "I noticed in the mud room you have some large maps of the trails located on your property."

"Yes," he acknowledged.

"After we clear the table following supper, could we lay out a map and tag it with all of your sightings?"

Toni, the younger sister, perked up and asked, "Can we still have our cake and ice cream?"

Everybody burst out with a laugh of agreement.

We all took a break to eat dessert. After the table was cleared, Charles rolled out a large map of the Prescott land, carefully using masking tape to tack down the curly edges. I'd gone to my room to get a package of small, yellow, sticky notes from my briefcase.

For the next hour everyone told me brief stories about the places they or other relatives had reported seeing the ghost. With each story and location, we placed a sticky note on the map.

There were numerous sightings spanning the roughly forty years the Prescott family had owned the property, with the ten most interesting having occurred in the past month.

Once that information was duly noted, I put the map away and participated in a board game with the family; Lucy won. Afterwards I approached Margaret and politely asked to be allowed to sleep in the carriage house. She frowned, saying, "It's a bit bare, and the heat is unpredictable at best."

I pointed out that the carriage house had a consistent number of sightings over the years, making it the ideal place for my stay. She nodded and said, "I guess you're right."

While she grabbed some fresh bedding and an electric blanket, I collected my things and carted them out to the carriage house.

As Margaret and I changed the sheets on the four-poster bed, she commented. "I hope it'll be warm enough out here. If it doesn't work out, we'll move you back into the house in the morning.

I thanked her and mentioned that I wanted to read before turning in. She bid me good night and left.

The space was not unlike a hotel suite. There was a clearly defined sitting room with older furniture worn from years of kids romping on it. A pair of doors opened into a bedroom space. I wondered if it had been a servant's quarters in another era.

I got ready for bed and settled in with a book, but the day had been a long one, and I quickly drifted off to sleep.

My dreams were haunted by my usual nightmares of mopping up after a roadside attack in Iraq. Then it was as if I was awake. I looked towards the foot of the bed and there was a little boy pointing out the window. I got out of bed and went to the window. Now the boy was outside in the parking area pointing down the trail that I had been on earlier.

I began to follow him down the trail.

The musical notes from the alarm clock woke me. After shutting it off, I stayed in bed, quietly thinking about the second part of my dream.

24 December 2012 – Christmas Eve morning, Prescott Preserve

Breakfast consisted of big, fluffy omelets, pastries, and terrific cups of coffee. The conversation was for the most part family chatter. As I sat enjoying a breakfast strudel, Lucy interrupted the chitchat to announce, "Roxy, I saw the ghost boy last night."

"When was this?" I sputtered.

The teen looked spooked as she explained, "I got up to go to the bathroom and glanced outside and saw him standing in the driveway, pointing down the trail."

Charles commented with a cough, "I think all this ghost talk has fed everyone's imagination."

His remark elicited a chorus of disagreement from the girls, and the conversation got less serious and soon frivolous. I excused myself from the table and gestured to Charles to join me in the kitchen.

"What's up, Roxy?" he asked as he entered the room.

"I still can't quite believe it, but I saw the boy, too," I revealed.

With a troubled look, he gently grabbed my arm and pointed me towards the mudroom. After we entered he closed the door.

"Roxy, please understand I'm trying to downplay the whole ghost thing." I was about to comment when he added, "But I can tell you: I've seen him, too, on the trail."

I waited for the story I knew would follow.

"It was the day after Thanksgiving."

I pointed at the parkas and asked, "Can we go for a walk?"

"Yes" he replied, as he handed me a parka, grabbed another for himself, and logged both numbers. In the parking lot, Charles pointed and said, "I saw him at the head of the trail."

"Did you follow him?"

"Yes, to the fork in the trail," he explained as we began to walk.

"Then what happened?"

"When I got to the fork, I noticed he was dressed in different clothes." Hudson hesitated before continuing. "When I first spotted him, he was in a T-shirt and shorts, but here at the fork in the trail he was clearly wearing a little girl's dress."

For the second time that evening I found myself sputtering: "Huh? Did you say dress?"

"Yes, a little girl's summer dress," he replied, with a look on his face that—as the saying goes—was as serious as a heart attack. "I know how strange that sounds."

"It's okay," I remarked. "It is what it is. And then what?"

"Then he went that way," he said, and pointed toward the overgrown, unmarked trail.

"Isn't that the way to the tree house?" I questioned.

"Yes, we don't use it and for good reason; during the summer months it's overgrown with poison ivy."

"Well, as I see it, he wanted you to go that way." I studied the trail for moment. "It's late fall now, so the trail should be clear of poison ivy." I gestured towards the beckoning trail with a simple "Shall we?"

"Let's," he agreed.

After walking through the defoliated brush for about fifteen minutes, we arrived at a large oak tree. Up among its huge, seasoned branches were the remnants of a long-decayed tree house. Charles studied it for a moment before saying, "I'm surprised that some of it is still up there."

As I looked around the small clearing, I noticed the barely visible remnants of a second trail and asked, "Where does that go?"

"What are you talking about?"

I pointed to the bare outline of a path leading up a grade from the tree house clearing and received a surprised look in response.

"Roxy, I have no idea, but I'm game to check it out." He paused, and with a glance at my left leg, asked, "Can you manage with your prosthetic?"

"You'd be surprised what I can do with this thing," I laughed. "Let's go."

Up the overgrown trail we went. After another ten or twelve minutes of hiking, we came to a small structure made of mortared cobblestones and almost completely hidden by a thicket of bushes and weeds.

"What's this?" I questioned.

Charles simply shrugged his shoulders in response. He looked every bit as surprised and perplexed as I was.

We stood silently studying the approximately eight-by-twelve-foot structure until Charles spoke. "Listen, do you hear water running?"

I did. I pushed through the brush at the front of the structure to reach a very weathered wood door. I lifted a broken latch and pulled, and the rusty hinges gave off a blood-curdling screech. The door only opened about six inches. I stepped back and looked at Charles. "I think it needs a harder yank," I grimaced. "I'm a bit limited in the bodyweight department. Can you do it?"

Charles pushed the brush aside, commenting, "Sure, I've got this covered." He grabbed the rusty handle and gave the door a hearty pull. The corroded hinges gave out another screeching moan as the door swung open.

We stepped inside onto a firm dirt floor. On the floor to the left was another wood door. On the right there was a very rusty array of some type of lead pipe configuration secured to the cobblestone wall with corroded iron supports.

In front of us was a boxlike stone structure with old, wood planks lying on top of it. Charles lifted the covering, revealing a cistern gurgling with crystal-clear water.

"This must have been the original springhouse," Hudson said.

"How do you get your water now?" I asked.

"We have a deep well that was put in sometime in the 1950s by the previous owner. But the original water source must've been this spring water and this cistern." He pointed to the cistern and then to a trough feeding to the old lead pipes. "The water in the cistern would have filled that trough, and the water was fed by gravity down to the house," Charles explained.

He looked down at the floor and pointed. "Before refrigeration they used these cold-water-fed springhouses as summer ice houses. I suspect that door on the floor opens up into a cold storage area."

He reached down and grabbed the rusty handle and attempted to lift the door, but it wouldn't move.

He gave me a pretend perturbed look, and then replaced it with a grin and the instructions, "Give me some room."

I backed up towards the front door. Again he reached down and pulled with all his strength. With a groan, he lifted the door, its rusty hinges screaming out like their front door cousins. As he looked into the lower area he let out a howl, "Oh, good Lord!"

I stepped over to his side and looked into the space. Lying below us on the dirt floor was a skeleton, clearly the remains of a child, clad in the ruins of a summer dress.

"My God, someone's little girl," he said in a somber tone. "Perhaps she fell in here and hit her head," he remarked.

I stood silently and studied the remains. Then I pointed down at them and said, "Notice how the body was laid out, how the hands are crossed over the chest. That was an act of care, an act of tenderness. This kid was carefully placed here."

"Why didn't the dress decay?" he asked.

I thought for a moment, and then remarked, "Judging from the paisley design I'd guess its double-knit polyester. It was the rage back in the 60s. It's mostly plastic and nearly indestructible unless it catches on fire."

Charles looked at me, the color drained from his face. "I suppose we should call the authorities," he said in a solemn tone.

It wasn't long before the Fremont County coroner and sheriff's department personnel were processing the scene. I commented to Charles with a sigh, "It's a grim thing to be doing on Christmas Eve. I feel sorry for them."

The authorities spent the afternoon documenting the scene and taking statements from both Charles and myself. An older, seasoned detective named Burger suggested these might be the remains of some long-ago kidnapped girl.

I took Burger aside and told him I had reason to believe the remains were those of the Wessex boy. Given the dress, of course he wondered why. I suggested that we put speculation aside until the medical examiner could rule on the gender and perhaps the cause of death. Due to the holidays, that might take a few days.

The detective wasn't happy with my answer and pressed me about why a private investigator was here in the first place. I led him away from the springhouse down the trail to the tree house clearing.

"Detective, do you believe in ghosts?" I inquired. He gave me an odd look before asking, "Off the record?"

I nodded to reassure him.

After a moment he spoke up, "I'm a Vietnam War veteran and I've seen some unbelievable things," he said in a reserved tone. He glanced at my lower left leg and my blade. "Afghanistan?"

"No, Iraq."

"OK, off the record," I repeated. He nodded.

"My clients were being haunted. They consulted a medium and I was called in to look into things," I explained.

He grinned, "Are you some sort of ghost hunter?"

"Nope, just a private investigator looking into a bigger question: Why the haunting?"

"What have you come up with?" he asked.

"Not much, just a few hunches and now, what might be a forty-year-old crime scene."

"That's enough for one day," he laughed.

He told me that the medical examiner would most likely examine the remains on December 26. I asked if I could be present, and he said he'd arrange it as a courtesy. I wished him a Merry Christmas and left the scene.

24 December 2012 – Christmas Eve, Prescott Preserve

The Christmas Eve dinner with the Hudsons was abuzz with chatter about the discovery of the body. I begged off when asked to reveal the gory details, citing the ongoing investigation. Charles was willing to talk about the springhouse and what we found but also would not expound on the grisly forensic scene.

After dinner I left the family to celebrate their Christmas Eve tradition and retired to the carriage house. There I enjoyed a quiet drink of Irish whiskey and Christmas music on the radio as I compiled my notes.

25 December 2012 – Christmas Day, the Prescott Preserve

On Christmas morning I joined the family for breakfast. All the presents had been opened on Christmas Eve, so there was none of the normal Christmas morning gift-opening hoo-ha. After we ate, the teens went out of their way to include me in all of their tabletop games. Later, the adults, being closer to my age, engaged me in kitchen talk as they prepared the holiday meal. To be honest, I've never exactly been handy with cooking. Mom always chased everyone out of the kitchen. My only successes have been with cookies. Even my efforts with cakes have been dismal at best. So I made a batch of Christmas cookies as part of my holiday offering.

In late afternoon I joined the family for a movie on their large-screen television. Afterwards Charles and Margaret made a point of thanking me for sacrificing my own holiday to stay with them. Charles poured drinks and the three of us began quietly discussing the extraordinary discovery and what would come next. Margaret wondered if I was going to be part of the investigation with the sheriff's office.

"Nope, the only reason I'm here is to work for you and Mrs. Devonshire. You folks wanted an explanation for your ghost mystery, and I believe we have our answer. I am of the opinion that the spirit of that kid was unsettled and wanted closure. Considering the nature of the case, I think we managed a reasonable resolution."

Margaret agreed, but Charles had a troubled look on his face when he spoke. "Roxy, you and I both noted how carefully that child was laid out. I get the impression there's more to it than just the accidental death of a child."

"I do as well," I said, sipping my whiskey.

Charles continued, "As the owner of the property where the death took place, I feel an obligation to understand the complete picture of what happened."

"Is there something you want from me?" I queried.

"Yes, I would like you to dig deeper."

I gently pushed back on what he was proposing. "Charles, this is a forty-year-old cold case," I reminded him. "The sheriff's office is better equipped to do this than I am."

"Exactly my point," he huffed. "Because it's a forty-year-old case, I'm guessing the sheriff is going to close the missing person case and that will be that."

I stared at the ice in my glass of whiskey for a moment before replying, "I believe that all depends on what the medical examiner finds."

"Well, then," he replied, "I'd like you to check it out tomorrow and see what she says, and then let's see what the sheriff's department does with the case. In the meantime, please keep an open mind.

"But Charles, you know my services aren't cheap."

I'm well aware of that, Roxy. But if that was my child, I'd hope someone would look into it.

26 December 2012 – The Fremont County Morgue

Sherrif's department detective Tom Berger and I met at the medical examiner's office and went together to the morgue, where the tech had counted and arranged the bones of the deceased on a stainless steel table.

Berger leaned toward me to say, "This should be a slam-dunk for identification if those remains are that missing boy. I'm told the county coroner has had the dental records for that Wessex kid for four decades."

Then he added, "At the department we've got a pool going. Most everybody thinks the remains are some kidnapped little girl. Only a few believe, like you do, that it's the Wessex kid. I wasn't sure where to put my money. In the end I sided with you."

"Nothing is ever as simple as it seems," was my only response.

The medical examiner walked in carrying two large envelopes. It was clear she was busy and focused on the business at hand when she barked, "Good morning, Berger; who is your friend?"

"This is Roxanne Kane, the private investigator who found the deceased. Roxanne, this is Dr. Rebecca Harris."

She looked over her glasses, giving me the once-over and a brief nod of acknowledgement, before turning away and placing x-ray films from the envelopes on a frosted light box. She studied the dental profile intently, tapping on each tooth with the back of her pen. "I'm told hundreds of men—police and military—looked for this kid forty years ago."

"Yes, that's right," Berger replied.

"I find it interesting that a private investigator—a woman with a peg leg, no less—reopened this cold case after all these years." She glanced back at me, "No insult intended, hon."

Understanding what she was implying I certainly wasn't insulted. I replied, "None taken."

The medical examiner shifted her focus to point at the x-rays of the newly found skull and a strip of old dental films. "Well, you were right. The lost kid's dental films match the skull. These are the remains of William A. Wessex."

Berger spoke up. "That's it; we've found the long-lost kid."

"Correct." She walked over to the stainless steel examination table and picked up the skull and turned it around. "But I have two important observations." She pointed at a pattern of cracks on the skull. Notice this fracture in the rear of the skull? These were perimortem, before or at the time of death."

She walked over to the table again and returned the skull.

Berger piped up, "Maybe the kid fell and hit his head."

Then she picked up a bone from the neck area and said, "This cervical vertebrae C-4 is broken, so no, detective, this was no accident. In my professional opinion, someone wrung this kid's neck and slammed his head against a hard surface, fracturing his skull."

Berger cut to the chase, "Cause of death, Doc?"

"Based on the skeletal evidence, I'd say clearly blunt force trauma complicated by a broken neck." She picked up a clipboard and began to write. "I'm ruling this case a homicide. Someone clearly throttled the kid to death."

I kept my silence and watched Berger as he sorted out implications in his head. Then he spoke up, saying, "Okay, Doc. But this is a forty-year-old case. I doubt the sheriff and the D.A. will want to burn modern resources trying to solve it."

Though Dr. Harris shook her head in disgust, her response was simply, "My clerk will fax my report to your office."

"Thanks, Doc."

Berger then looked to me, "I guess we're done here. The sheriff asked me to thank you for your assistance in this matter."

I did my best to be gracious, "And I thank you, Detective Berger. Do you mind if I chat with the medical examiner for a few moments?"

He shrugged his shoulders. "It's your dime." As we shook hands, he said, "Nice working with you, Ms. Kane." And with that, Berger turned and left the room.

Before I could open my mouth, the doctor spoke up. "Ms. Kane. You obviously still have questions. What's your continued interest?"

"Well," I said with a smile, "As a private investigator, I'm a hired hand, and as such I do what my client wants me to do—within reason, of course. And my client wants me to get to the bottom of this, almost as if this was his own kid."

"That's rather noble of him—and generous, considering what your fees must be," she responded with a look of surprise. "How long have you been working on the case?"

"Four…" I started before she cut me off.

"Four months?"

"No, four days," I said. "I had a lucky break."

She unclipped the x-rays from the light box and started returning them to their envelopes, before saying, "That would ordinarily mean you would close the case, right?"

"Not this time."

She gave me a quizzical look, "You found the kid; what else is there?"

"Dr. Harris, let me ask you a question. Say the boy just died and they rolled him in here today with these injuries. How would you have handled that?"

"Pretty much the same way except that I would do a standard autopsy. The examination of soft tissues might give us forensic info like bruising around the neck, perhaps hand impressions of the perpetrator, etc."

I thought for a second before asking, "And if that boy was brought in here today in a little girl's dress, what would you say?"

Harris thought for a moment, "Well, if I had a young boy brought in today who was throttled like this kid I would consider it a crime of passion." She glanced over at the bones with a look of sudden realization, "My God, it was a hate crime. But those laws weren't in effect forty years ago."

I nodded in agreement, "Yes, but laws about murder *were* in effect then, and as you know, there is no statute of limitations on murder, and the fact this boy was wearing a dress speaks to motive. Back then, being perceived as a homosexual could result in harassment or worse."

With that, I concluded my business with the medical examiner and went to a coffee shop and made a few phone calls.

27 December 2012 – Plattsburgh, New York

The Fremont County Sheriff's office gave me permission to do the family notification in person since I found the remains of the Wessex boy, so I drove up to Plattsburgh, New York, to meet with surviving members of the Wessex family.

I arrived at the home of Willie's older sister, Elizabeth Wessex Matthews, at dinner time. From my car, I studied the house for a few minutes; the residence was certainly upscale. My online research had revealed that Mrs. Matthews' husband came from money and then proceeded to make more in the natural gas futures business.

I had called ahead and indicated that the Hudson family wanted me to speak to her. When she tried to put me off to a much later date, I was forced to reveal that some significant clues about her little brother's disappearance had turned up. She put me on hold for a few minutes, and then returned to suggest I visit her later that day.

As I approached the front door I thought carefully about how I was going to reveal the news. I took a deep breath and pressed the doorbell. Inside I heard a chime, one of a much higher quality than what I have in my residence.

After a few moments, a woman opened the door.

"Mrs. Matthews?" I asked.

"No. I'm Mrs. Ulster, her personal assistant. Are you Ms. Kane?"

"Yes," I replied.

Ulster motioned for me to enter. My first impression was *What a ritzy place!* I was ushered down a hall into a library lined with books from floor to ceiling, complete with several ladders for accessing those on higher shelves.

"Mrs. Matthews will be with you in a few moments. Please make yourself comfortable." And with that, Ulster left me in the library.

I took advantage of my time alone to browse and study the book titles. The collection was predominantly nonfiction and extremely impressive.

"Are you a big reader, Ms. Kane?" a woman's voice spoke from behind me. I turned to see a tall, attractive woman, elegantly dressed, who could have been cast in a Nordic movie as a warrior queen.

"Yes, I am. And you are Mrs. Matthews, I presume?"

"Correct." She gestured towards an overstuffed leather chair, and she sat down on a velvet loveseat.

"So, Ms. Kane, what after forty years is so pressing that I had to change my very busy schedule?" she commented with a tone that suggested perturbation instead of interest. I decided to be blunt.

"I found your brother," I said.

I waited a moment for a reaction. Strangely, my words seemed to go right over her. Then I added, "I'm sorry for your loss."

Mrs. Mathews sat there in what I thought was a state of shock. After perhaps a couple minutes of quiet, I broke the silence to ask, "Mrs. Matthews, are you all right?"

She snapped back to reality, saying, "I wondered if this day would ever come."

She reached into her pocket for her cell phone and pressed a single key. Just a couple seconds later, she said, "Daddy, can you come to the library right now? It's important."

She disconnected the call and turned to me to say, "My father lives here. I thought he should be present."

"I completely understand," I replied.

While we waited for her father to join us I made small talk, complimenting the extensive library. For a few moments the conversation was cordial and trivial—odd, I thought, considering the news I had just delivered.

The library door opened, and a vital-looking man in his 70s or early 80s entered the room, closing the door behind him.

"Good evening, Liz; what is so important?" he asked his daughter.

"Daddy, please take a seat. This is Ms. Kane, a private investigator." Mrs. Matthews patted the empty loveseat space next to her, and her father joined her on the small couch.

"Okay, what's this all about?" he asked.

Mrs. Matthews looked to me for the answer.

"Mr. Wessex, we found your son Willie."

His face registered his shock before he cried out, "Good lord; is he alive or dead?"

"Long dead sir. I'm sorry."

He seemed to take the news in stride, although I could see his eyes tear up. He looked at his daughter and softly said, "I guess this gives us the closure we've long waited for."

She just nodded, still not expressing any emotion. Mr. Wessex looked at me and asked, "You are a private detective and not the police?"

"That's correct," I responded.

"How did you become involved?" he asked.

"Mr. Hudson, the current owner of the Prescott Preserve, hired me."

"Why would Charlie Hudson do that after all these years?" he inquired.

I didn't want to divulge the story of the ghost, so I simply said, "It's a long story, but suffice it to say, we found your son, and the medical examiner has confirmed that the remains are his. The Fremont County sheriff's department authorized me to notify you since I discovered the remains.

The old man nodded, and then turned to his daughter to say, "I'll call the Fredrickson Funeral Home. Willie must have a proper burial."

"How long before we can get his body?" he asked me.

"Sir, there's a complication."

"What kind of complication?"

"I'm sorry to have to tell you this, but it appears there was foul play," I explained.

"Goodness, no!" Wessex moaned. "I always thought he'd been kidnapped, perhaps grew up somewhere else. Or that he'd fallen in the bog and was swallowed up by the muck."

While Mr. Wessex was talking, I made a mental note regarding Elizabeth Matthews. She was silent and seemingly distracted. I decided to try to figure out why.

"The police report states that the family was going to go on a hike when Willie was lost."

"Oh yes," Mr. Wessex agreed. "We had just finished a picnic lunch by the boathouse. My wife suggested that Willie change out of his shorts into long pants to avoid poison ivy. He went up to the main house to do that, but he didn't come back, so I sent Liz up to the house to get him. She came back and said she couldn't find him anywhere. We all started walking the trails looking for him."

"Where did you look, sir, and Mrs. Matthews, where did you look?"

Wessex didn't blink, "I went to the east lakeside area and looked in the bogs. My wife walked the trail around the lake. Liz checked the tree house and the fairy circle. By suppertime we decided to call the authorities. Soon there were hundreds of people searching the grounds and dragging the lake. They did everything they knew how to do. A few days later, some Army mountain rangers even came and scoured the landscape."

I remained silent for a few moments, thinking, and then I decided to go for it. "Sir, did your son ever give you an indication that he might be gay?"

Mr. Wessex stood up with a shocked look and loudly pronounced, "My son Willie was a boy scout and quite a junior woodsman. Certainly he had a soft heart like his mother. He would cry at sad movies. But I assure you he was all boy, through and through. Hell! He was even blooded with me and his uncles the previous fall when we shot a 10-point buck.

"Shut up, Daddy. He was nothing of the kind. He was a dandy boy and you know it," Liz barked, coming out of her trance-like state.

"What are you talking about?" the old man whimpered.

"Willie was a faggot, Daddy, a swishy faggot!" she shouted.

Wessex rose to his feet and yelled back at his daughter, "Don't call him that!"

That's when I made my move. "Liz, I'm guessing you went up to the house and caught your little brother in one of your dresses."

Mr. Wessex turned to me with a look of shock.

Liz sprang to her feet, shouting angrily, "Yes, I caught the little bastard in my best Sunday dress."

"I suppose you screamed at him" I asked.

She went off on another rant, exclaiming, "Yes, I screamed at him, the little queer! He was prancing around in my heels, too!"

I pressed my edge, "Why were you so angry at him?"

"He threatened to tell Dad!"

"Tell him what?" I prodded.

"He threatened to tell Dad that I was sneaking out of the compound to see a boyfriend. He taunted me that Dad would believe him and not me," she barked.

"So what happened?"

"I grabbed him, pushed him down, and started pounding his head on the floor."

"Is that when he went limp?" I asked.

"Yes." She collapsed onto the loveseat.

"So how did he end up in the spring house?"

Mr. Wessex had been silent all this time, seemingly aghast at the revelations. "The spring house?" he questioned.

The still-agitated Liz continued, "While the rest of the family was out looking for him, I did a fireman's carry like they showed us in scouts. I took him to the spring house. Then I put him in the space down below."

Mr. Wessex was stunned, his jaw gaping.

That's when I spoke up, "That's where we found him. He looked to be laid out with care."

At this point she was still talking, but obviously very distant in her thoughts. "I guess I was feeling a bit sad. He was my brother, after all. I knew nobody ever went to the spring house, so I figured he'd be there forever, undiscovered."

Mr. Wessex got up and walked to the other side of the library, mumbling over and over again, "I don't know you."

I stood up and announced: "Elizabeth Wessex Matthews, as an officer of the court, I'm placing you under arrest for the murder of your brother William Wessex III."

Mrs. Matthews snapback to her arrogant self and coughed, "You're not a cop!"

"I am a licensed New York State private investigator and an officer of the court. I assure you, you are under arrest."

She glared at me and said, "It's my word against yours. My father will not testify against me."

I reached into my pocket and removed a small digital recorder. "It doesn't matter what your father says, your confession has been recorded."

Mr. Wessex shook his head and stormed out of the library, slamming the door behind him. Elizabeth sat down, stunned and speechless.

I took out my cell phone and pressed 911.

5 January 2013 – The Celtic Harp Restaurant and Pub, Utica

I had lunch with Alice Devonshire and filled her in on the whole sordid affair. She informed me that the Hudsons were delighted with my services and handed me a generous check.

"See, I told you I needed a detective and not a ghost hunter," Devonshire said with a look of satisfaction.

"But I saw a ghost and that gave me the lead I needed," I commented.

"Roxy," she said with a smirk," a ghost hunter might have simply logged the sighting and left it at that. You followed up like the investigative professional you are and cracked a forty-year-old case wide open. Congratulations!"

While driving back to Old Forge, I could only wonder if discovering Willie Wessex's remains and apprehending his murderous sister was going to put his spirit to rest. Maybe I'll contact the Hudson family someday and find out.

Dolls of Potsdam

by Marie Hannan-Mandel

Esme picked a tiny crumb from the seat of the funeral home waiting-room couch. The place didn't look very clean, but she supposed her mother wouldn't mind now. Esme had made all the arrangements, and soon she and her mother would make their last trip together.

There wasn't one decent crime show as she flicked through the hundreds of channels on the television. The young male employee had told her it could take an hour or more for them to finish with her mother, and she had settled down to wait. She needed something to take her mind off her task. She wasn't fussy. She'd watch a rerun. And then she saw her sister Martha. On television. All dressed up and preening while a young man with a whole lot of hair—though none on his face—introduced a home-makeover show. Esme had noticed there weren't many men on television with hair on their faces anymore, unless it was cut short and tight around the mouth and nose like Christmas wrapping.

Martha didn't have a home of her own to make over. Martha couldn't be about to mess up their mother's house in front of the entire world—or at least the part of it that liked watching places being torn apart—could she?

Esme thought it was typical of her sister to pretend that Potsdam, New York, was in the Adirondacks. It wasn't. It was in the foothills, beyond the foothills, but of course it sounded better on television to pretend it was somewhere really pretty, or alongside of somewhere really pretty. The pretense wasn't even necessary, because Potsdam was a lovely little town with the Raquette River running through it. The river sprang from Raquette Lake, which was in the Adirondacks, and it emptied into the St. Lawrence River, which was a very nice place to end, Esme thought. She and Martha, two years younger, had gone to a camp at Raquette Lake every year as children. She'd liked it, but she had always been so happy to return home to Potsdam. Esme keenly resented the way Martha had tried to make Potsdam sound better than it was when there was nothing wrong with it to begin with. Esme dreaded Martha's determination. If she didn't like something, she changed it.

Esme was nearer sixty than fifty, but she didn't look it. And not just because she was a little plump. She didn't look her age because she'd decided a long time before to never move her face more than necessary—no wide smiles, no frowns, and certainly no pulling of faces the way Martha and their mother did. She hadn't given the wrinkles, dimples, and lines a chance to form. It made it difficult for people to know what she was thinking, and that was good, too. No one looking at her in that room, seated on that grubby couch, would have known that her heart was being broken all over again.

Martha was on television, laughing at their house, her parents' house—Esme's house, really, since Martha had left years before. It was the house where Esme had lived all her life, the house to which she would return when she left this place on the New York-Pennsylvania border. Their mother was coming home. Their mother, who had been foolish enough to marry a man and move away when she was old enough to know better. When they were all old enough to know better. Martha had encouraged her with all that "you only live once" nonsense. Yes, you only live once, but you don't have to be foolish while doing it, Esme had told her mother, who'd looked at Esme as if she'd squashed a kitten.

"Look at this crazy thing," Martha said, holding up one of the crocheted armchair covers—an antimacassar, though Martha didn't know the correct name, and neither, of course, did the young man. Esme had made it herself using a very difficult yarn that gave it texture and movement. The shades of red and green just sang out. The young man laughed and rolled his eyes, and his hair never moved. "These are all over the place," Martha added as the camera came close.

The carpet in the parlor, blue with swirls of green, was the next target. Esme had picked it, knowing it would enhance the old leather couch. Esme had to admit that it didn't film well, but then, neither did Martha, who looked like a gorgon on camera. But that did little to make Esme feel better.

"The former owner had, shall we say, a unique sense of style." Martha's voice was too loud. Esme had told her so many times, but it seemed to work wonderfully on television.

The former owner? Since when was she "former"? Unless Martha had confused her sister with their dead mother, Esme was still half owner of that house. Esme wasn't sure how long it took for these shows to get on the air, but Martha must have arranged to have it done the minute Esme left town. Or more likely she'd talked to the film people the week Esme went to see their cousin Ruth, who had insisted she needed help settling her dead husband's affairs. Martha had urged her to go to Ruth because she was "good at that kind of thing," and then Ruth hadn't taken one word of advice from Esme the entire time she was there. Maybe Ruth had been in on it.

But Martha couldn't have known exactly when their mother would die, so she must have told them she'd let them know. She would let them know when her mother died, and they could come and tear up the poor woman's house. Talk about making death arrangements. Martha was a cold woman, Esme thought.

"Can you say 'hoarder'?" Martha asked.

The young man laughed. "You could say that."

Esme remembered all the times Martha had said to her, "Esme, there's no one works a crochet hook as well as you," and "That's just the right shade of carpet for this room. You're so good at everything you do."

"Have you ever seen anything like this?" Martha asked, waving her arm at the china cabinet which contained Esme's doll collection. She missed her dolls, and there Martha was, the young man, too, laughing at them and pulling out her Marie Osmond special order Huggs & Kissy Mistle Ho Ho Ho dolls. The boy and girl were dressed in Christmas colors, and they looked just like Marie and her brother Donny except for the bright red noses. Martha took Kissy and the young man took Huggs, and they danced them in the air as if they were playthings. Not content with this, Martha grabbed up another doll—the Kestner Hilda doll—and began to theatrically blow away the dust, as if Esme would have left her that way. Martha had promised to keep everything dusted, and now she huffed and puffed on the tiny porcelain face, its tongue just showing through two teeth surrounded by sweet baby lips. Esme gasped as Martha pulled at the doll's gently curling brown hair and plucked at the original dress. Martha and the young man sneered at Esme and everything she loved.

Esme had always worked from home, a home she shared with her parents and Martha, and then just her parents, then just her mother, and then just herself. After college, Martha had packed up and moved to the city, while Esme had stayed. The house became her creation. Neither their mother nor Martha cared much about it, but Esme loved the Victorian grandeur of the place, passed from father to son through the generations of their father's family.

Martha, the young man, and a whole slew of people tore the house apart right in front of her, and gave away—no, threw away—all Esme's beautiful things. They made the house look like every other house on television. Esme couldn't stop herself from watching, even though it was almost as painful as watching her mother die. She felt like a specimen pinned to a felt mat, watching the final pin approaching, the one that would kill her.

Martha hadn't come down for their mother's service. She'd said, "Well, you'll have to bring her ashes back here anyway, so I'll see you then."

"Ashes? What ashes?" Esme had asked.

"Mother wanted to be cremated. You remember she told us that?"

Esme didn't remember, but this was before the TV show, so she'd believed Martha. For all Esme knew, Mother had wanted to be put into a mausoleum or shot into space or frozen in case they someday figured out how to make old people young again.

Once everything was finished at the funeral home, Esme took the Adirondack Trailways bus to Potsdam on a route which didn't even travel Adirondack roads. Esme remained angry at Martha for lying about their town, their house, their lives. Martha had changed the house, and probably the locks. Esme pondered the way her life had been tossed, just like her hand-sewn cushions, into a dumpster. She didn't understand the whole "let's throw it away and get new" attitude she'd been noticing for a while now. Fashions changed, and just because a person didn't happen to want to change with them, just because someone got herself a style and wanted to stick with it, didn't make that person crazy, did it? How crazy were those women who held onto all their old clothes and were now selling them for big money or giving them to their daughters when the fashion came around again? Since when did being faithful and constant and reliable and loyal mean being crazy? Esme didn't know.

Esme rode in the brilliant spring sunshine through one town after another, a nine-hour trip that involved two buses and multiple stops along the way. Her large tartan carryall was heavy, for it contained her mother's ashes in a large cardboard box, along with all the other things she'd had to carry with her.

Despite what she would have to deal with when she arrived, Esme was calm as the bus pulled up on Market Street in front of the historic buildings with their embellishments and excesses. At least Martha didn't have control over the downtown area. Esme was finally home. Although she felt like crying, she stopped up her tears because she didn't want anyone to see her and believe what Martha had been telling the entire country—that she was nuts.

Potsdam had been named for the town in Germany, but now it was mainly known for having two universities and a whole lot of students, groups of whom came towards Esme as they headed out for the evening. The sun shone and the river rollicked high against its banks as Esme walked across the bridge and down Maple Street. She thought briefly of the lake from whence the river came and the happy days at the camp before her life was stolen from her. Esme closed her eyes and saw that place where she had been just Esme—not Martha's sister, nor her parents' child, but just Esme.

She walked briskly along their block and watched their large Victorian house, with its striking grey, green, and peach paint, come into view. Esme had noticed that neither Martha nor that young presenter had ever mentioned the fact that the house was Victorian as they laughed at her dolls and antimacassars, which actually fit in perfectly with the architecture. They hadn't even mentioned all the original woodwork.

Esme stopped as if on the edge of a large gaping hole, smacking herself in the thigh with her carryall. She considered the possibility that they had painted the woodwork. She hadn't seen them do it, but she'd been in shock, after all, and couldn't remember everything they'd said. She and Martha had once watched one of these types of shows in which an idiot designer had painted all the original woodwork "sparkling" white while some loud, young couple egged her on. If Martha has painted even one inch of the original cherry wood paneling or the chestnut wood stairs, Esme would kill her.

Esme walked down the side of the house to the back door. Tall evergreens circled their yard and provided total privacy. The door was unlocked, as it always was. At least Martha hadn't replaced the broken latch.

"We're home," Esme called as she let herself in.

"Hello, Esme," Martha said, coming towards her, all smiles. She looked quizzically behind Esme.

"We're home," Esme repeated, holding up the tartan bag with their mother's ashes.

She was relieved to see that the kitchen hadn't been "improved." She looked in the cabinet which held all the glasses, some of them quite old, and saw they hadn't been touched either. She ran her hand along the old wooden cabinets and pulls, which dated back to when their parents had first moved in, and opened the large catch-all drawer and again saw that nothing had been changed. Nothing had been discarded or altered.

"What are you looking for?" Martha asked.

"Nothing, just checking whether you'd changed things in here as well," Esme said.

"As well as what?" Martha snapped.

Esme walked past Martha and into the front hallway, which had been swept clean of the paintings of seascapes their grandfather had collected over years of travelling the country as a tire salesman. The wood had not been painted, and for a moment Esme softened toward her sister. Anyone could be swept up in the desire to be famous, after all. And it wasn't as if Martha would ever get another chance to shine the way she had next to that young man.

Martha walked into the dining room and Esme followed. The antique glass cabinet was gone, as were all Esme's dolls. In its place was a thin table made of dark wood so heavily lacquered that it looked plastic. On it rested a mismatched group of the most boring vases Esme had ever seen.

"Where are my dolls?" Esme asked. Until that moment she hadn't allowed herself to consider their fate.

"They were so creepy, Esme. I mean, a woman your age with all those dolls," Martha said as if she expected Esme to agree with her, as if Esme was another young, stupid person who thought anything that wasn't bought yesterday was only fit for the garbage.

"Where are my dolls?" Esme asked again, trying so hard not to show how much they mattered to her, trying not to give Martha the satisfaction of seeing her comments hurt.

"Don't worry. They're packed up and stacked out in the carriage house. Most of them, anyway. I threw away the tatty ones." Martha laughed gaily as if they'd shared a joke.

"The tatty ones? Not the one with the porcelain face and brown curly hair?" Esme whispered.

"Yes, it was a mess." Martha wouldn't look at her, turning her head every time Esme tried to catch her eye.

"It was one of a kind." Esme felt her head swim, and she sat on the edge of a modern dining room chair whose wood was as fake looking as the sideboard.

"What?" Martha snapped.

"It was worth a lot of money."

"How much?" Martha demanded.

"Thousands," Esme whispered. She didn't care about the money. She cared about her Hilda doll, which she had found at the back of an antique store in Old Forge. She had bought it because she'd loved it, and it was only later that she'd realized its monetary value. She thought of her possessions, her treasures, mishandled and abused.

"Oh. Sorry about that. I could have—we could have—used the money," Martha said.

"We?" Esme grasped the tartan bag again and only realized which "we" Martha was talking about when she saw the smile on Martha's face, the smile of a sane person humoring a lunatic.

"How long before I left did you arrange for that television program to come here?" Esme asked. "I know these things take time."

Martha didn't look the way she had on the show. She was back to wearing the shirtwaist dresses she'd worn all her life—not the same ones, obviously, but the same style. They kept things in their family—and it wasn't just Esme who did so.

"Don't worry about that now. Come and see what they've done," Martha said as if Esme's question was insignificant, which to her, of course, it was.

The parlor looked like a discount furniture showroom.

"Isn't it wonderful?" Martha asked. With that question, Esme saw the gay, lighthearted person she'd seen on television.

"Where are all Mother's things? Where are all my things? Don't you think you should have asked before inviting those television people to come in here and change everything around?" Esme considered these to be perfectly reasonable questions.

"I didn't want to bother you. And I thought it would be a wonderful surprise," Martha said.

"You knew I was coming back with our dead mother and you thought after that shock I would want to walk in and find my whole house changed? Did you really think that, Martha?" Esme truly wanted to know if her sister was that oblivious to the person she should have been closest to. Neither of them had ever married. They had no children, and now, no parents, yet Martha didn't care about Esme at all. How could that be? Esme wondered.

Martha looked puzzled, running her hand along the top of the new, brown leather sofa that stood just away from the wall. Why replace one leather sofa with another? And one that wouldn't last five minutes if the way it was responding to Martha's touch was any indication. Cheap goods. Cheap goods for a tacky, careless woman. Esme noticed that all of the furniture was standing away from the walls, just like in furniture stores, so you could walk around each piece and check if something had happened to it, or if there was any damage that might mean you could ask for a discount for taking the floor model.

"I suppose it never occurred to you that I'd see you on television. What were you going to say? That someone broke in here and redecorated? That's what it looks like." Esme was still wearing all her outdoor clothes and carrying the heavy bag.

"What do you mean?" Martha asked. She seemed surprised.

"This place looks like someone broke in, stole everything of value, and then redecorated it with shoddy goods, hoping the owners wouldn't notice. It's no better than those thugs who smash the furniture and spray-paint the walls. What have you done to my house?" Esme swung herself around, the tartan bag almost clipping a hideous stainless-steel table lamp.

"You are a bit scatty, you know, and once everyone saw the inside of the house with all those handicrafts and things you had everywhere, it was clear you needed help. I even heard whispers of a hoarding problem." Martha was clearly very pleased with herself.

"What whispers? You said it yourself to that young man with the sprayed-down hair," Esme protested. She wanted to remain calm, in control, but found her voice rising.

"Wasn't he divine?" Martha asked as if they were teenagers again and Martha was discussing a boy Esme liked and Martha intended to take away from her. Now Esme realized that's how it had always been with Martha.

"Divine is not the word I would use. He looked as fake as all this tacky stuff you've got packed in here." Esme couldn't stop herself from tapping the heavy bag with the box of ashes against her leg, even though it was really beginning to hurt.

"Do you hear the way you talk? It's positively old-fashioned. And those gloves. Who wears cotton gloves anymore?"

Esme looked at her sister standing across the room, so triumphant she was vibrating, but on a very different frequency from the throb of fury that pulsed through Esme's brain.

Martha walked away, into the kitchen. Esme followed her. She was running around the house as if she could shake Esme off.

At least in the kitchen nothing had been thrown away.

"This house is half mine. More than half. You've lived here rent free for years. The way I see it, it's mine now. It's time you found your own place to live," Martha said.

Esme opened the drawer she'd checked earlier and pulled out her father's fully loaded gun from its hiding place under dozens of dish towels. She held it behind her back, out of Martha's sight.

"Martha!" Esme called in a voice so commanding that Martha stopped and turned.

"You're crazy," Martha almost shouted, her face red.

"Maybe. Certainly I was crazy to give up my life so that you could have yours. I was crazy to love you enough to sacrifice so you could be free." Martha's sneer pushed her on. "But I'm not crazy enough to let you cheat me out of what is mine."

"So, what are you going to do? You're not going to do anything," Martha barked as if issuing an order.

"I'm going to kill you. I'm killing you and taking back my house. With Mother dead, and you dead, it's all mine." Esme took the gun from behind her back. The nickel plating glinted in the shaft of light that danced though the window. Her gloved hand tightened around the grip.

"But, you can't. You can't kill me." Martha's voice sounded the note of emotion Esme had been waiting for. Finally, Martha took her seriously.

"Yes, I can. I'm going to make it look like suicide." Esme waited for pity, for sorrow to overwhelm her, but it didn't. She pulled the tartan bag containing the box of ashes high up on her arm. Esme thought she might as well keep her mother near as she finished their journey.

"No one will believe that. I wouldn't shoot myself." Martha looked about to turn, but perhaps afraid Esme would shoot her in the back, didn't.

"Yes, they will. 'Poor Martha made a fool of herself on television, threw away dolls worth a fortune, and discovered she couldn't live with the shame of making such a clown of herself.' No one here knows you, but they all know me. They all know the woman who took care of her parents and volunteered at the food bank and the library. They all know me. All they know about you is that you came in here and made fun of this house and acted like you knew what you were doing when you didn't. And they know you're someone who wasn't very nice about our hometown. Nobody here will appreciate you pretending this is the Adirondacks, like Potsdam isn't pretty enough on its own. Oh yes, and there's also a picture of you winning the shooting contest at the lake."

"What?" Martha seemed to have forgotten.

"Lake Raquette Camp for Girls. You were the winner of the shooting contest every year."

Martha's eyes widened as she remembered. "Now Esme, I know you've had a rough time, dealing with Mother and all of that. Why don't you go upstairs and rest?" Martha was so confident that Esme would do what she said that she didn't even look at the gun.

Esme grasped Martha by the arm. They hadn't hugged when she'd arrived, and Esme realized she hadn't hugged her sister in years. Martha had never liked to be touched. Esme dragged her into the parlor and pushed her down onto the leather couch, grabbing her around the neck.

"Please, Esme, don't. I'll go. I'll go away, and you'll never see me again," Martha whispered, but even in that moment, that important moment, she didn't look Esme in the eyes. Even in that moment she was lying.

Martha struggled, and Esme's arm swung out, catching Martha on the side of the head with the heavy bag full of their mother's ashes. Esme felt bad about involving her mother, and she put the tartan bag down on the floor. The blow had stunned Martha enough to make it easy to stick the gun into her mouth and aim down, towards the back of her head. So many surprises—that she, little, pudgy, timid Esme could hold down her taller, flamboyant sister. In the end, all Martha's strength had been in her fierce desire to get her own way. For once, Esme had wanted something enough to fight her.

Esme pulled the trigger. The noise was shockingly loud, but these old houses had thick walls, and this house, *her* house, was far enough away from its neighbors that no one would hear it.

Hot Containment

by G. Miki Hayden

This might be the moment. He eased himself over to Lila's side of the bed and started to edge onto her, but she pushed him away. "Get off me, Jack," she said. Then, burying her head underneath her hand, "It's so hot," she added.

"The air is on," he answered meekly.

"I feel like crap."

Get off me, fat boy, she thought. She'd said it once.

He loved his wife. Adored her, in fact, and he couldn't blame her for feeling that she'd married beneath herself, in spite of all his science awards and the money that kept on piling in. Dr. Jack Credway—with an M.D. and a couple of Ph.D.s—was a star within his very limited sphere, but Lila had been the only one to accept him — first as a boy, then as a man. She'd gone with him to two of their seventh-grade dances, when she was already a student athlete and (to his eyes, anyway) a great beauty.

"What can I do for you, honey?" he asked. Poor thing. He could almost feel her suffering, and he felt guilty.

"Please, let's sleep now," Lila said.

Wasn't he lucky simply to be able to lie beside her? She was his queen.

This year he'd been awarded the Heineken Prize in biochemistry, and how many Heineken winners went on to capture the Nobel? He could practically count on it.

Curled on his side there in the dark, he smiled at the possiblity of the

Big Win. But it didn't really matter, did it? He already had just about all the recognition he'd ever wanted, and he was able to pursue his research on his own terms. Who else could claim something like that? Enders? Durue? No, neither of them. Only Credway.

In a moment, he began to drowse lightly.

But then he was jarred awake by a noise downstairs. Maybe it was their schnauzer, Baxter. Jack glanced over at the dog's bed and saw that Baxter, too, had been roused by the sudden clatter.

Quiet resumed, and both man and dog returned their heads to their memory foam pillows.

Thump!

That could only be the sound of a human stumble.

Jack pushed back the covers on his side of the bed. "What?" asked Lila.

"You stay here."

He stood and found the baseball bat he kept right outside the closet for any such frightening occasion. And he was frightened. His coordination had gone awry, and a flush of fear ran up and down his spine and through his not inconsiderable gut.

Though, clearly, this far out in the backcountry of the Adirondacks, nefarious visitors were going to be few and far between. What the hell had happened to his security system? Well, he'd suppressed the pings from rabbits and other small animals. If someone was in the house, he must have come on foot.

Jack kept listening to the sound he'd heard, now repeating inside his head. He must have misinterpreted it.

He crept down the stairs, but at the bottom was confronted by the illumination of the desk light shining from inside the den. He never left the desk light on. Or tonight he had, and he was just scaring himself.

Near the entrance to the den, a bout of full-on terror gripped him. A redheaded young man stood rifling through the papers in Jack's desk and throwing them to the floor like so much trash.

This can't be happening. Can not.

The intruder glanced up, retrieved a nasty-looking gun from the desktop and pointed it at Jack, then snickered. "I've heard of bringing a knife to a gunfight but never bringing a baseball bat." Then he shouted, "Ivan. Ivan. Get your butt in here!"

The man gestured with the gun, indicating that Jack needed to drop the bat.

Jack saw no choice—besides which, his hands were trembling too badly for him to want to continue holding the thing. He rolled the metal club onto the blue and beige Persian carpet, his heart banging somewhere deep inside his fat-boy chest, his brain all but frozen. He stared dully at the knotted-wool scimitars and elaborate, ancient flagons depicted beneath his feet. Maybe Lila had married him for his money, but she'd never wanted to live out here where he could earn it. Lila yearned for city life.

She was so precious, and how had he paid her back? He wanted to hurl on the sixty-thousand-dollar antique rug.

Another man—young and slight and short—popped his head through the door from the back guest suite. He stared at Jack as if observing a dangerous animal, a grizzly, rather than a castrated human. "There wasn't... we didn't see... no car in the driveway... no garage..." He stuttered the words out.

Jack and Lila's driver, H.J., would be the one to find their bodies.

But no, Jack was smarter than these thugs. That was a sure thing. Jack had brought his brains to a gunfight. In the movies, of course, cleverness worked. But now his thoughts faltered. His mouth was dry, and adrenaline coursed through shaking muscles.

"Quite a house you have here," stammered the one named Ivan. "You must be rich."

"No," said Jack. He didn't want to bear the brunt of their idea of class warfare. "We don't own it." And he didn't quite own it. The house was held by his corporation, Baxter, Inc., his business that licensed the manufacture of the latest and greatest vaccines for nearly everything humans vaccinated against. The old standbys were improved in Jack's updated and less-expensive versions, for which he took in astounding royalties.

I've made the planet a safer place to live, he told himself, though he wasn't ever sure he believed exactly that. What, to be precise, was unsafe and out of control?—the microbes, or the men making money from warding them off, Jack included? He felt faint.

He heard her light step on the stairs. "No," he called out to Lila sharply. But really, they were too late to save themselves, weren't they? Would these men be merciful? That was always possible, of course. But not very.

"Come on down," the red-haired man countered loudly enough to be heard where she stood. She walked down slowly—slowly, because she obviously wasn't very well, which Jack observed in clear-cut detail when she entered the room. Her eyes were sunken in her head, her hair seemed thin; in fact, she appeared thin in general, had lost too much weight. His chest tightened in worry over her safety. Worry about all the care he hadn't taken of her, couldn't take of her now.

And he didn't like the predatory way the redhead stared at her—oh, god, spare them the indignities.

"What's going on?" Lila asked. She seemed to try to take the scene in sensibly, but the equation didn't calculate.

And what could Jack say? That she shouldn't be afraid? That he had the situation well in hand? He groaned.

Baxter trotted down the stairs, no doubt confused that their night had turned so quickly into day.

Inside the den, the schnauzer commenced to bark in an angry tone. The little dog wasn't used to strangers and disliked them.

"Baxter," Jack hissed firmly to make the dog shut up.

But a split second later, the man's pistol went off with an incredible explosion, and Baxter lay flat on the rug, his life's blood gushing out from seemingly everywhere. A puff of smoke sent the bitter smell of gunfire floating across the room.

Jack's heart cracked.

He and Lila were going to die—because only a madman would shoot and kill such a pretty little dog.

Lila screamed and dropped to the floor—as if she could help what was far beyond any human repair. She stared up at Jack, and he started to cry. Baxter was their child. When they cared for him, it was as though they were building a family of their own.

"What... the hell!" said Ivan with a pause, but no stuttering—and a look of shock as great as Jack's must have been.

Jack hadn't meant... Of course he hadn't caused *this*, but he had done too many things...not quite right things. And the result was his punishment. Perhaps an avenging universe was a lawful and proper construction, though he couldn't say he liked the way it was turning out.

Baxter's blood soaked through his wife's nightgown, exposing her slender, naked form. Jack shrugged off his pajama top, leaned down and pulled her up off the floor, and dressed her in the cotton flannel.

"What a gentleman," the redhead cooed.

Jack wore a white t-shirt underneath his pajamas. Would he have been so thoughtful if he'd had to reveal his sad rolls of fat?

"Now to business. Pay to play—pay to go on living, that is. Cash? Jewelry? Buy your lives here."

Jack looked around. They had so many expensive things, but nothing immediate and negotiable. Sniffling in the last of his tears for a much-loved dog, he took off his platinum wedding band and put it on the end table closest him. Then he removed the diamond ring from Lila's cold and quaking finger and added it to the unimpressive offering. Though it didn't look like much, he'd spent more than a million for the Australian pink gem. Should he tell the thieves? Maybe then they'd be satisfied. Or it would ignite them even further.

"Not enough," said the redhead. "People like you always have a safe."

"I don't have money in the house," Jack explained.

He didn't like the look the redhead gave him.

"Let's just go," said Ivan. He glanced around as had Jack before him, trying to find an object that would be worth this improbable journey.

"Pay now and go on living. Pay now before you're too late."

Lila reached out her hand and clutched at Jack's forearm. She depended on him.

"Live or die. Life or death."

Jack's legs weighed as heavily on him as might the trunk on an ancient redwood. How tired he felt. "You can have my credit cards," he said. "I won't cancel."

"Oh, you promise?" asked the redhead.

Jack's usual life was arranged like the ticking of a clock, down to the crossing of his t's and dotting of his i's. Neither he nor Lila needed cash.

"Last chance," said the redhead. "How about you, my lovely—some nice necklaces?"

"The blue and white flask on the table near the window is worth about a hundred and twenty thousand," said Lila, speaking for only the second time since she'd come into the room. "Take that."

The redhead snatched the vase off the table and flung it onto the floor. The carpet softened the blow and the artifact was spared, but then the man stepped down on this piece of antiquity with a heavy boot, and the fifteenth-century Ming porcelain broke audibly.

"No jewelry, bitch?"

She pulled the Victorian ivory cameo off her neck and gave it to Jack, who placed it alongside both their rings. It couldn't be worth much—a thousand or two?

The redhead pocketed the three pieces, then, without warning, he turned and shot the gun again.

At first Jack thought no damage had been done, but a second later Lila crumpled and fell straight back onto the carpet, propelled violently by the force of the tearing projectile.

He opened his mouth to scream but no sound came out. If Jack's heart had cracked in two with the killing of Baxter, it now fissured into ten-thousand pieces. He knelt beside her. She was still alive, but wouldn't be for long. He took her hand.

"I'm sorry," she whispered and tried to say more. But sorry for what? What had Lila to apologize for, when all the fault from start to finish lay with Jack—for loving her, for pursuing her, for marrying her, for wanting to have her always by his side. No matter the cost.

And he, for all that he knew about life and death and all the lives he tried each day to save, couldn't do a thing to stop her from leaving him.

"Christ, Chasen," said the stuttering man, "what the hell have you done?"

But the redhead laughed. "All right, then, Mr. Homeowner Man. You wouldn't pay to save your wife, but how about kicking in some of the big bucks to save yourself?"

Did Jack care whether he lived or died? Wouldn't death be a haven? Life without Lila wasn't a possibility.

The agony that flooded through him was too cruel to tolerate.

He held her hand, and alongside the pain, he began to feel anger. He'd brought some intelligence to the gunfight, hadn't he?

Jack shivered from the powerful and conflicting emotions cascading up and down his nervous system all at once. "The cash, the coins…did you see a building to our west when you came in?"

"Ye…yeees," agreed the slight one Chasen had called Ivan.

"That's where we keep everything of real value." Jack took a last look around this room of his, a room he loved because Lila had chosen every item in it.

The fragments of his heart joined together and sobbed to their depths, but Jack kept his face as cold as stone.

They trudged over the dry, fall woodland floor, pine needles crackling underfoot. Or rather Jack was the one who struggled to trudge. The lab, surrounded by a ten-foot-high electric fence topped with barbed wire, wasn't far, but it was a great distance for a man—even one not very old—who was driven daily to the front of the small facility.

"You need to work out, get yourself in shape," said the madman. But he seemed more irritable and tired than bent on twitting Jack for the fat man's lack of fitness. "Cut out the Twinkies. Get yourself a new wife." The shadow of a smile appeared on his face.

"I bet he has an alarm on the place," Ivan warned his partner.

Jack paused to catch his breath. Even in the chill of the night and wearing only his pajama bottoms and t-shirt, he was sweating.

"No, I enter a code," he told Ivan. "You can wait and shoot me and run if I'm lying and an alarm goes off. But I'm not."

"What is this place?" asked Chasen, though not with more than idle curiosity.

"Where I work," said Jack.

“It’s like a top secret thing…barbed wire. Like a military thing.”

Jack started walking again, eager to get there. “No, it’s corporate. But with secrets.” He turned around and looked back through the trees at the house. His family was there. Baxter and Lila. He had stolen a little bit of happiness with them.

“She said she was sorry,” Chasen went on. “It was for letting me screw her. I guess she needed some.” He glanced sideways at Jack. “And she said you had lots of money in the house. I killed her for you, pal. That lying bitch.”

The words came without warning, like the shot that had brought Lila down.

Jack trembled, felt as if he could vomit, fought for a moment to catch his breath.

I realize you could have whatever man you want, but I love you more than any of them could.

Oh, Jack, I’m not as wonderful as you always seem to think. I’m just completely ordinary. And of course I love you too.

And she *had* loved him, hadn’t she? She sometimes acted as if she did. Their lives were simple, quiet ones. Too quiet for her? Of course it was too dull with him, too quiet… And so she’d found at least one afternoon’s entertainment with this rabid criminal?

He pictured her naked with this vile hoodlum. Despicable but trim, and sexually proficient, Jack was sure.

He snapped out of it. These were crazy thoughts that Chasen had put in his head. Jack was a logical man, a man of science. “When did you meet her?” he asked softly. He almost couldn’t force out the words.

“In town,” said Chasen. “A couple of weeks ago. In the Prairie Bar and Grill. She was smokin’ hot to trot.”

“Oh, wow,” added Ivan leaning over toward them. “I didn’t know.”

“Yeah,” said Chasen, and he smirked.

Jack didn’t answer—because whatever he told these two wouldn’t matter a bit. But every evening he always asked H.J. “Did my wife at least go out for a drive?”

“No, sir, she didn’t feel up to it, just sent me to the diner for your meal.”

She hadn't met Chasen, hadn't betrayed Jack, hadn't suggested Chasen rob their home.

The three men had crossed the divide—the half-mile of woodland between the house and the lab. He'd made it this far. Again, he looked back at what he could see of the house. Lila's grave. He thought he might have a heart attack, and, yes, he was very willing to die sometime soon, but he had to hold on.

He used the key, and then input the code—pi squared to ten digits, with each digit minus a geometric progression of numbers. Who else but Jack could know the frequently changing algorithm? No one would be able to cut off his fingers or dig out his eyeball to enter the premises, and no one but he and a computer in Omaha knew the current cipher formula.

"Don't worry," he said, and walked in first.

"Leave the door open," ordered Chasen.

Jack shrugged and left the heavy steel door ajar.

He ushered the two past a set of five blue, positive-pressure suits.

"What's that, uh, symbol?" Ivan asked, pointing at a metal plaque on the wall.

"Nothing," said Jack. "Just tells the garbage people that this might be biological waste." Though no trash left the lab except as ash.

"It's a nuclear thing," exclaimed Chasen, finally becoming aware that he might have to confront something that wasn't within his range of control.

Jack shook his head. "No. A completely different symbol."

The heavy steel door slammed behind them and Chasen jumped. "Just the wind," lied Jack. The door was on a timer and wouldn't stay open for longer than twenty-five seconds—just long enough for him to bring in a box of supplies.

His territory, this; Jack again entered a complex equation into the lock on the outer area of the lab proper, after which he walked past the showers, the vacuum room, and the ultraviolet-light room into the main area of the level four, hot-containment lab, where he breathed deeply in relief.

Close. He was close. He heard the sigh of little Baxter's last breath, Lila's final words of apology. *What, Lila? What? You did me no wrong.*

No, it was always the other way around. I wanted you, but I caged you in, so callously, so unfairly.

He went directly to the refrigeration unit ahead and keyed in the ultimate set of numbers.

"What're you doing?" asked Chasen, nervous now just as Jack had grown calm, almost relaxed, over the impending outcome.

"A refrigerator, but I use it as a safe. Everything's in here." He took a test tube from its rack and dropped it clumsily. Accidentally on purpose, of course, so that the pathogen-detection system would set off the alarm, and three dead men found themselves entrapped in absolute lockdown. There would be no going back.

This was the equivalent of a biological Chernobyl, except the general public would remain safe and never know. Did it matter if the authorities had to firebomb the lab to assure the most judicious outcome?

Chasen had his gun pointed straight at Jack. "You disappoint me, Mr. Man."

"Actually, I've done more than that." Jack found his way to his computer chair, where he slumped down. "I've just killed you." He looked toward the one the redhead had called Ivan. "Killed you both with a virus so virulent that no one survives it—even, or especially, the strong and the young."

Jack watched the redhead turn pale, then red, then, alternately, several shades of green.

"You must have an antidote, or you wouldn't have let it loose in here," shrilled the stranger who'd murdered Jack's dearest companions.

"Why would I want to live without my wife?" Jack asked him, incredulous. "Get used to the idea that the three of us are infected with one hundred percent certainty and will die in a matter of minutes or hours." Live without Lila and not exact his revenge? That had never been a possible option.

"Nooooo," spat out the stuttering Ivan.

"Yes, and with such horrible effects you won't want to live even as long as that." In fact, Jack felt his breath begin to catch.

Chasen's gun still pointed at the scientist.

"Go ahead and kill me," Jack said calmly. "You'll only spare me some of the suffering."

Ivan ran toward the door. "Too late," called out Jack. "We're in lock-down. The multiple airlock doors are all ten-inch steel and can't be pried open even with a crowbar. It would take you days to drill through, if that's even possible." The air supply was internally circulated—the microbes, too, were imprisoned here.

In a minute he heard Chasen and Ivan making feeble attempts in the outer area to drag open the door. Good luck to them.

Being almost dead took away much of the mystery that life's end holds for those still living, and all of the fear.

Jack had only one regret, one that made him sick with anxiety and terrible guilt, despite the uselessness of such emotions. He had infected Lila with a virus, one just strong enough to make her ill, to keep her home and by his side.

He never meant to make her quite as sick as she'd become.

He slid down to the floor and stretched out full length. The great thing about being in such miserable physical shape was the fact that it wouldn't take him long to die.

All he'd wanted was to keep his beautiful wife contained, a sort of biological detention that she would neither understand nor violate.

Was that love, true love? "I love you, Lila."

Given enough time, he could have forced the secrets from this other, most-dreadful Marburg virus and created a vaccine that would have eventually saved lives.

It was extremely hot in here. His blood had already started to boil, and his mind began to drift… toward Lila, who was waiting for him.

It's all right, darling. You did nothing wrong. She would say that to him, and he to her.

Sampson Home For Girls

by Jordan Elizabeth Mierek

December 29, 1925

Wind crawled through the window Henrietta had left open, fluttering the lace curtains. Snowflakes danced into the dorm room to settle over the rug on the center of the floor. White covered the intricate, Oriental pattern. Her mother had owned that rug. Henrietta could remember lying beside her on it in the front parlor, listening to the fire crackle and her mother's rhythmic voice as she read aloud from *Uncle Tom's Cabin.*

They'd never gotten to finish it.

The novel sat above the dorm room hearth with a ribbon poking from the middle. The photographs of her parents rested on either end of the wooden shelf, along with the picture of Henrietta and her brother seated on the front steps of the boarding school. He had his arm over her shoulders, both of them grinning. She blinked back tears. He'd promised her the Sampson Home for Girls would be the best, the safest place.

How he'd been mistaken.

Henrietta swung her legs off the bed with its maroon coverlet and padded to the window in her stockings. Below her stretched the Adirondack woods; the trees, naked of leaves, shone with layers of snow and ice. Beyond them lay the village, where smoke coiled upwards from chimneys. The lake glistened as if covered with diamonds.

The road might be passable as soon as the sun crept higher into the cloudless sky. She could make it if she bundled up enough.

She pushed the window up higher. Frigid air slapped her cheeks as she studied the north wing bedrooms opposite from hers. Each window was dark, empty. Shut. No one moved beyond the glass. Snow, inches deep, covered the furniture on the porches. Footprints from yesterday filled in as if no one except ghosts walked the grounds.

Henrietta chewed a strand of her ginger-colored hair. What if she was a ghost, trapped forever within the brick walls, alone?

How long before someone ventured to the boarding house? Normally, the servants went into town every Monday for supplies. If no one went, the villagers might come looking. She could survive alone for a week. It might be safer than being plucked off the road by a wolf or bear.

Her brother wouldn't come for her until July, their summer holiday.

The mansion moaned as the wind blew harder. Snow melted through her socks to nip her feet.

Something else moaned, too.

Henrietta froze. Could there be another survivor?

A girl called through the hallway, her voice high pitched and whiny. "*She* did it. She'll do it again. Can't stop her. They'll kill us all."

Henrietta stared at the bedroom door as the girl's cries grew louder.

Maria. How had Maria gotten out? The headmistress had sent for the authorities.

Henrietta's room didn't lock; few of the doors did. She glanced at her brass bed, the dresser, and her wardrobe. The desk. The nightstand. All seemed too heavy for her to use to block the entrance; she wouldn't be able to push them. Henrietta's heart pounded and her breathing quickened. Her lungs felt tight, a wheeze in them.

No, calm down. If she didn't, she might have one of the attacks the good doctor had diagnosed as asthma. Henrietta gripped the window frame with her trembling hands.

The floorboards outside her door creaked and fingernails scraped over the wood near the brass handle.

"Anyone left?" Maria cackled.

July 1, 2010

Marissa stretched her legs beneath the table and drummed her fingertips against the top. The hazelnut coffee in her pink ceramic mug vibrated. Everyone else in the living room guzzled their drink as if hazelnut-flavored anything wasn't the foulest concoction. Not only did Marissa hate coffee, but nuts made her feel sick. Not allergic sick, just gross sick. Why couldn't it have been at least French vanilla?

She chewed a strand of her hair and wished she could taste the ginger in its color.

"Funerals are normally held the week the person dies," her mother said.

Marissa glanced up from glaring at her mug. Her mother was on her second cup and still chugging. Disgusting.

"I still think we should wait until all of the family is here," Marissa's uncle insisted. His gray beard jiggled as he moved his jaw. Some cake crumbs clung to the wiry strands. The cake, too, had been hazelnut. "They should be home by the first week in August."

They—his wife and two sons. Marissa's aunt was from Germany. Every summer she visited her parents for a month and took her kids along for an adventure of quaint villages and sauerkraut.

Marissa peered at her dad, the other occupant of her uncle's living room. Her father hadn't touched his coffee. At least she wasn't the only one to find it revolting.

He coughed into his fist. "We could start planning everything. We'll have the service at the Presbyterian Church. The reception can be at a café, or in one of our houses."

Marissa hoped it wouldn't be in her uncle's living room. He might serve more coffee.

"We'll have her cremated," Marissa's mother said. "She left enough money in her will to cover the expense."

"A small stone." Her uncle nodded. "Aunt Henrietta never wanted anything fancy."

"I have the boxes from the nursing home in the car," Marissa said. When she'd visited her great-aunt, she'd never thought about how little Henrietta had: the clothes in the wardrobe, stuffed animals on the bed, black-and-white photographs on the walls, and the small television on the nightstand. The nurses had packed everything into two cardboard boxes.

"Henrietta was such a sweetheart," the female nurse had said. "She never had a rude thing to say to anyone."

"Poor thing never said much of anything," the male nurse had added.

Thinking back, Marissa couldn't remember her great-aunt ever saying more than a few words.

"See what you think we should keep," her mother said. "We can take the clothes to the Salvation Army." She rested her hand on Marissa's shoulder. "Maybe you can put together a collage from the old pictures for us to display at the funeral. There are more in your grandfather's things."

"Sure." Marissa grinned. "Leave it to the history major to play with old photos." Maybe she could find something interesting for her thesis.

Marissa laid the dollar-store poster board on her bedroom floor. She'd gotten the biggest sheet of black they had—black would bring out the photographs more. White tended to make them appear washed out and more faded.

She wrote 100 YEARS across the top using a marker. Few people lived that long, but Henrietta had made it before passing in her sleep. According to the nurse at the nursing home, Henrietta had told her, the night before she died, that Maria had come to visit. Probably someone from her childhood.

Her grandfather's photos were kept in albums, but great-aunt Henrietta had hers in a tin cigar box. Marissa lifted a handful. The edges were torn and wrinkling, but most of the images were still legible. She flipped over a picture of a woman holding a baby and read aloud, "Mother and I, 1911." Henrietta would've been a year old.

There were more photos of Marissa's grandfather and Henrietta as children. He'd been ten years older, so in most of them, he held her on his lap or clutched her hand.

As Henrietta aged, she became the sole focus. Teenage Henrietta stood beside a car. She leaned against a tree in the woods. She sat in a boat on a lake.

She held a door open at a large establishment. The same establishment, with tower rooms and four stories, surrounded by a forest, was in most of the older pictures.

Marissa dumped out the box. Henrietta hadn't kept any modern photos. The final ones had been of that building. She flipped them over and read aloud, "Sampson Home for Girls." The dates, written in pencil in the lower corners, ranged from 1920 to 1925.

"Mom?" Marissa wandered into the kitchen where her mother arranged flowers in a crystal vase. "What was the Sampson Home for Girls?" She held up a photograph of Henrietta sitting on the front steps beside a young man. The back labeled him as Henrietta's brother, Marissa's grandfather.

"Hmm." Her mother glanced at it. "Oh, right. It was a boarding school in the Adirondacks. Henrietta went there after their parents died."

"They were orphans?" Marissa frowned. No one had mentioned that.

"She was ten and my father was twenty. Their parents passed in an automobile accident. My father was already working at the bank. He kept the house, but he thought Henrietta should be around women. She agreed to go to Sampson during the winters. Lots of wealthy orphans went there. Think of it as the school's specialty."

"No other family?" Marissa studied the smiles in the photograph. Henrietta leaned against her brother's shoulder and he had his arm around her. They both laughed. According to the date, 1921, Henrietta would have been there a year.

"Their parents were the only ones to emigrate here from England. Henrietta didn't want to go all the way there. She was still only a child."

"She never mentioned it." Then again, Henrietta hadn't said more than pleasantries. *How are you? Lovely weather.*

"I only knew from my father. At first, she loved it there, but something happened to change that, so he brought her home. Hired a tutor."

"What happened?" All of the photographs of the home had appeared pleasant.

"He never said. I suppose she lost a friend. Young girls can be touchy. Maybe had a falling out with another resident. Perhaps she didn't do well on some exams."

Henrietta had never married. She'd lived with her brother until he'd died from a severe asthma attack and she went into assisted living.

When Henrietta's asthma had worsened, she'd been transferred into the nursing home section of the facility.

"You'd think she would've mentioned this at least once." It must have been a major part of her childhood.

Her mother shrugged. "Henrietta was a very private person."

Marissa grinned. "I know what I'm going to do for the photo collage. I'll take some modern pictures of the school to compare and contrast."

Her mother set the vase on the windowsill over the sink. "I'm sure it's not still there."

"The ruins might be." The poster would be creative and historical. Sampson Home for Girls could even work for her master's thesis.

"It's in the Adirondacks, over an hour away."

"I'll make it a weekend trip." Marissa returned to her bedroom and read the photograph backs until she found one that told her the name of the town: Sampson, New York. Duh. She laughed to herself as she Googled the location.

Sampson, New York, was an hour and fifteen minutes away. She found a little motel on Sampson Lake that rented rooms for seventy dollars a night.

Nothing mentioned an old boarding school for orphans, though.

Marissa turned onto Apple Street and headed into Sampson. Quaint shops lined the roadway: bakeries, furniture stores, cafes, and a bookseller with a polka-dot awning. Visitors wandered the sidewalk, chatting to each other and licking ice cream cones. Marissa stopped her Subaru at the light and glanced at the map she'd printed off the internet. The Snow Pine Motel would be on her right, up another block, beside the lake.

The street light turned to green and she eased into traffic until she turned into the parking lot for the motel. The one-story building made a horseshoe shape. The brown paint matched the shingles, and each door had a cement patio with two green Adirondack chairs. Two little boys ran across the mowed lawn with Spiderman kites fluttering above.

Marissa parked outside the main entrance and headed inside. A stuffed bear stood on its hind legs beside the front desk, its claws outstretched and mouth open in a snarl. She shuddered. Animals from taxidermists reminded her too much of death.

The teenage girl behind the counter looked up from her magazine. "Hello. What can I do for you?" She toyed with a silver oval locket hanging around her neck. How cool. Lockets seemed so historical.

"Reservation for Marissa Etienne."

The girl called it up on her computer. "I still have your credit card in the system from when you called last week, so you can pay with that tomorrow at checkout or with cash." She slid a key on a plastic tag across the maple desk. "You're in room 18. You can rent a row boat here and I also have brochures about the hiking trails."

Marissa tucked the key into the pocket of her jean shorts. "Thanks, but I'm actually here looking for the Sampson Home for Girls."

"The what?" She blinked.

Marissa opened her purse and pulled out the envelope of photographs. She shifted through until she found a clear shot of the boarding school. "This place. My aunt used to go there in the 1920s."

The girl held it up. "Oh, that old place. It's off in the woods. You can't drive there anymore."

Marissa's heartbeat picked up. She'd pictured it as boarded up, abandoned, forgotten, but on a main road. "I don't mind a good walk."

"Like, it's practically impossible. She handed the photo back. "Sorry."

Maybe she meant it was off limits to tourists. "I'm studying it for my master's thesis." That should earn special points.

The girl shrugged. "Check at the library. They do a lot of history things, so they might know something." She pulled a town map from under the desk. "It's here." She pointed at a cartoon building. "I'll ask my brother about it too. Sometimes people go up there at Halloween. I think he's gone once."

"Thanks." Marissa folded the map in half. "I bet its fun at Halloween. Empty hallways. Holes to let wind whistle through."

"Plus, it's haunted."

"Isn't every old building?" Marissa chuckled. People liked to make ghosts from the simplest shadows.

"It's really haunted." The girl frowned. "Everyone died."

The hairs on Marissa's arm lifted. "Huh?"

"That's why they closed it. Someone poisoned everyone there."

December 30, 1925

Sheriff Daniels kicked the double front doors of the Sampson Home for Girls. The lock snapped and they swung inward. Snow blew in around him, whirling through the hallway.

A girl lay slumped beside the main stairs. Her chin rested on her chest and her arms hung limp. Frothy vomit covered the front of her red dress. Her brown hair stirred in the wind and he thought he caught a glimpse of her unseeing black eyes before the curls hid them again.

One of the asylum workers whistled from behind him. "What in the name of..."

"Heck," the other worker muttered, "She's dead, ain't she?"

Sheriff Daniels tucked his gloved hands into his jacket pockets. When the two men from the state mental asylum had told him no one answered at the school, he hadn't believed them. Someone was always here. The girls were orphans, and even though they were wealthy, few went home at the holidays. There were school workers and the headmistress, who lived in Sampson year round.

"Dead as a door nail," Sheriff Daniels whispered. He lifted his voice. "Hello?" The word bounced back.

"Witchcraft," one of the workers said. "Ain't natural to live way out here in the middle of nowhere."

"No witches." Sheriff Daniels drew his baton and edged down the hallway. The air stank of death—he recognized it from the time the old hunter got trapped in his shack in a snowstorm.

He stopped in the first doorway, which opened into the ballroom. He'd visited for the early December Christmas pageant every year since the school opened. Instead of girls dressed alike in green velvet gowns, he found a servant lying on her belly with vomit around her face.

Sheriff Daniels steeled his nerves. When he was home, he could break down. Now, he had to stay stiff. Emotionless. There might be a killer, but he would have to check for survivors before summoning reinforcements.

With the asylum workers at his heels, he scoured the boarding school. Most of the girls were dead in the dining hall with half-eaten bowls of oatmeal on the table.

"Something in the food," he guessed aloud. If it were spoiled, though, they would be sick, not perished.

In the library, a girl sat in one of the velvet, high-backed chairs. She wore a blue dress with a high collar and white lace around the black buttons. Blood stained the cotton cloth, and dried smears covered her cheeks. Her red hair puffed around her face. She'd covered her lap with a quilt, and she failed to look up from the book in her lap.

Sheriff Daniels sighed through his teeth.

"Witch," an asylum worker said.

The sheriff glared at him before crossing to the girl. She kept reading, her lips moving silently along with the words printed on the pages. She was probably in shock.

"I'm Sheriff Daniels." He stopped in front of her chair. "Are you hurt? Is that blood yours?"

She slid one hand off the book to clutch the locket hanging around her neck. Her lips stilled, but her gaze remained on the novel. He lifted it from her hands slowly to avoid startling her. *Uncle Tom's Cabin*, the pages bent and the spine worn.

"Do you know what happened here?" He closed the book and crouched in front of her.

"I hate oatmeal," she whispered. "Maria always eats mine."

"Do you know where Maria is?"

She shook her head. A tear slid down her cheek, leaving a trail in the blood. "What's your name?" He rested his hand on her leg, careful to keep the touch light. Fatherly. She couldn't be much older than his fifteen-year-old son.

She shifted her gaze to an open door in the back of the room. "Henrietta."

July 8, 2010

"Brandon Daniels." The man unlocked the display case in the rear of the

Sampson Town Library. "You could say my family founded this town. We've been here since the 1700s. Fought in the Revolutionary War. I'm an honorary S.A.R.—Sons of the Revolution."

Marissa nodded. She'd learned about the S.A.R. in one of her history classes. "It should be called Daniels Town, then." She meant it as a joke, so she laughed, but he frowned.

"The Sampson family was here even longer." He looked to be in his early thirties, probably about ten years older than she was. Black hair hung to his shoulders, and he wore a plaid button-up shirt with green jeans.

Brandon lifted the largest photograph from the display case and handed it to her. "Careful. It's old."

The photographer had captured a panoramic view of the Sampson Home for Girls. The windows seemed to sparkle, and she could almost picture the bushes flowering around the veranda. "Wow."

"That was taken when the home first opened. 1915. Mr. Sampson had just died from what they referred to as consumption, and Mrs. Sampson needed a way to keep the house. Her husband's family had built it in the early 1800s."

"They were rich." Marissa handed the photograph back. "Anyone who owned such a gigantic house would have to be. Do you know how many rooms?"

"Over one hundred. The ballroom was famous in the community. Even before it became a boarding school, people rented it for functions. The village held elections there every year."

"Not enough money to keep the lifestyle Mrs. Sampson wanted?"

"Her husband was a bit of an infamous gambler." Brandon Daniels relocked the display case. "The teacup is from there. The Sampsons had their own china pattern. See the lily of the valley in a heart painted around the outside?"

Marissa nodded. It was outlined in gold, and the pattern decorated the saucer as well. "Beautiful."

"They had it on every door, and every girl who went to the school was given a locket with her name engraved on the back and the heart-flower on the front. Mrs. Sampson encouraged them to keep pictures of their parents inside. From what I can understand, she'd been orphaned as a child and knew what it felt like."

"That's a wonderful mission." Marissa had heard horror stories of historical orphanages. Henrietta's photos of the home had looked peaceful and cozy—a way for the girls to heal and mature.

"Mrs. Sampson kept tutors for languages and for the arts—music, painting, drawing, gardening. She also made sure they learned manners and the usual subjects such as reading and writing."

"And arithmetic?" Marissa grinned. "I'm glad my great-aunt got to go there. It must've been really hard for her when her parents died."

"Death affects the rich and the poor." Brandon Daniels moved on to the next display case. "These are local postcards. We only have that one from the home." It was another photograph of the mansion, with "Sampson's Home for Girls 1923" printed across the top.

Marissa bent to study the details. "What happened to it? The girl at the motel said everyone was poisoned."

Brandon scratched his head. "My great-grandpa was the one who actually found everyone dead, and my grandfather was one of the men who helped remove the bodies. Far as anyone can figure, someone put arsenic in the morning oatmeal."

Marissa gasped. She hadn't expected actual murder, or that everyone had literally died. She'd assumed the motel clerk had exaggerated. "Why would someone do that?" Bile rose in her throat. Her great-aunt might've been poisoned.

"They probably had a rat problem and someone wasn't careful enough."

"How many people survived?"

"They found eight girls and the gardener. After that, the town boarded the place up. A couple years ago, some paranormal investigators went up there. They didn't find anything, but the local news channels hosted the special. I think the actual documentary was on some reality show about ghost hunters."

"Can we go there?" Marissa realized her hands trembled, so she clasped them behind her back. "I'd love a picture of the place."

Brandon glanced out the library's front picture window. "It's a really overgrown trail through the woods."

"I can go change into jeans and sneakers." When she'd put on her shorts and sandals that morning back home, she hadn't expected a hike.

"It's town property, but it should be okay as long as we're careful and don't hurt anything. Meet me back here in an hour?"

Marissa held out her hand. "Thank you, on behalf of me and my great-aunt.

He shook it. "And your curiosity?"

"That, too."

Marissa stumbled over a root. Her legs ached as if they'd caught fire. She paused to lean against a maple tree and stretch her calves. She might visit the gym every Friday evening, but she'd never trekked through the woods for an hour straight. It was taking almost as long as it had taken her to drive to Sampson.

"Almost there." Brandon took a swig from his water bottle. "You don't think it'll be morbid to compare your aunt's picture from back then to the way it looks now? Like, this place is dead and so is she?"

Marissa swatted a horsefly off her neck before it could bite her. "It's symbolic. Time keeps moving and nature takes over. The dust-to-dust thing."

"Don't be too disappointed. It's a real dump now."

They followed the "path" onward, up the slight mountainous incline. It had been the only road from the Sampson house to the village, but without upkeep, weeds had grown over the dirt and gravel. The only things to guide their way were the ancient trees on either side. Saplings grew up the middle, but the tall ones remained where they had thrived for centuries.

At the end, the mansion rose up from the woods. The four stories were still intact, but with holes in the roof and broken windows. Vines crawled up the brick sides. One of the towers had crumbled.

Marissa rubbed her arms, suddenly cold. Perhaps Brandon had been right. This did seem like an eerie location, something meant to be forgotten. It wasn't just an abandoned building. Innocent people had died here.

"We can go in a little ways." Brandon pushed through a bush toward the front steps, stones pressed into the hill. "Kids come up all the time around Halloween."

Her sneakers crunched over the debris of sticks and decaying leaves. Weeds caught on her jeans as if pulling her back. "It seems wrong that no one ever found out who put the arsenic in the food."

"Detective work wasn't very high tech back then." He led the way up the crumbling stone steps.

"Hang on." She pulled her camera from her purse, slung it over her shoulder, and snapped a picture of the mansion's entrance. Despite the weathered state, it would be the same angle as the photo of Henrietta and her brother. Marissa pictured girls running around the house, laughing, with their skirts fluttering. Okay, so maybe it wasn't considered ladylike to run back then, but they would've taken strolls around the grounds. In Henrietta's pictures the land appeared well kept, with trimmed bushes and flower patches.

Brandon pushed the front door open. The hinges squealed, and the door only opened a few feet before it stuck.

"Not locked?" She lifted her eyebrows.

"Sheriff broke the lock when he barged in. No one ever paid to get it fixed."

"No wonder people come in here." Her shoes squeaked against the floor. The hardwood had warped. Water spots covered the ceiling and paint peeled off the walls. Someone had smashed the hallway table. Pieces of a vase lay amongst the remains, reminding her of her mother's handiwork with flowers at home.

Each room held the same state of disrepair. More peeling paint. Holes in the walls. Mice and rats scampering across the ruined wood floors. Faded, threadbare carpets remained as evidence of a glamorous life.

"It feels like a tomb," Marissa whispered. Every noise bounced back to them, from the birds twittering in the rafters to the wind rushing through nooks.

The reception hall had caved in and someone had written RAGE across the floor in the ballroom. The chandelier lay smashed in the middle of the room.

"I see what you mean about the symbol." Marissa pointed at a heart-flower carved above the dining hall doorway. "It's over every room."

"Let's not go in there." He continued down the hallway. "I hate thinking about how so many people died in there."

Marissa shuddered, leaving the shut door alone.

"This is my favorite room," Daniel said when they entered the library. Floor to ceiling shelves lined the walls. "By the time my grandfather brought me here, the books were already ruined, but I always imaged curling up in here." He pointed at one of the high-backed chairs where someone had left a crumpled quilt.

"Too bad they can't build this into a hotel or something. It seems like such a waste."

"It's too far gone to be repaired now." Brandon sighed. "I'll show you some of the bedrooms upstairs. I've almost never gone to the second floor. Too many holes to fall through."

Marissa nodded toward a door in the back of the library. "What's through there?"

"I think it was the headmistress's office."

As Marissa wandered across the library, it felt as though people watched. Ghosts held their breath. She giggled. Ghosts didn't exist, and even if they did, they didn't still breathe.

She peered into the little room. Decaying, yellowed papers covered the floor as if they'd blown off the desk. The chair had toppled and someone had thrown a porcelain tea set against the wall, the broken pieces scattered.

As she turned to leave, she noticed a painting over the door. Someone had spray-painted a red line across it, but the image beneath still shone through. A woman in a high-collared black dress held a baby. Two little girls in matching black dresses stood at her side. Marissa snapped a picture of the elegance, set against the cracked, watermarked ceiling and peeling, white walls.

"Know who that is?" she asked when Brandon joined her.

"Mrs. Sampson. See the mole on her chin?" He tapped the cleft in his chin where the woman in the painting had a mole the size of a penny.

"We have some photos of her in the library. Those are her daughters."

Marissa's stomach cramped. "Were they here when it happened?"

"No, they died with her husband. Tuberculosis. We have a photograph of them too."

Marissa blinked away tears. That poor woman. She'd lost her family and then tried to help orphans, only to have an accident—or murder—ruin the rest of her life.

She took a step back and her heel felt something beneath the rug. Marissa used the toe of her sneaker to move a corner of it, revealing a locked trapdoor. "What do you think that went to?"

"Storage maybe? I'm sure there was a cellar for storing food."

Marissa crouched to take a picture of the metal lock. If Mrs. Sampson had gone to the trouble of locking the trapdoor, it probably was for storage. Maybe she'd kept confidential records in there. It would be cool to fish them out, but time would've ruined them.

Brandon led the way up the main stairs. "The other ones have too many holes. These were built the strongest, so they're still safe."

Someone had drawn a pentagram on one of the bedroom floors. Another bedroom contained empty beer cans. Graffiti marred the walls.

Marissa fished the envelope of Henrietta's pictures from her purse and flipped through them while Brandon held her camera.

"This one's from the ballroom." Henrietta stood on the stage holding a wreath. Marissa flipped the photograph over. Christmas Pageant, 1924.

"Most of them were taken outdoors," Brandon observed.

"This one's in a bedroom." Henrietta sat on a bed between two girls. They seemed to be working on a quilt. She read the back. Maria, Henrietta, Norma. 1925. "Their names all ended in an A. That's cool."

"Let's wander around the outside. I bet you can get some great shots. Tonight I'll make some phone calls and maybe you can do some interviews tomorrow."

"Oh?" She tucked the pictures away.

"The nurse and the gardener stayed in town even after the place closed. I can see if their descendants have any information you can use."

"Wow, thanks!" She almost hugged him, but realized how odd that would seem from a stranger.

"No problem. I've always felt like this was my town, so I like all this history stuff."

Marissa took one last glance into the nearest bedroom and wondered which one had been Henrietta's.

When they returned to the library, Brandon worked on filing at the circulation desk and Marissa settled at one of the three computers in the back. She Googled paranormal investigators and ghost hunter TV shows until she found the one that had studied the building. She took her iPod from her purse and plugged the headphones into the computer so she could listen to the episode online.

The team of five males and two females, one of them a psychic, explored the mansion, including the cellar and upper floors. They set up video cameras and walked with EMF readers. When they played back the footage, they caught a white glimpse in the dining room, which they claimed to be a ghost. Marissa had a feeling it was more a trick of the light.

The EMF readers danced around every corner, but Marissa wasn't sure how accurate they were. She'd never researched how to hunt for ghosts.

The psychic claimed to feel hands pulling on her and said she sensed girls in every room.

"I can feel one of the girls the strongest here," the psychic said from the little room off the library. "She's scared and afraid she'll die. She said that someone is suffocating her with a rag. It's someone she trusts."

Marissa shivered. She'd been in that room about two hours ago, but she hadn't sensed anything apart from the eerie stillness.

"When I first came in, it felt as though someone had pushed me," the psychic added. "It was as if the entity wanted me on the floor."

The team had also caught some "spectral" noises on their tape recorders. Most of the sounds reminded Marissa of wind howling or floorboards creaking, but one made the hairs on her arms stand up.

It distinctly sounded like a little girl crying out, "Mrs. Sampson wants to replace us!"

December 29, 1925

Doors slammed against the walls in the hallway. Maria cackled, lifting the hairs on Henrietta's arms. She fought down her asthma. *Calm. No panic.*

"Come out! You can," Maria screamed. "We won't be safe. Never be safe."

Henrietta's bedroom door burst open and Maria staggered inside. Blood dripped from her hands. She'd curled her fingers into claws.

"Never safe!" Her voice rose in a piercing wail.

Henrietta grabbed her stylus off the desk where she'd been doing her calligraphy class work. "Get back!" The point would be sharp enough to pierce skin if she drove it into Maria hard enough.

"Henri, I know you love me." Maria grabbed the doorknob to swing it. "I'm not crazy. She's lying. She knows I know." Her green eyes softened. "You're my best friend."

"Maria," Henrietta wheezed. "No one's going to hurt you. They're going to help you."

"Mrs. Sampson wants to kill me." Maria slapped her hand against the wall leaving a print in blood. "I saw what she did to Norma!"

"You're just sad. We're all sad, but Norma had to go home." The day their other best friend had returned to her grandparents in Connecticut, Maria had started raving. The nurse had given her a calming tonic, but Maria had become violent, so Mrs. Sampson had locked her in the closet downstairs and sent for state aid. The mental institute would have to take her.

Henrietta blinked away tears. Ever since she'd arrived at the Home, Norma and Maria had been her constant companions. Now, she'd lost them both within the same week.

"At least Norma got better," Henrietta whispered. Ever since Norma's grandparents had sent word that, now that she'd turned sixteen, she would return to their house to stay, Norma had suffered stomach pains. They'd passed the day she left, but Mrs. Sampson kept everyone away from her in case it was contagious. They'd had to send Norma farewell letters instead.

"Norma is dead!" Maria fell to her knees and dragged her hands across her cheeks. "Listen. You'll believe me. I was visiting Norma. I wanted to say goodnight. I wasn't supposed to be there. It was too late. Curfew. Mrs. Sampson came in, so I hid under the bed."

Henrietta shook her head. Maria might do crazy things, but would she risk catching Norma's illness? "How did you hurt your hands?" Maria had lost her mind. Mrs. Sampson had told them.

"Mrs. Sampson took Norma into her office. The one behind the library. She put a rag over her mouth and killed her."

Henrietta lifted the stylus over her head. "Mrs. Sampson wouldn't have killed anyone."

"Then she stuffed her through a trapdoor. I saw her!"

"No. Maria, you need help. You're bleeding."

"I had to break though the closet door. One of the hinges didn't sit right." Maria laughed. "I wouldn't let Mrs. Sampson do that to you. You might be next. I put rat poison in the oatmeal. I killed her!"

Henrietta gasped. Could it be true?

"Everyone's dead. Everyone ate the oatmeal," Maria continued. Almost everyone. She'd skipped it and nibbled on toast. Other girls might have, too.

"Listen to me." Maria lunged at Henrietta.

Screaming, Henrietta rammed the stylus into Maria's chest and shoved her toward the bed. Her friend's gasps haunted her footsteps as she raced through the open door and down the hallway.

"Henri!" Maria's staggering cries nipped at her.

Henrietta turned at the end of the hall and shoved open the door to the porch. In her battered state, Maria might not be able to follow her down the fire escape. Snow soaked through Henrietta's socks and weighted the hem of her dress.

No, the snow was too deep. It slowed her as she wove around the furniture to get to the metal stairs.

"Henri." Maria seized her arm.

Henrietta screamed, whirling away. Her back hit the wooden railing. She grabbed it, but felt herself falling. Maria clung to her, blood dripping from her chest, evidence of the stylus wound.

Then, Maria's bleeding hands slipped off. Her mouth opened in a howl as she tumbled over the railing to fall three floors onto the cement patio at the entrance to the building.

June 9, 2010

Marissa awoke to find two voicemails on her cell phone.

"Hi, Marissa," her mother said as caller number one. "If you don't mind, I'd like to meet you in Sampson today. I thought about your poster and decided I'd like to see the Home in person. I looked through your grandfather's old things and I came across a few of Henrietta's. He had a pouch with her diary, a copy of Uncle Tom's Cabin, and a silver locket in it. Maybe you can add those things to the display. There was a paper pinned to the outside of the pouch that said 'Sampson things.' Anyway, call me when you get up. Love you."

Marissa leaned into the pillow of her motel bed and closed her eyes. The locket might be the one every girl had been given. She pictured it with a heart-flower on the front.

"This is Brandon, you gave me this number," said caller number two. "I spoke to the old nurse's family. They said we can meet them this afternoon. The great-grandson didn't know too much. The nurse had been home with her family that Christmas, but she always talked about three girls who'd gotten really sick when they found out they had to go home. On the day they left, they got well again, fast. She always thought it was strange. Let me know if you want to meet up before you head out." He left his cell phone number and hung up.

Marissa tossed the phone onto the foot of the bed. The voice from the ghost hunter episode lingered in her mind. When she closed her eyes, she pictured the trapdoor.

Before she left, she'd find out what was under there.

"Hey." Marissa waved at the same girl behind the motel counter. "I'm going to pay with the credit card."

"No problem." She typed on her computer before printing out a bill.

Marissa signed the paper and passed it back. As the girl leaned over, her locket caught the sunlight, illuminating the engraving of a heart-flower.

"That's really cool." Marissa pointed at it. "Is that from the Sampson Home for Girls?"

"I don't think so." The girl took it off and held it out. "It was my grandmother's. She gave it me when I was little. I have no idea where she got it."

Marissa turned it over and read the name on the back. Norma. Could the girl's grandmother have been Henrietta's friend? Marissa took out that picture for the girl to see. "Is this your grandmother?"

The girl squinted at it. "Her name was Norma, but she didn't look like that. I know she used to live in Connecticut before she bought a summer camp up here with my grandfather."

"Was she an orphan?"

"Nobody ever said."

Marissa snapped the locket open. On the right was a photograph of a man in a top hat. On the other side, a photograph of…Mrs. Sampson. The mole on her chin was unmistakable.

"Grandma said those were her parents."

Marissa frowned. "I thought Mrs. Sampson's daughters died of tuberculosis."

The girl took the locket back and snapped it shut. "I dunno. Grandma never talked much about the past. Oh, I asked my brother about the Home. He said you shouldn't go up there. It isn't safe."

"I'm only going to go one more time." Marissa pictured the hammer she kept in her car's emergency kit. "There was this really cool trapdoor I want to explore."

Marissa fit the pronged end of the hammer beneath the edge of the trapdoor and pushed down. The wood cracked, but it didn't budge. She held her breath, waiting for a ghostly hand to push her or a spectral voice to wail.

A crow cawed somewhere in the mansion and boards creaked with age.

She shoved the hammer in deeper and pushed harder. The wood cracked and the lock snapped. She pushed the trapdoor back. It slammed the floor in a fury of dust motes. A reek of damp earth and decay slapped her nose.

Marissa snapped on her flashlight and aimed it into the hole. A ladder led downward. Marissa lay on the floor to peer in deeper. The beam illuminated earthen walls and…cloth bundles. They leaned against the sides as if propped up.

A footstep sounded beside her, and Marissa jerked upright, screaming. She lifted the flashlight as her heartbeat quickened.

A young man stood next to her, wearing jeans and a stained T-shirt. He smiled, but the smile didn't reach his eyes beneath his glasses.

"Who are you?" Her breath wheezed. No, not an asthma attack. Why had she come alone? She should've waited for her mother or gotten Brandon.

"My sister called me from the motel," he drawled. "She's the receptionist there."

"Oh." Marissa sighed and pressed her hand over her racing heart. "Thank goodness; you had me scared for a minute there." He must have come to make sure she stayed safe.

"She mentioned you were looking at a trapdoor. That's the only one here."

"It's really cool. There's a tunnel under here." Marissa aimed the beam down. "Take a look."

"It's from the Underground Railroad. They used to hide runaway slaves."

Marissa's eyes widened. "Wow. How cool. No one mentioned that."

"Consider it family lore. My grandmother only told me. My parents and my sister wouldn't care. My dad owns the motel."

"Cool! Did your grandmother go here?"

He tucked his hands into his pockets. "The real Norma did."

"Huh?" Marissa stood and brushed broken plaster off her jeans.

"There was an orphan named Norma Smith who came here because her rich grandparents didn't want to bother with her. When they finally did want her back, Norma got really sick. Then she went home." He smiled wider. "Only, the real Norma didn't go anywhere. She's in that tunnel all wrapped up in muslin."

Marissa's stomach clenched and her hands trembled around the flashlight and hammer. Those cloth bundles. People?

"How?" Her airways felt tighter.

He leaned against the doorway, her only exit from the office. "Dear

Mrs. Sampson loved being rich. She'd been so poor before she got married. Then when her husband died, she lost so much. She wanted her daughters to have better lives, so she pretended they had died too. She called it tuberculosis, but even her husband didn't have it. A few drops of poison and he was gone. No one suspected she would have done it."

Marissa tried to laugh. Maybe it was all made up. "What a story." Her voice squeaked.

He shook his head. "My grandmother told me everything. Mrs. Sampson made her daughters dress as servants. None of the orphans noticed servants. They'd all come from well off families. Then, one girl had to go home. She'd been there so long, no one on the outside would really remember her. Mrs. Sampson poisoned her to put her in the infirmary. Then she offed her the night before her departure and her oldest took her place. She did that with the other two daughters too. My grandmother's real name was Joan."

"Your grandmother was okay with that?" Marissa rasped.

"Of course. She got a privileged life. She could keep in touch with her sisters. School buddies are encouraged to write to each other."

She gulped. What would he do now? Why had he told her? So she wouldn't report the bodies to the authorities?

He dove across the space to pin her to the wall, his hands clamped around her wrists. Marissa kicked at him, but he dug the toe of his hiking boot into her shin.

"Sorry you had to find out," he growled.

"Let me go! I won't tell anyone." Blurriness bit at her vision as her asthma worsened. The attack nipped at her.

She had to fight it off, had to stop him.

He dragged her toward the trapdoor. If he threw her down…

A gun went off. He yelped and shoved her away. Blood welled from a wound in his leg.

"What the…" He growled as a hand grabbed him by the collar of his shirt and knocked him through the open trapdoor. His body disappeared into the darkness.

Brandon tucked his pistol into his holster. "Are you okay? Marissa!"

She sagged against the desk, panting. "Why…how…?"

"I always carry a gun. Never know what animals you'll meet in the woods." He pulled his cell phone from his pocket and punched three buttons. "Yes, 911. This is Brandon Daniels. I have an emergency at the old Sampson Home for Girls."

"Marissa!" Her mother charged into the room to seize her daughter into a hug. "When I told Brandon you were already up here, he wanted to meet you. Why did you come alone? That man could've murdered you!"

Marissa kept gulping for air until her mother found her inhaler in her purse and helped her take it.

"Come outside with me." Her arm over Marissa's shoulders, she edged her out to the veranda.

Marissa paused on the top steps to inhale the crisp Adirondack air. Despite her blurry vision, she glanced back at the front door.

Three teenage girls stood in the doorway with linked arms.

A leaf blew across them and they vanished.

Mother, May I?

by Jenny Milchman

Maggie Ferris hated the snow. Her mother had died on a snowy day, which should've been reason enough. But in truth, Maggie didn't remember all that much about her mother. She did remember her mother kissing her goodnight, because her mother liked to kiss her on the nose, and the sound of her voice, although Maggie might've been thinking of TV moms more than her own. And she remembered one other thing, more like a detail from a dream, which indeed came back to Maggie in dreams on bad nights. It was the pond in back of their house, filling with red.

The reason Maggie hated snow was because it covered up the pond, which outside of her dreams wasn't red, but a place to collect frogs in the summer and slide on in the winter. When it snowed, all the cracks and fissures in the ice, the rotten spot over to the left, were hidden. Heavy, falling snow stopped her if she wanted to go out for a few minutes to get to where the lights of the living room couldn't shine.

"Maggie! Mags!"

Her father was sitting on the living room couch, the afghan her mother had knit parachuting down over his knees. *Parachuting.* Good description of the way the afghan poofed out, as if her father had just lifted it into the air. Reading was Maggie's favorite subject in school because of the words. Words that said one thing but meant another. Words that meant one thing but said another.

"Yes, Daddy?"

"The blanket got twisted," her father said in his cranky, querulous way.

Querulous. That was another good word. Maggie used to think it meant fearful, uncertain. Kind of like tremulous. But then she learned it meant almost the exact opposite. It was the argumentative tone her father got whenever something bothered him.

"I'm sorry, Daddy," Maggie said. "Looks like you got it straight."

She went to him anyway, and fluttered around, drawing the soft wool down, tucking the edges around her father's frail legs. For a while after her mother died he had still been able to walk slowly; now the meat on his bones was so wasted that he hardly moved at all. Nights he slept on this couch; days he spent sitting on it. Her father said he had some kind of disease named after a ballplayer named Lou something, which made no kind of sense to Maggie. A sports star had to run, not just walk. And whoever heard of a sickness that got called a man's name? When you got the flu, it wasn't like the doctor said, "Looks like you've got Harry." Besides, her father never went to a doctor. How would he even know what was wrong? Whenever Maggie heard rumblings in town—people talking as she left a store after doing her shopping—they were always saying that nothing was wrong with her father. And it *was* awfully strange that his sickness had started the very same day her mother died.

"Warm enough, Daddy?"

Her father gave a jerk of his chin. Then he lifted his head, like a dog scenting something.

"School bus," he said.

After a moment passed, Maggie heard the groan of the engine as the bus rounded the bend. Her father couldn't walk, but he could hear very well.

She checked that the tray on the table was close enough for her father to reach. She touched the coffee with one fingertip, and then blew on her reddened skin. Hot enough to stay that way for a while. Maggie trotted to the refrigerator and took out a sandwich wrapped in wax paper and a plate of fruit. If she removed these any earlier, they would spend too much time warming up before lunchtime. Her father was afraid of bacteria collecting, and from science class Maggie knew that was a real hazard, not like the sports-star disease.

She glanced out the kitchen window. As soon as the yellow tail of the school bus drew even with the porch, it would mean she had thirty seconds to get out, or the bus would leave without her.

Maggie slept in her clothes to save time in the morning. It took a while to attend to her father, set things out the way he needed. For a while she had tried sleeping in her coat and boots, but that was too uncomfortable.

No flash of yellow yet. Maggie snatched a box of muffins out of the pantry and dumped one on a plate. Coffee, sandwich, fruit, muffin. She took a last look around, satisfied. And then she remembered.

"Mags! The bus!"

The last time she'd served these muffins, her father had complained. They were the healthy kind and needed jam. "Dry as dust," he'd said, which wasn't a particularly good use of language. Mr. McCarthy would've called it a cliché.

Cliché or not, her father hadn't taken more than one bite of the gritty muffin—now *there* was a good word for it—which was what concerned Maggie now. If her father didn't eat breakfast, he would get even more shrunken. He might never walk again. He might even die.

She snatched a jar of jam from the cupboard.

The humped rear of the bus caught her attention, and the jam jar fell in a blistering pool around her feet. Some splashed up and spattered the jeans she'd slept in last night. The school bus doors sighed audibly, unless that was just the wind brushing against the snow.

Maggie was paralyzed, staring at the lake of red.

Paralyzed, a cliché.

Frozen, even worse.

The bubbles of jam hooked her eyes and she couldn't blink.

"Mags!" Her father's voice, suddenly strong. "You're gonna miss it!"

Maggie stooped down and scooped up a dollop of jam, edging it onto the muffin plate with her hand. The floor would have to wait. Not like her father would get off the couch and see the mess anyway. Maggie ran, setting the plate on the table in front of the couch at the same time she grabbed for her books.

"Bye, Daddy," she said breathlessly. "See you this afternoon."

She was still licking jam off her hand as she clambered up onto the bus.

Maggie fell asleep in class.

That happened a lot.

It was uncomfortable sleeping in her clothes. Winters were cold in Wedeskyull, colder and snowier than in other places; she knew that from books. And so Maggie had learned to wear layers, and that made rolling around in bed difficult. Plus there were her dreams. But mostly Maggie stayed awake because she was listening for noises downstairs. The couch was narrow, even for a man as slight as her father had become. What if he fell off? Or worse? It had been a long time since Maggie was able to believe, like most kids did, that parents lasted forever. Kids thought of parents as characters in a video game. They could be shot and get right back up again. Always there the next time the device powered on. But Maggie knew that wasn't so.

"Margaret?"

Mr. McCarthy was the strongest man she'd ever seen, with muscles like rubble all over him, but his voice was kind.

"Did you hear what I said?"

Maggie's mind rumbled. She rubbed sleep from her eyes—she'd really fallen deep—ignoring the kids who were taking out their cell phones and texting without looking to be sure the teacher was distracted.

"No after-school activities today. Everybody's to go straight home."

Maggie blinked.

"There's a...situation in town that the police are coping with."

Situation. The kind of word that gave no information at all. Maggie noted the time on the clock on the wall across the room. If everyone rode the bus instead of sticking around for their activities, then she would have less time than usual to fix dinner before she had to start getting things ready for tomorrow.

Mr. McCarthy gave a clap of his hands, which after a moment silenced the clicking and clacking of tiny keys.

"All right, everyone. Go home and talk about it on Facebook."

Maggie clomped snow off her boots on the porch, took a deep breath, and stepped inside. The house was warm. One time the furnace had busted—Maggie hadn't been able to think of an elegant word for *broken*; she still sometimes felt the cold claw of fear that had gripped her throat as soon as she had registered the temperature inside—and her father had lain shivering on the couch all day. Now Maggie made sure that her father's cell phone was always fully charged, even though service at their house was a little like how the kids at school acted toward her, on and off. She kept the landline by her father, too, though in winter that sometimes went out without their even knowing it.

"Mags?"

Maggie crept close. Sometimes her father said her name in his sleep.

"Bus had extra kids on it today. There was yelling when you got off."

Her father's amazing hearing again. "No band practice today and no hockey, Daddy," Maggie said. "The bus was full up."

She pulled the afghan up from where it had pooled around her father's legs, at the same time gauging the amount of food he had eaten, and the level of pee in the bottle.

"Why no band?"

When he wasn't being querulous, her father reminded her of a lizard, poking his head out, constantly checking on things that weren't there.

"I don't know, Daddy." Mr. McCarthy's words came back to her. "I'll go and see if I can find out." That would delay emptying the bottle, her most hated task. Before her father could say anything else, she added, "Then I'll make dinner. Spaghetti tonight."

"I don't like the brown kind."

Back to querulous.

Maggie had read that whole grains were important, but she said "I'll make white," and trotted upstairs.

Everyone was talking about the situation. It was hard to figure out what was really going on. Someone said that a murderer was on the loose, the kind of bright, transparent comment that got a hundred likes but no one really believed. But it did seem true that someone had escaped from the prison on the outskirts of Wedeskyull. That didn't worry Maggie overly much. What kinds of crimes did anyone commit up here? Stealing lift passes?

She typed, "The murderer's probably on the summit of Marcy right now," and instantly got four likes.

Then she went downstairs to fix dinner.

Maggie was heating water when someone knocked on their front door.

"Mags!"

Maggie came running. A visitor was an unusual enough occurrence that it might make her father struggle to get up, and if he did, he'd be shaky for hours.

She put her hand on the doorknob. For one crazy second, she thought it might be Mr. McCarthy, here to tell her father that he'd had to wake Maggie up in class for the fourth time this month.

She opened the door. The cold was a solid wall outside, though at least it wasn't snowing. A man pushed inside. The wind did most of the work closing the door.

The man was wearing the strangest outfit, orange pants and an orange shirt. No coat, which in winter up here was the same thing as trying to commit suicide.

Maggie turned around. Some things she couldn't do. Some things only her father still could. Like tell her who this man was and why he had come to their house.

"Mags?" Her father's voice didn't sound querulous now. It was thin, like his legs. "Do you have a big pot of water on to boil?"

Maggie frowned. Her father was doing the strangest thing with his hands behind the man's back. It looked like he was throwing something. Like a pantomime.

"Yes, Daddy." Then she figured it out. "You mean I should serve dinner? Is he staying?"

The man looked at her father. "I thank you for the invitation," he said. His voice sounded croggy, unused. He coughed, then said, "Why don't I help you with that big pot of hot water, little girl? I wouldn't want it to spill on anyone accidentally."

They ate around the table in front of the couch, after Maggie directed the man to pull up two chairs. Maggie's father's plate rested on his lap. The table was too small for three. Her father's knees were clacking with the tension of holding onto the plate. Maggie noticed spots of tomato sauce on her mother's afghan, and she ticked through the cleaning options in her mind. Options—a small but better word for possibilities. Cold water was the key to removing stains from wool.

The man who had come to visit cleared his throat and spoke for the first time since he had asked Maggie which bowl she wanted him to get down for the pasta. Might as well make use of a big, tall man to help her with the hard parts, the ones most eleven year olds would never be called on to do. Like Mr. McCarthy, this man was stony and humped with muscle. His voice wasn't kind, though.

"I'm going to need me a change of clothes."

Maggie looked up from the worm of noodle she was slurping.

Her father's eyes closed. "Upstairs. There's a dresser in the room at the back of the hall."

Maggie frowned. She could understand why the man would want to change out of his ugly, orange outfit. What she didn't get was why her father would be directing him to her parents' old room. Maggie had long ago brought all of her father's clothes downstairs. She kept them on top of the washer and dryer in the mudroom.

"No, they're not," she said.

The man looked at her. Then he looked at her father.

"They're in the laundry room."

Her father's eyes were still closed. "I thought—" His voice did a hiccup hitch. "I thought he might want something nice."

The man sat back in his chair, big fingers laced across his belly. "Well," he said, "that's mighty nice of you. To think about how I should look. My appearance, you might say." He turned to Maggie. "And that was a very nice meal."

Maggie didn't sit back in her chair. She leaned forward. "Who are you?" she asked.

The man stood, scraping his chair legs so loudly that Maggie jumped.

"Why don't you run and get me that change of clothes, little girl?" he said. "Then your father can tell you who I am."

Maggie walked upstairs slowly. Something nice. Did her father mean khakis, a button down shirt, the kind of thing he used to wear back when her mother was still alive and they went to church?

She opened up the closet door, greeted by a musty smell and a starry burst of dust. She pulled pants and a shirt from hangers, then turned and contemplated the dresser. Did the man need underwear, too, and socks? Certainly he needed a coat.

Maggie went back downstairs, clothes in hand. The man was standing before her father by the couch. From the feel in the air, she could tell they had been talking. She thought about the situation. Why didn't adults use words that told a kid anything? That was the good thing about books. What was in them was the same for everybody.

She held out her arms, and the man stepped forward. And then, to Maggie's complete and utter disbelief—no clever way to say *this*—he started to undress.

"Don't you want to use the john?" her father asked, still in that weebly voice.

The man looked up. He was shirtless. His chest had a rough mat of hair on it.

"Nossir," he said. "Think I prefer to stay right here. So I can hear in case you two get to talking." He said it as if eavesdropping on them was a perfectly normal thing to do. Then he busied himself with the buttons on the shirt.

Maggie looked down at her father.

His eyes were closed again. He didn't want to look at the man while he was dressing either. The man started tugging down his pants and Maggie spun around so fast she nearly fell.

"All right," her father was saying from the couch. "Why don't you go take a coat, the biggest and thickest, from the hall closet? Then you can be on your way."

Maggie started for the hall closet herself. She wanted to get there first. The biggest and thickest coat was her father's. If the man took that one, her father might never go outside again. She tugged open the door. "How about this one?"

She turned, holding out the jacket her father used to hike in, back when he'd taken hikes.

The man smiled down at her. "Now, that doesn't look very warm." He pulled a curtain aside and peered out into the night. "Cold out there."

"Maggie," her father said, and his voice carried all the way to the entry hall, "give the man my ski coat."

They used to ski too. The poles were still wedged in the closet. Maggie had to move them aside to get out her father's coat.

"Thank you kindly, little girl," the man said. "But I don't think I'll be needing that as of this moment. No one in their right mind would go outside tonight."

On the couch, Maggie saw her father lower himself back—which meant he had been trying to sit up.

"Who are you?" Maggie said again.

"Maggie," her father said quietly, "that isn't polite."

He hadn't called her *Mags* since the man had arrived, Maggie realized.

"I never was a big believer in that 'children should be seen and not heard' philosophy," said the man.

Philosophy, Maggie thought. Good word. He said it as if it were three words, though: *phil-oso-phy.*

"Go on and tell the little girl who I am."

Her father shifted on the couch. Maggie half-rose to help him, but the man spoke so loudly, she dropped back down in her seat.

"I said, tell her!"

Her father jumped. He didn't quite jump *up*, but his body bounced on the couch. It was the most Maggie had seen him move all year.

"Okay," her father said. "Okay. Maggie, this is..." He stopped. "He's..."

"I was a friend of your mother's," the man said, voice back to normal now, like a flat, untouched lake. Gray and depthless.

Maggie raised her head. She hadn't looked at the man much since he had first come in, but now she did. Would her mother have had a friend like this? With eyes full of crushed glass? Her mother's eyes—Maggie knew she wasn't getting this mixed up from television—had caressed you, like a silk scarf.

"A good friend," the man went on, as if sensing Maggie's doubt.

"Maggie," her father said, low, "go upstairs."

"Now, David," the man said.

So he did know her father.

"We were just starting to talk."

Her father's legs twitched beneath the afghan. Suddenly, he leaned over and pushed the blanket to the floor. When he sat back, his chest was rising and falling.

"Daddy," Maggie said. "Lie still."

"I think that would be best," the man agreed.

"You're wearing new clothes," Maggie's father said. "You have a coat. You don't want to squander the time."

Squander. To do away with unnecessarily.

"Haste makes waste," the man countered.

"Not in this kind of situation."

Maggie had no idea what they were talking about, but there was that word again. *Situation.* And suddenly she did want to go upstairs.

There were too many posts on Facebook to catch up with. Maggie sat at her computer, idly scrolling through the comment stream. Lots of complaints about having to miss hockey practice that afternoon. Lots of jubilation—if toneless voices on the screen could convey rejoicing—about choir rehearsal being cancelled and extra help with homework put off.

Maggie kept scrolling.

People had gotten back to the topic on everyone's mind.

Sux.

Anybody hear anything?

Another rectangle jumped out on the screen.

Just look for a man in a jumpsuit...

I know what I'm going as for next Halloween...

That was the word for that outfit. Maggie hadn't known it. Stupid, motherless Maggie, who didn't go to movies, or even watch that much TV, now that she had so many tasks to attend to for her father. The other kids knew things that teenagers did, and Maggie knew more than any of them, but so much less too.

The man downstairs had been wearing a jumpsuit.

The kind worn by men in prison.

He was the situation.

And they were his prisoners.

Pretend you don't know anything.

The words came to her in her mother's lilting voice, like a stream of ribbon candy.

Maggie sat back down.

What could she type that wouldn't get laughed off, or receive a dozen likes and no real attention before the next kid updated and eyes veered away?

The prisoner is in my house.

Someone had called him a murderer, and Maggie had immediately done what she didn't want anyone else to do right now: Assumed it was a joke, or at least an exaggeration. But what if they were right? What if this man had killed someone?

Send the police.

Like anybody would do that.

I know what happened. I know what's going on.

But she didn't have time to wait and see if anybody wanted to chat or ask her any questions. She had to get back downstairs. She had to check on her dad.

Maggie's hands flew across the screen, typing, deleting, as she collected her thoughts.

She settled on just one word.

Help.

Not one person liked it, nor typed a comment in return.

Maggie watched as the screen clock added a minute.

In this climate, silence, no response at all, spoke louder than anything.

Someone had seen what she'd written…and was deciding what to do.

Maggie had just started to head for the stairs when she heard voices. It was her father, speaking through gritted teeth as if he were in pain. "This is the first place anyone will look for you. I'm surprised the cops haven't been here yet."

Even having figured it out, having learned to trust herself more than anybody else, Maggie startled at having it confirmed.

"Road's closed," the man said.

Maggie looked out the hall window. She hadn't noticed it was snowing, which said something about her state of mind. She was always the first to realize when that choking, white veil started coming down. But indeed snow was falling in great, white sheets, the flakes so close you couldn't see night between them.

"Storm'll be your best cover," her father said.

"I don't need any cover."

Silence before the man spoke again, as if in answer to an unspoken question.

"I'm not going anywhere. Not without her."

Maggie's heart started up a soldier's march in her chest. She took a step backward, then one more.

"No," she heard her father say.

There was a hanging pause.

The man laughed. "Doesn't look like you'll be much good at stopping me."

A sudden loud scramble then, the sound of plastic skittering across the table, before Maggie heard a violent shatter.

Then a mean laugh. "Phones weren't working anyway. But I don't mind a little extra insurance. No way to call even after I take the little girl outta here."

"I'll—"

Another jagged burst of laughter. "You'll what? There's nothing you can do. Not now. And not then either."

"You murderous son of a bitch—"

And then came the sound of a great weight falling, and Maggie had to clap her hand over her mouth to keep from screeching. That was her father, and when she peeked over the rail, she saw half his body, just his torso, dangling over the sofa, arms extended helplessly toward the man's legs. The man stepped easily out of her father's reach.

"Let me help you back onto that couch."

The man bent down, repositioning Maggie's father.

Maggie wrenched her head around. The snow was a solid wall of white now. She wouldn't get far on the road, and the road would be the first place the man would go anyway.

But if she could get out back, she'd just have to cross the pond. Then there'd be plenty of hiding places.

The stairs went straight into the living room. In order to get to either door, she'd have to run right by the man. He was big. He'd just picked her father off the floor as if he were a broomstick.

And then she realized.

She didn't have to get by him.

She had to lead him.

If only her father would fall again. The man would be distracted for a second, lifting him up, and Maggie could make her escape.

Unless the man didn't lift her father this time.

Maggie settled on something more basic. She scuttled back into her room and grabbed two books off the shelf. Big, hardcover ones. Then she tiptoed back to the stairs, creeping down as many as she could without being detected. She was so intent that she caught only snatches of what the man and her father were saying.

"—never had any fight in you—"

"—she was my fight and you took her—"

Any closer to the bottom and Maggie would be seen, or else the stair would creak, or her shoes would be heard. Maggie raised her arms and hurtled the books as far as she could. She didn't hear the thuds until she was already halfway to the kitchen. But as she ran, she did glimpse out of the corner of her eye—what a cliché—the man taking a step in the direction of the noise, and her father rising to see.

Her father rising?

That was impossible, a trick of Maggie's fevered imagination.

She kept running toward the back door.

She didn't have her coat, of course. A shard of thought about not having a coat during an Adirondack winter came back to her. Suicide, she'd called it.

But the alternative was kidnapping by a murderer, presuming the kids at school were right. Who had the man killed?

She could hear the drum of boots behind her.

She grabbed for the door and slipped out, not taking time to yank it shut.

She ran for the frozen pond.

Snow was still coming down in great waves, and the ice was covered. But that didn't matter as much as Maggie had always feared. She knew the pond well enough to avoid the deep ruts that could trip her. And she knew where the rotten spot was, how thinly the ice lay over it. If only she weren't shivering so hard.

The cold had assaulted her instantly, giving her no time to get used to it. Her body was flapping like a sheet.

"Margaret!" the man roared.

Maggie halted, shoes slipping on the ice.

Nobody called her Margaret except for her teachers.

The man didn't look quite as big several paces behind her.

"Stop," he said. "Come with me."

Maggie walked backward now, not wanting to turn her back on the man. She was halfway across, which meant almost to the forest. Her boots cleared a trail in the snow, and she saw the pocked and opaque sheet of ice that held her up. She took another step, but the man was walking too now, closing the gap she'd managed to gain.

"Margaret," he said again. "You belong to me. That's how your mother wanted it."

Maggie's teeth were chattering so fiercely it was difficult to talk. "Yuh-you d-d-d-didn't know my mother."

The man's face split into a fractured grin that looked like it hurt. His eyes danced wildly in the night. "I loved her. We were going to be a family."

Maggie tried to control the shaking of her head.

There came a cry from far away. "Mags!"

Maggie whirled suddenly on the ice. She slipped and her bare palm raked across the rough surface, leaving a black streak behind. How had her father gotten to the kitchen?

"Don't believe him!" he shouted. "Your mother didn't want anything to do with him!"

His uncanny hearing at work again; he had heard the man's every word.

Then Maggie saw something that made her mind crack apart like small slivers of ice. Her father, taking herky-jerky steps toward the pond.

"Daddy?" Maggie tried to call. "Yuh-you c-c-c-can walk?"

Whatever response her father made didn't reach her. But suddenly time had gone still, frozen in place like the pond. Maggie was five and the water before her was turning red. Something was being dragged down the bank—no, it was someone, too awful for Maggie to see—and her father was running after, but he wasn't going to get there in time. And though Maggie hadn't known it then, that was the last time she would ever see her father take a step.

Until now.

Her gaze shot down to the pure and sheeting expanse of white around her.

The man was withdrawing something from his pocket.

A knife that he must've taken from their kitchen.

The kitchen where Maggie had cooked ever since her mother had died. Killed; she was killed, Maggie knew that now. After which her father got the Lou whatever-it-was disease. Only he didn't really have it, did he? Maggie knew that now too.

The man was starting toward her father, who wasn't going to be fast enough again. He stood so uncertainly that he canted forward.

Maggie let out a trembling yell. "Okay! I'll come with you!"

The man turned.

Maggie took one step sideways. She held out her arms, as if she needed help.

Where exactly did the snow sag, hinting at the sogginess beneath? A spring-fed soft patch in the ice that persisted despite winter's rough assault. She felt something give, just a little dip, before she snatched her foot away. And then she waited.

Stutter-stitched words emerged from her mouth. “We c-c-can stuh-still be a family.”

The man’s grin broke apart. He took a step, reaching for her.

Then another.

Maggie sidled as close to the rotten patch as she dared. The man kept walking. When the soft ice buckled and broke, his body torpedoed down with a soundless splash before the water whisked him away.

And Maggie’s father stumbled toward her.

Good Luck Lake

by W.K. Pomeroy

Even above the other scents in the cranberry bog, the too-familiar scent of decay assaulted Damir's nose. Before getting close, he knew it was not a doll or a dummy. The black, matted hair bobbing in and out of the water belonged to a decomposing human body.

He felt a strong sense of déjà vu when he said to himself, "Today started so well. This is not how today was supposed to go."

Damir took one final photo of the glorious reds, oranges, and yellows shimmering in the last reflected rays of the sunrise off misty Spectacle Lake and the smaller Dry Lake, both visible from the top of Good Luck Cliff. For a change, the local weather report had actually been right—it had been a perfect sunrise for taking pictures of the late-fall foliage. He turned to slip his camera back into his backpack when he noticed what some locals called a destroying angel, but Damir knew from his research as an Amanita bisporigera, growing out of the base of a dead tree behind him. Despite bad memories of someone using a different variety of Amanita to kill people this past spring, the morning dew dripping off the fungus was so beautiful he couldn't resist the urge to snap a few high-resolution pictures of it. After the final shot, where he could actually see the meniscus of the water bulging before it would break and fall to the ground, Damir began his climb down the mountain.

Looking down the first steeper section of the path he had climbed up in near darkness, an itch made him realize his headlamp was still strapped around his forehead.

The thought came into his mind that even for the much simpler climb up Panther Mountain, Bisera would not have been willing to come with him so early in the morning. He shook his head violently, removing the lamp and stuffing it into the right side pocket of his backpack. He didn't want to think about Bisera, yet as he climbed down the mountain he found himself picturing her. He wondered if she had kept her hair the same bright, bleached blonde it had been the last time he had seen her, or if she had changed it again for her American boyfriend, now that she had been with him in Boston for a few years.

Thoughts of her distracted him enough he half fell while scrambling down some steep rocks. His hip scraped on a small glacial boulder, but not enough to rip his faded jeans. He caught his balance at a small plateau directly across from a little cave. The hole in the stone looked like it would be a perfect resting place for a small bear.

Warm from the effort of climbing down, despite the early morning fall cool, Damir took off his jacket and tied its arms around his waist. Not taking all his attention from the hole in the rock, he took a bottle of water from his backpack and sipped at it.

More than six years it had been since Bisera left, and he still found himself thinking about her. He knew he had some obsessive tendencies; usually he made them work for him, rather than letting them become so distracting. Continuing down the mountain, he could feel burning in his thighs from using muscles for breaking his decent rather than climbing.

At the turn to the left, where he could go to the road or fork right over to Good Luck Lake, he heard what sounded like Bisera's laughter echoing up the path. Without even a conscious decision, he turned toward the lake.

Out on the cranberry bog, she jumped up and down, laughing and happy, obviously enjoying the springy feel of the thick, floating moss. He quickly realized she seemed younger than Bisera, probably not even twenty-five. Her blonde hair fell much further past her shoulders than Bisera's had when last he saw her. This girl's happiness felt contagious, and Damir allowed himself a controlled smile.

He had just decided not to interrupt her fun and to go back to his car, when she stopped laughing. Her footsteps made almost no noise as she ran over to the edge of the lake and started babbling, "Oh my god, oh my god, oh my god, oh my god…."

Damir realized he had moved toward her when he felt the bounce of the suspended bog beneath his feet. He stepped around a ragged hole in the surface to get close enough to her to ask without shouting, "What is wrong?"

If she was startled by his appearance, it did not show. She twisted her neck to look up at him and say, "Oh my god," one more time, then pointed at what looked like hair bobbing in the water, just off the edge of the bog.

Ten years and two days earlier, Nhat Huu Quan felt prepared to die.

He looked at the five cigarette burn scars on the back of his right hand in a pattern exactly like the number five on a standard six-sided die. In Vietnamese the symbol translated to, "Tu hai giai nuynh de." The English equivalent would be "One person, protected by a group of friends."

Nhat let his open hand fall to his side. Without making eye contact, his gaze shifted to the heavily muscled arm of Jimmy Li. An ebony panther tattoo curled around the bicep, tongue sticking out licking one red claw. Nhat didn't look around the dusty warehouse, or at the other four hard-core members of the Vee Boyz circled around him. He knew the others would use homemade weapons, except maybe Too Shy, who preferred to use his feet. Saito probably had that little blackjack of his. They would all hurt, but Nhat felt sure the brass knuckles wrapped around Jimmy's hand would do the most damage.

Jimmy flexed his arm making the panther ripple. "Ready?"

Nhat's deep nod seemed almost a deferential bow.

A kick hit the back of his knees. He stumbled forward without quite falling. Someone, probably Cam, whipped a bicycle chain against his left side, going right through the loose, hooded Syracuse University sweatshirt he bought in the secondhand store, hoping it would cushion some of their blows.

Nhat remembered thinking, *Too Shy hit first,* just before Jimmy's brass knuckles connected with the left side of his jaw. The cracking noise was followed by a crunching sensation under his skin; then nothing.

"Oh my god, it's a..., oh my god...." She didn't seem to be able to get her breath.

"Calm down." Damir's tone held steel reassurance. "What is your name?"

For a moment, a completely confused expression took control of the girl's face, like either the question or her name made no sense. Two more breaths brought sense back. "I'm Nadine."

"Nadine, it is nice to meet you, despite the circumstances. I am Damir."

She pointed out into the lake, everything from her shoulders down quivering with angst. "That's a, that's a...."

"Body," Damir finished for her. He let her take that in, and then continued. "My friend Aleksandra is coroner." He grimaced hearing his Bosnian accent slip out. "I vill call her now."

"OK." Nadine's trembling slowed a little.

Damir removed his cell phone from the clip on his belt. To avoid being interrupted while taking his photos, he had not turned it on after charging it the previous night. The reassuring power-up music told him his little skid down the rocks hadn't damaged it too much. His second relief occurred when he saw three bars of signal appear on his display. He found Aleksandra's number in his contacts and pressed send.

She answered on the fourth ring. Her throat had the dry sound of someone barely awake. "Dis had better be good."

"*Dobroye utro,* Aleksandra."

"It is not good morning, and your Russian is still awful, Mr. Hemnon."

As she was speaking, Damir heard from her end of the phone a male voice speaking at a volume he obviously was not supposed to hear, "What is he doing calling you at this time of the morning?"

A soft grunt followed that might have been one of Aleksandra's sharp elbows impacting the man's gut.

Damir turned his body away from Nadine, who kept alternating her attention from Damir to the body and back. "Is Good Luck Lake in your territory?"

Aleksandra stifled a sleepy laugh, "If you asking me if Good Luck Lake is in my jurisdiction as coroner, the answer is *da*. You found body?"

Damir consciously made himself not imitate her *da*, since he knew she was self-conscious about using her Russian instead of English. His voice took on a scientific detachment as he replied, "In the lake, floating, just off the cranberry bog; long enough so there is a definite decomposition odor. You will need divers, I think. Probably best to request a SCUBA team from Uniform Special Services. From what I can see of the clothing and hair, I believe the body was female."

"You don't think this another body from that Kiralynn's camp thing?" Aleksandra sounded suddenly wide awake.

Nadine moved away from the edge of the lake, closer to Damir, obviously trying to listen to the phone call and not look at the corpse any more.

"I doubt it is related. It is a good twenty-five minute drive to Piseco from here, and both those bodies belonged to people who were on foot."

"Accidental drowning, then?"

"Could be, but I have not seen many people who come up here of their own will wearing a cocktail dress."

Aleksandra sighed, "Don't leave; I will have officers on scene as soon as possible."

"Do not make Mr. Murphy get out of bed. I am sure there are other state police investigators that would be just as good for my purposes."

Aleksandra took a long pause. "I will call you back when I have arrival time of officers," she finally said, and she disconnected the call before he could speak.

"Thank you," Damir said to the cell phone static.

"Well, what's the deal?" asked Nadine.

He looked at her young, pixie-like features and decided there were worse places he could be. "We have to wait for the police."

Eight years earlier, Nhat Huu Quan stood, with only the aid of an ornate, brass-handled cane, in front of an audience of over two hundred refugees, at-risk students, and local politicians gathered for an evening of anti-gang presentations.

"And despite what it cost me," he concluded, "despite the coma, despite the scars, despite the limp, one of the proudest achievements of my life was getting out alive, while I still could."

Surprisingly powerful emotions washed over Nhat as the entire audience rose to their feet applauding.

A dark-haired Somali girl in the front row, with large tears flowing down her face, caught his attention. Something about her pierced nose, her long, thin body, the way her dark lips quivered, made Nhat wonder how he had not noticed her while giving his speech.

Damir stood up from the large log in the makeshift camp area he and Nadine had moved to while waiting for the police. He glanced at his watch, noting forty-five minutes had passed since he called. Despite what she said, Aleksandra had not phoned him back.

Damir did not let impatience show on his face when he spotted the first policeman, wearing the tan felt hat with the purple band of a New York State trooper, walking down toward them. By his gait, Damir knew this trooper did not have the same military training as the only trooper he was well acquainted with, Brian Murphy.

"I am Officer Sternan. I understand you folks have found something?"

"Yes, sir. It is this way." Damir led the way down to the lake with Nadine and the trooper following.

Sternan paused when they reached the bog. After watching it support the weight of the taller Damir for a few steps, the officer shrugged his shoulders and followed.

Damir stepped around the ragged hole in the bog, offering a balancing hand to Nadine. She smiled at him, but did not take his hand.

After a few more steps Damir pointed out the bobbing corpse to Officer Sternan.

The officer's face revealed nothing, and when he spoke it was with a professional tone. "Okay, I am going to need the two of you to stick around a little while to answer some questions."

Damir shook his head almost imperceptibly. "You will also need divers, and possibly ground-penetrating radar."

Officer Sternan turned away from the body, seeming to measure Damir's tall, cool exterior for the first time.

"And why, sir, would we need radar?"

"Because I suspect this isn't the only body dumped in this bog."

Four years earlier, walking with the fingers of his right hand entwined with Samena's and no weight supported by the cane in his other hand, Nhat did not see the young man approaching them down the brightly lit Poland Junior-Senior High School hallway as any kind of a threat, even though he had no bodyguard with him.

"Mr. Quan," the boy, obviously at least half Vietnamese, said as he held out his hand to shake and lowered his eyes deferentially, "It is a great honor to meet you."

Reluctantly, Nhat released the warmth of Samena's hand to shake the hand of the young man.

"My name is Bao Hau. Tonight is the third time I heard you speak. Your jumping out story is ..." Bao paused, obviously struggling for the word.

In a soft, low tone, Samena volunteered, "Inspiring?"

Nhat glanced at her. A tinge of surprise registered on his face, not expecting she would finish someone else's sentence.

Bao looked up at Samena's dark face and pierced nose. "Yes, inspiring. Thank you." Bao stuck his smooth non-workman hands in the pockets of his jeans, seeming nervous.

"Bao, this is my fiancé, Samena."

Bao looked up at her again. She stood at least a foot taller than he did, and a solid four inches taller than Nhat. "You are a very lucky man, Mr. Quan."

"Luck is the residue of hard work and good design," Nhat quoted from one of his own speeches.

"But aren't you a little more likely to be lucky with a family like the Vee Boyz behind you?"

"I don't believe in taking orders from men that will eventually get me killed."

"But the way you keep speaking out against them, aren't you afraid they'll come after you again?"

Nhat evaluated the young man. He made assumptions about Bao's strength of character, lack of parental guidance, and how close to the edge he might be. Nhat stepped closer to the young man, inside what most people would consider their zone of comfort.

Bao had a little room to step back before he would have hit the lockers lining the hall, but he stood his ground.

"No," Nhat said loudly enough it echoed down the hall to a small group of people gathered by the exit door, "I am not afraid." Then, so quietly even Samena could not hear, he whispered, "I know where the bodies are buried."

Although still tired from a half day of answering police questions, Damir dressed for his medical transcriptionist job at Saint Luke's Hospital the morning after he and Nadine discovered the body. He had half buttoned his shirt when his cell phone buzzed and began to dance the vibrate-mode shuffle on the little table by the door.

Damir glanced at the caller ID, and paused only a moment before answering with a flat toned, "*Spasibo za zvanok mne obratmo.*"

Alexandra ignored his half-hearted thanks, asking, "How did you know there would be other bodies?"

"I did not know for sure."

"But you guessed because…?"

"The hole someone cut in the bog that was a good distance from the body in the lake, and the fact that the preservative properties of cranberry bogs can make some forensics difficult."

"True. Time of death for the bog bodies will be difficult to determine. I will be doing full autopsies later today, but I do have preliminary COD, TOD, and ID for body in lake. She bled out from multiple stab wounds to abdomen. Dead thirty-two to forty-eight hours. Her name was Samena Raama."

The silence went on for a few seconds more than comfortable, even for two old friends. Alexandra broke it, "You remember her, don't you?"

"Yes, she and Nhat Huu Quan have been very active with the Refugee Center."

"They were a couple, yes?"

"For a long time." Damir's answer sounded hollow in his own ears. "Does he know?"

"Police should have visited him last night."

The quiet static of the phone line stretched out between them, and again Alexandra's voice broke the silence. "You will go see him?"

"Why would I do that? I barely know him."

"You are both intelligent men, both from another country, with similar pains in your past, and you found her."

"Nadine found her." The protest came out automatically and felt weak even as the words left his mouth.

"I understand. You have dealt with death too much. I just thought…" Her voice faded out.

Damir sighed, knowing he was defeated. "Give me his address. I will go visit him after work."

Damir stood outside the thick, unpainted wood door, knowing his presence would not help Nhat, but he had promised Aleksandra. He reached for a brass knocker that could have belonged on any 1950s house. He lifted it up and let it thunk back against the door.

A half-Vietnamese teenager Damir thought for a moment might be Nhat's son opened the door. Damir quickly realized the boy did not look much like Nhat, not at all like Samena, and the boy's age would not be correct from what little he knew of their timeline together.

"Hi. My name is Damir, and I know Mr. Quan through the Refugee Center. I know this is a difficult time, but I was hoping to speak with him."

"Come in." He waved Damir in with his hand.

Damir glanced at a nine-foot-long, folding table in the first room they passed through and counted four sandwich trays, three fruit trays, and at least five different dessert trays piled there. None of the plastic wrap covering the food had been broken.

In the next room, Nhat and another man stood from a brown leather couch facing a flat-screen TV mounted into the wall, but not turned on.

"Mr. Hemnon, forgive me for not meeting you at the door. I guessed it was another food tray being delivered."

Damir hunched his shoulders slightly. "There is nothing to forgive."

"Have you met my," Nhat paused, almost seeming to soundlessly clear his throat, "my associate Bao Hau?"

Bao extended his hand. Damir reached down, clasped it firmly in his, and looked him in the eye. The back of the man's hand felt oddly rough to Damir's touch, but he did not look at it then.

"The boy who answered the door is Jae." Nhat paused. "This is hard on him. Samena and I were going to adopt him after we got married."

Damir nodded, not sure what to say. When he nodded, he got a look at Bao's hand: five black scars, four surrounding one. Without being obvious, he examined the man. Bao stood much shorter than Nhat, with wiry muscles. A barely healed scratch showed from the edge of his shirt sleeve running almost all the way down into the pattern of burn marks.

"I wanted to let you know I was the one who found her body."

"I thought the police said a couple found it?" Nhat's somber face now showed curiosity.

"Not a couple, though a girl did spot her first." They all sat on the couch. Damir told them the whole story of his climb down Good Luck Cliff, his meeting with Nadine, Samena's body floating in the lake, the long wait for the police, and the longer period of questioning.

"I'm sorry you had to go through that." Nhat held a hand to his temple as if holding a memory in. "She would not have wanted you to see her like that."

"I will choose to remember her as I knew her from the Refugee Center and as the chairperson of so many wonderful events at the mosque."

"Do the police have any suspects?" Bao asked, speaking for the first time.

Nhat turned on him, "What difference do suspects make? Neither justice nor revenge will bring her back."

Bao dropped his eyes. "You are right."

Damir chose the pause following this exchange to ask, "I cannot help noticing the burns on the back of your hand. If I hadn't heard Nhat speak, I would not have known they were gang markings. Are you still in?"

Bao's hand darted to his pocket, though his words came out slowly, "I am…"

Nhat cut him off gently, "I have been working for two years to get him out, without him going through the beating, without him going through what I went through." His voice grew quieter, "Though of late, I have begun to think this may not be possible. The Vee Boyz current leader, a man who goes by the nickname, Too Shy, seems completely unwilling to be reasonable."

In the same quiet tone, Damir replied, "I think I understand."

Outside Nhat's house, Damir considered what he knew, what he thought he knew, and whom he should call about it. He knew Samena's death was a state police case. He could call Brian Murphy, but he didn't think Brian would know much about it, since he had not been on the scene.

Pieces of information did not fit together quite right in Damir's mind. He folded his long body into his Hyundai Sonata. As he reached to put the key in the ignition, his cell phone started playing Aleksandra's custom ring.

Before he was able to get out his greeting in Russian, she started in. "It is gang dumping ground. The Utica police gang expert says every body we have identified so far is someone Vee Boyz were connected with; two were former members."

Damir nodded to his cell phone even though she could not see him.

She continued as if she had seen the nod, "They think the Vee Boyz killed Samena, though they not sure which boy it was."

"I am sitting in front of Nhat's house. I was just in there. Nhat has a gang member with him right now."

"Is he safe?"

"I think he is, but the police will want to pick up Bao Hau for questioning. Can you tell me, did you find anything under Samena's finger nails?"

"Nothing usable. She was in the water too long. Why?"

"Bao Hau has a scratch on his arm."

"And you think?"

"It would have been nice to be able to check. You said this morning she died of stab wounds; could they have been caused by a pocket knife?"

"Yes, by the depth of the wounds, I would say no more than a three-inch blade."

"If there is a state police officer near me that you can trust, I may be able to use what you have told me to catch Samena's killer tonight."

"How soon would you like someone there?"

Twenty minutes later Brian Murphy's patrol car pulled in behind Damir's Sonata. The large man moved like an overweight mountain lion, still powerful and graceful, but slightly out of balance with himself. Brian's cheeks glowed bright cherry in a reflection of the late evening sunset.

"Damir, so good to be working with you again."

"How much do you know?"

"I think I'm pretty much up to speed. You've figured out who killed the woman in the lake up in the Adirondacks, and you have a plan to prove it. You need me here to make sure the victim's husband doesn't get hurt and to make the arrest. Protect and arrest, kinda my standard role with you."

If the situation had not been so serious, Damir would have laughed in appreciation. Instead he corrected, "Nhat is not ...was not her husband. I have a guess on the killer, but all the facts don't quite fit. If my guess is right, this may not take long. If I am wrong, I may add to Nhat's pain. Are you all right with that?"

Brian tugged at the brim of his hat, smiled his toothy smile, and nodded.

"One more thing—do you have a swab and an evidence bag?"

Once again Damir let the heavy knocker hit the door. This time Nhat did answer it.

"Did you forget something?"

"No, I have new things to tell you. This is my friend, State Police Inspector Brian Murphy."

Nhat cocked his head sideways like a bird. "Come in, officer."

This time Damir noticed the typically American décor of the house. He saw no evidence of Vietnamese or Sudanese art with the exception of one Sudanese woven basket on the floor under the table full of food trays. "I believe you know that I have consulted with the police on several occasions."

Nhat's face did not show any reaction. "You have made the news more than once."

"When I got out to my car, Mr. Murphy was waiting for me with some interesting information."

Brian's body stiffened when he heard Damir lie, but he gave nothing away.

"Is Mr. Hau still here?"

Nhat clenched his right hand into a tight fist. "Bao," he called into the other room, "come in here."

Bao and Jae came into the room together.

"Jae, go upstairs please," Nhat ordered.

"But…" the teenager pleaded.

Nhat gave him that parental *Do It Now* stare. Jae turned his head to Bao, who gave him the slightest of nods. Obviously not happy, the boy stomped out of the room. His heavy footsteps on an unseen stairway could be heard echoing through the house.

"Inspector Murphy told me that Samena scratched her killer, and he was waiting for a warrant to get a DNA sample from you." Damir's eyes focused on Bao.

Self-consciously Bao covered his right wrist with his left hand.

"I told him that a warrant would not be necessary, as you would certainly volunteer something like that. This would clear you, and let the police get back to finding the real murderer."

Brian took a swab covered in a plastic container from his pocket.

"I am not sure if I should?" Bao looked at Nhat.

Nhat looked back at him, "If it will clear you, what is the harm?"

"What if it is wrong? What if they make a mistake?"

"This isn't like TV," Brian spoke for the first time. "Our labs triple check stuff to make sure they get it right."

Bao looked like a trapped animal.

Damir tightened the trap, "The other part of the warrant will be for your pocket knife. You see," Damir turned his attention to Nhat,

"Samena was killed by a short-bladed knife much like the one Bao keeps in his right front pocket."

Nhat turned to Bao, his voice low with a quiet rage. "Did you do this?"

"I…I…I…"

Nhat stopped his stuttering with a loud, open-hand slap.

Brain started to step toward them, but Damir put a hand out.

"I had no choice. I had to kill her or you. Do you understand? Or else they would have killed you, her, and Jae."

Nhat's hand pumped in and out of a fist several times; then he stepped back out of Bao's space.

Bao looked up at Brian, "I want to make a deal. I can give you names, dates, places."

Brian stepped forward with his handcuffs now out. "That will be up to the district attorney. You are under arrest."

Five months later, Damir got a phone call from Brian.

"It's over. The last of the Vee Boyz took a plea today. Too Shy is in for two concurrent sentences of twenty-five years for murder and drug trafficking. He'll be parole eligible after fifteen. Bao's deal is eleven years, isolated custody, eligible for release in seven years."

Brian laughed, "Someday you will have to tell me how you know so many people in such interesting places."

"Because, like you, I value my friends most highly."

"I think that was almost a compliment. Thank you, Damir. At some point, we'll have to get together again and have a cup of that sludge you call coffee."

"I am meeting Nhat for lunch today. I will tell him everything."

"Are you sure you still want to do that?"

"Yes."

Damir walked through the restaurant entrance area, noting the small knot of patrons sitting at the bar.

"Welcome to the Lotus Garden," a thin waitress with cute, angular features clutched a handful of lunch menus. "Can I help you?"

"I am supposed to be meeting someone."

"Ahh, right this way." She led him into the Carriage Room.

Nhat waved to him from the left, rear corner of the room, sitting with his back to the sushi bar.

Slightly uncomfortable with the lack of sight lines, Damir sat with his back to the entrance.

"Can I get you anything to drink?" The waitress handed him a menu.

Damir glanced at the cup of hot tea in front of Nhat. "A cold Thai tea?"

She nodded and moved back toward the bar.

"It is busy in here."

Nhat nodded, "I think there is a play or something over at the Stanley."

Damir nodded, "That makes sense."

"You said you wanted to talk about some things."

"Yes, I do." Damir took a deep breath. "How is Jae? You told me that you and Samena were going to adopt him?"

"We were, but the state doesn't like single adoptive fathers."

"But he still lives with you?"

"Yes."

"And he is Bao's brother?"

Nhat only paused for a fraction of a second. "We don't advertise that, in fear of what's left of the Vee Boyz coming after him, but yes, that is true."

"You will raise him?"

"Yes."

"Even though his brother killed Samena?"

"Bao was in an impossible situation. He made the wrong choice. It would have been better if he killed me." Nhat's flat tone made it sound like he had said this a thousand times and wished he could stop saying it.

"I understand what you are saying, but I don't understand why Bao would have kept that pocket knife instead of getting rid of it, or why he would have stabbed her in the abdomen instead of someplace that would have killed her more quickly."

Nhat considered Damir's words a long time before saying, "Even if Bao will answer those questions, I am not sure we will ever really know."

"Are you ready to order?" the waitress asked.

Damir shook his head.

Nhat glanced at his menu, "Not yet. Can you give us a few minutes?"

She bobbed her head and moved to another table.

"When were you with the Vee Boyz?"

"More than a decade ago," Nhat replied.

"They sold drugs?"

"Yes."

"According to what my friends close to your case tell me, they were still selling drugs before all this happened."

"That would make sense, but I wouldn't know that for sure."

"Here is the odd thing. After the Vee Boyz got picked up, the police expected some real problems with addicts not getting their fixes, and they anticipated fights among the other local gangs for their market. None of that happened. Almost like someone was ready to fill the void before it was even there."

"Mr. Hemnon, are you wearing a wire?"

"No."

"For the purposes of this conversation, I am going to assume you are. So I am going to talk in hypotheticals."

Damir nodded.

"If I had the resources to fill that void, perhaps from my old days running with the Vee Boyz, that would mean I ordered the brother of a boy I am raising as my son to infiltrate the Vee Boyz, then kill my fiancé, just to get the Vee Boyz out of my way." He paused taking a sip from his hot tea. "Do you really think that kind of evil exists in our little corner of upstate New York?"

Images of the dead he had seen in Bosnia and the dead he had seen since coming to New York flashed in front of Damir's eyes. "I think it can be anywhere."

Nhat swallowed the last of his hot tea in a fast gulp before replying, "I guess it can be, but in this case it isn't. He put his teacup down on the table. "I was so looking forward to a nice meal here."

Damir turned to watch Nhat walk out, and then he watched as the bodyguard separated himself from the bar to follow his boss out the door.

The Rebel

by Woody Sins

Frank Stabb sniffed the air as he crawled out of his small tent. It was a force of habit. He hadn't actually smelled anything since that awful day in 1918.

He answered the call of duty in 1917, when President Wilson announced that the United States was entering the Great War to assist the French and British in their titanic efforts to end the most terrible war in history. He left his home on Tug Hill and made it through the training required of the soldiers of the American Expeditionary Force. In addition to combat training, he took observation and surveying classes, and then he shipped off to France in the summer of 1918 with the 42nd Infantry Division. Under Major General Pershing, he fought on the front line at St. Mihiel, only to be caught in a gas attack while preparing for the last offensive at Argonne. He was invalided back to the states and given only a few years to live. The last thing he ever smelled was the odor of mustard gas as it seeped into the communication trench where his unit was mustering. The war ended only two weeks later. He had just turned nineteen.

He struck his tent and kicked up the embers of his fire to cook a bit of the bacon he had wrapped in waxed paper in his knapsack. As he went to retrieve the pack, which he had hung in a tree to keep it away from the bears, he saw that it had been opened where it hung. Most of the bacon and flour he had brought with him was gone. He softly cursed the critters that stole it and resigned himself to the walk back to the advance camp to resupply.

After the war, Frank had gone back to the family farm near West Leyden. Although he could walk for miles still, the rigors of farm life were too much for him. He would have to stop many times in the course of a day in a fit of coughing, bringing up more and more blood each time. In 1919, he left his family and his beloved Ethel, whom he had planned to marry, to seek his fortune elsewhere. After eventually traveling to Lyons Falls, he signed on with the Gould Paper Company as a surveyor and was sent to assess the tract of lumber south of Old Forge. The mountain air worked as a panacea to his injuries and, thus far, he was able to keep his condition from his employers. He was working the stretch of land to the south of Limekiln Lake. His job was to map the area and determine the best locations for camps, trails, and river landings where logs could be rolled into the water. Today, however, he needed to take time from his work to get more supplies.

"Yer not the only one to lose supplies," the sutler said. "Ol' Jim just came back missing his mess kit and most of his provender. He thinks the woods are haunted. Some laundry also goes missin' now and again, right off the line when everyone's in the woods."

Frank scoffed. "What would a ghost want with a mess kit? It's probably just squirrels."

But what would a squirrel want with a mess kit? Frank thought as he left with his supplies.

Frank walked along the bank of a small creek, keeping an eye on the mud for the hoof prints of the whitetail deer that proliferated in the area. They would lead him to a deer trail that he could use to penetrate farther into the underbrush and speed his progress. His backpack was hitched on his back, his rifle in a sling built into the pack.

Soon, in the mud near an outcropping of flinty stone that the water tumbled over, he saw what he was looking for—many different tracks in the mud indicating it was the watering spot of the local deer. He examined the area for the faint signs of the trail he knew should be nearby. Suddenly, he spotted another print in the mud. An indentation unmistakably made by a human foot. The print looked fresh, perhaps made the day before. It was not the print of a heavy boot, nor was it the mark of a bare foot. It seemed to be made by a softly clad foot, as if by a moccasin. Nearby were flakes of the flinty stone from the outcrop. They seemed to have been chipped off by force.

Frank sometimes met hunters during the fall, but in the spring he wouldn't expect to see anyone until he went back to camp. But he did not spend much time puzzling over the secret the mud and stone held. He soon found the trail he was looking for and followed it back into the woods, updating his map and frequently consulting his compass as he went.

Frank walked along the trail for about a half mile, slowing his pace as it got harder and harder to follow. He pushed his way into a small clearing, startling a quail that was nesting there. It took off with a *whop-whopwhop* and flew into the underbrush behind him. He turned around to watch its progress, and as he did, he took a step backward.

WHOOOMPH!

Frank was suddenly knocked off his feet. When he finally collected his wits, he discovered that he was hovering several inches above the ground. Something had him by his pack. Terror briefly overcame him, and he twisted around in a futile attempt to see what it was. He fumbled with the clasp on his pack and finally was able to undo it, after which he tumbled to the ground with a thud. He lay there, gasping for breath, waiting for whatever had grabbed him to make its next move. After lying there for what seemed like hours, he decided that, since nothing had happened yet, he was not in any immediate danger and got to his feet.

His pack was hanging on the end of a sapling that had been cut down and fixed horizontally to a larger tree with what looked like homemade rope. With some effort, he dislodged his pack, which had been pierced by a sharpened piece of flint attached to the free end of the sapling with more of the rope. Frank examined the setup and realized that he had walked into a booby trap. No phantasm built this, he thought. He unsheathed his rifle, and loaded it from a small collection of bullets he kept in his vest pocket.

Frank found where the trail left the clearing and continued to follow it, well to the side in case there was another trap. The trail seemed to become more defined, as if it was more heavily traveled. A coughing fit suddenly overcame him. He spat blood as he doubled over in pain. As the pain subsided, he stood up, and suddenly found himself face to face with another person.

A strange apparition stood several feet before him. A man of indeterminate, ancient age and the countenance of a carved and dried apple stared into his eyes. He was dressed in buckskin trousers, moccasins, and a white shirt that looked clean and neat compared to the tattered coat he wore over it. The coat looked like part of a military uniform, with the remains of gold piping around the collar and shoulders. It may have been gray at one time. The man's long, white beard hung wildly from his brown, wrinkled chin. In his hand he held an old saber, raised as if to strike. He looked just as startled to see Frank as Frank was to see him. Frank had grabbed his gun and pointed it in the man's general direction, ready for action.

The two men considered each other for a moment. Then the strange apparition lowered his saber. "Well, Yank, it seems my knife can't win in a gun fight." He spoke with a thick Southern drawl that Frank could barely make out, and his voice sounded as if it hadn't been used in a generation. A nearly toothless smile spread under his crooked nose.

"Pardon?" Frank was now more puzzled than wary.

"Well, you found me. I s'pose yer going to take me in. 'Bout time you did. I'm mighty tired of running."

"I haven't been looking for you. In fact I didn't expect to see anyone at all," said Frank. "Are you an escaped criminal or something?"

The old man stood upright, stuck the saber into the ground at Frank's feet, and saluted. "Beggin' your pardon. Name's Virgil Kane, of Bennet Young's Irregulars, Confederate States Army." His smile broadened.

"Confederate States Army," echoed Frank. "You aren't an escaped criminal, you're a loon is what you are, and not the good kind."

The old man sighed. "C'mon, it looks like I got some explaining to do. If you got any of that there bacon left, we can have a bit o' dinner. Follow me."

The old man began to walk off into the woods. Frank stood for a moment, shrugged his shoulders, and followed. At least he now knew what the Phantom of the Woods was.

The two men walked through the undergrowth beneath the tall spruce trees back to the small stream that Frank had found earlier. They were farther upstream, where the waters fell over another outcropping that formed a sheltered cove facing the south branch of the Moose River. Frank could see the valley where the river ran. Virgil went to the left side of the cove, which was overgrown with pine brambles. He pulled a root that was sticking out, which served as a handle for a cleverly hidden door. "C'mon in, Yank!"

"The name's Frank." He had to stoop low to enter the small hole in the bramble. He found himself in a room built into an overhang in the rock. The front wall was made of stone mortared with dried mud. The outside was, evidently, covered in dirt and planted with brambles to hide the crude but clever dwelling. At one end of the roughly oblong room was a fireplace built from flat stones. A larger rock was placed across the top as a mantle to support a chimney made the same way as the fireplace, taking advantage of a fissure in the overhanging rock. Deer skins hung on the outside walls, and dried venison and herbs and roots hung from poles arranged like rafters. Bedding was arranged near the fire, as was a table built from a log cut lengthways. A chair made from a cross section of log was next to it. A large Stars and Bars hung on the inside wall, somewhat faded and showing signs of repair, but obviously well cared for. An old musket leaned on the wall next to it. A holster with an old black powder pistol hung on a peg jammed into a crack in the wall.

"Have a seat. Y'all wouldn't have any coffee, or something stronger?"

Frank rummaged in his pack for his pouch of coffee without saying a word. Virgil smiled broadly, took a pot that looked suspiciously like part of a modern mess kit, and went to fill it in the creek. Soon, the smell of brewing coffee filled the dwelling, although Frank could only imagine it. Virgil filled some smaller pots with the brew, and offered one to Frank, who was now sitting at the low table. Virgil sat on his bedding and began his story.

"I grew up in the woods of Tennessee, as you probably can tell. In 1862, I signed up to fight the Yankees and wound up serving under General Longstreet with the Army of Virginia. In the spring of '63,

General Lee marched us north to invade Pennsylvania, in the hopes of intimidating the Yanks into giving up the war and letting the Confederacy be. Instead, we ran into the Yankee army in a little crossroads named Gettysburg. I was captured on the second of July.

"I was marched off and loaded on a train that would take me to a prison in Elmira, New York. I am proud to say that I never went to that hellhole. I managed to escape from the transport train, and I made my way to Canada. There, I was recruited by Lieutenant Young for a raid into Vermont to rob the banks in St Alban's to get funds for our noble cause. We were to check into hotels in the village in ones and twos so as not to arouse suspicion.

"It was October tenth of '64 that we were finally ready. At three o'clock, we started our operation. I was assigned to round up some horses for our escape, but some of the townsfolk resisted, and I wound up shooting one. I knew I had to make a getaway, so I hopped on one of the horses and made a run for it. I was passing another band of our soldiers, who were trying to set fire to the town, when my horse was spooked, and bolted. When I finally fell off, I was far out of town. I made my way back, but the rest of the band had skedaddled, and the local law was after me for murder.

"I hid out until dark. I knew I had to leave Vermont, so I went to Lake Champlain and stole a rowboat. I crossed by the light of the moon and made my way to the mountains I could see from shore. I was able to avoid people, but I had to move every so often, when loggers or other folk made things too crowded for my tastes.

"I survived, as you can see, by my wits and the skills my daddy taught me in Tennessee. I 'borrowed' some items when I could, mostly from camps when the owners weren't around. I hunted deer and other critters until I couldn't get no more powder, then I switched to gins and other traps."

"I've seen your handiwork," said Frank, now seeing the booby-trapped trail for what it really was: a deer snare.

Virgil paid him no mind. "I've been meaning to head back to the Confederacy, but these mountains seem to have a spell on me. I don't recollect how long I've been here."

"Seems about fifty-six years. Did it occur to you to nick a newspaper?"

"Aw, I cain't read!" said Virgil with a grin.

"Well, let me bring you up to date," Frank said.

The shadows were beginning to get long when Frank finished his story. Virgil sat in silence, his hands on his knees. A tear formed in his eye when he learned that his beloved Confederacy had fallen and General Lee, the hero of the South, had been defeated. He sat expressionless as Frank described his experiences in the Great War and the terrible, terrible weapons that man had invented to kill his fellows.

Frank finished speaking. The two war veterans sat staring at the floor at their feet, each lost in his own thoughts. Finally, Virgil looked up and spoke.

"I can't go back. Everything I knew is gone. Different. Changed forever. But I'm tired, old. I don't think I can hold out much longer. Winters are fierce. Summers are hot an' full of skeeters and chiggers that gnaw through everything to get at you. I can't go on like this."

At this, Frank looked up. "Well, I can't do anything about the bugs, but I can help you stay out here as long as you want. The mill just bought this tract, and I'll be here as long as there are trees to cut. The company won't miss the supplies that one old woodsman would need, and I'll report this area as all swamp with no standing timber. That'll keep the loggers out. You should be fixed for as long as you need."

Virgil's countenance slowly melted into a smile as he contemplated these words. "That'll do just fine. I'm mighty grateful."

The two men rose to their feet and shook hands. Suddenly, Frank was seized in a coughing fit. He collapsed, blood flowing from the corners of his mouth. He gasped and coughed as Virgil stood by, helpless. Finally, the coughing stopped. Frank had no more energy. He closed his eyes, his gurgling breath coming in gasps. Soon this also stopped. Virgil realized that the poison gas Frank had told him about had finally claimed another victim.

The old warrior moved Frank's body as best he could up the bank to a small clearing. Although they had only known each other for a few short hours, Virgil regarded him as a close friend after his years of solitude. He dug a shallow grave in the sandy soil and laid Frank to rest in it. He fashioned a cross from some pine sticks from the nearby woods and placed it, unadorned, at the head of the grave.

Virgil sat deep in thought and prayer until the light began to fail. He went back to his home and found Frank's rifle, still loaded from their earlier encounter. As the moon rose above the spruce, Virgil walked slowly up the bank again and disappeared into the forest.

Rides With Strangers

by Gigi Vernon

The key to getting picked up was good eye contact. The less traffic there was, like on this empty stretch of Route 30 bisecting the Adirondack wilderness, the more important it was to really focus on the occupants of the occasional car.

Fortunately, it was a good day for hitching. The sky was blue and the air crisp and clean. It was warm in the sun and cool in the shade, and the leaves were already turning a splendid quilt of red and gold. Just like a postcard. On a day like this, Jenna wouldn't have minded hiking to the closest town's bus station, but Steve made that impossible.

A white van came noisily around the curve heading north. Jenna stuck out her thumb. Through the bug-splattered windshield, Jenna locked eyes with a woman in the passenger seat.

The van whizzed by without stopping.

Jenna dropped her thumb and shielded her mouth, nose, and eyes with a hand against the grit and dry leaves stirred up by its passing. The driver couldn't even be bothered to slow down.

She could understand them passing her by. Though she'd tried to make herself as presentable as she could, they saw a scruffy young woman. She'd braided her none-too-clean hair into pigtails and mashed a baseball cap over it to hide its state. There wasn't much she could do about her clothes, which were much the worse for weeks of wear. Despite the pleasant warmth of the September day, she wore a tee shirt under three faded, flannel shirts so she didn't have to carry them. Her jeans had streaks of greasy dirt on the thighs and one knee was ripped. Her cheap sneakers were run down at the heel. On her back was a big, old, grimy, orange pack with a sleeping bag and water bottles strapped to it.

In the van's passenger seat, Susan gripped Gary's arm. "Honey, what are you doing? Don't stop. Honey! Seriously?"

"We can't just leave her, sweetheart," Gary said as he braked. "It's not safe out here in the wilderness for a young woman alone. What if a serial killer picks her up?"

The van slammed to a halt with a screech of brakes and a squeal of rubber, and then began to back toward Jenna.

Now that she got a better look at it, she realized it was the biggest, oldest van she'd ever seen—like some kind of hippie-mobile. The lower half was so eaten away by rust it looked like dried-up Swiss cheese, or lace, brown with age.

When it reached her, the driver, a thirtyish guy with glasses and a ponytail, wearing a straw cowboy hat and a Hawaiian button-down shirt, rolled down the window and asked with a grin, "Need a lift?"

Before she answered, Jenna peered inside, checking it out. The woman sitting next to him was plump, with short, curly, dark hair and a large gold pentacle prominently displayed above the scooped neckline of her pink blouse. Behind them were windows and two rows of back seats. A teenage girl with shoulder-length, fuzzy red hair was squeezed onto the first row with a fat-cheeked baby in a car seat and a panting golden retriever. It seemed obvious they were a family on summer vacation heading to the High Peaks region of the Adirondacks or Saranac Lake. Perfectly safe.

"Yeah, thanks. I do need a ride," Jenna said. "Do you have room for my friend?" She turned and beckoned to Steve.

He emerged from behind a fir tree, cradling a bandaged wrist.

An apprehensive look passed between the couple.

Jenna had to admit it wasn't just the hasty bandage that made Steve look odd. It was the huge, bug-eyed, mirrored sunglasses, the twigs and bits of leaves stuck in the shaggy hair and beard, the worn business suit, and the expensive, new hiking boots covered in dried mud.

"Um," the woman hesitated.

"We sure appreciate you stopping," Jenna preempted.

"Yeah, sure," the man said, grinning, his eyes a watery blue. When he reached back and unlatched the door, Jenna noticed a sprawling, green, dragon tattoo on his bicep. "Kelsey, sweetheart, you and Ripper climb in the back, okay?" he said to the teen.

The dogs name was Ripper?

Sullenly but without argument, the girl got on one knee and dove over the seat's top, her long, scratched legs in their shorts pouring over it like a diver into water. Taking hold of Ripper's collar, she tugged and the dog followed, and the two of them curled up together on the back seat.

Jenna went around to the other side, unslung her backpack, and slid in next to the baby. The cracks in the seat vinyl were repaired with duct tape. The baby wore a pink onesie patterned with blue ducks and matching pink booties. With a grin of happiness, she pumped her arms and legs vigorously like she was doing a dance. A sippy cup rolled around on the floor.

On the other side, Steve got in and shut the door.

With a big goofy smile, the driver extended his hand. "Hi, I'm Gary."

"I'm Jenna and this is Steve," Jenna replied, reaching out to shake his hand.

Steve stared straight ahead like a blind man.

Rebuffed, Gary's smile dimmed, and he withdrew his hand.

The dog stuck its snout in Jenna's hair and sniffed with great interest, and then began to lick her neck with gusto. It didn't feel bad, but it was distracting.

"Ripper, stop," the woman reprimanded. "Sorry about that. She's very nice. Too nice, sometimes. She can be a total pain. Just push her away."

"No problem," Jenna said, moving out of reach of the friendly canine.

Ripper moved her snuffling investigation to Steve, though apparently she didn't find his neck worth licking.

The woman turned sideways, so she could get a better look at them. "I'm Susan," she introduced herself with a prim, little, secret smile like the Madonna. "And that little sweetie next to you is my daughter, Dorothea."

"What are you two doing out here? Camping?" Gary asked in a friendly tone as he put the van into gear.

"Yeah, camping," Jenna said, but didn't elaborate.

"Are you all right, Steve?" Susan asked with concern. "What happened to you? Does that wrist need to be seen to?"

Steve didn't reply.

"It's nothing. Just a scratch. He's fine," Jenna answered for him.

Gary pulled back onto the road. "Warm, huh? How about more air?" he asked, as he fiddled with the knob and the air conditioning wheezed loudly.

Artificially frigid air blasted Jenna. The speed of the van was frightening, exhilarating, mesmerizing. She felt dazed. It seemed like it'd been forever since she'd experienced being in a vehicle. She became aware of being completely surrounded by people, too many people, in a small space, too small.

"Where are you headed?" Susan asked with her secret smile.

"Canada," Jenna said vaguely, and turned the conversation to them. "How about you?"

"We are too!" Gary said, glancing in the rearview mirror at her, his idiotic grin getting even wider, if that were possible. "What a coincidence!"

Susan shot him a look.

Jenna decided he was weird. "Sure is," she agreed, suppressing the urge to rudely roll her eyes.

"You two are friends?" Susan prodded, curious, darting another quick glance at Steve.

"Uh huh," Jenna said, brightly. It was a bit hard to explain, and she didn't think they'd understand. Besides, Steve had asked her not to say anything to anyone.

Susan regretted letting Gary stop for the two hitchhikers. Steve was creepy. The sunglasses and his lack of response were unnerving.

Spooky. He made her think of serial killers. Or spies. Cops. She shivered. They shouldn't have picked them up. When they realized the young woman wasn't alone, they should've changed their minds and driven off.

She, Jenna, wasn't much better. Her hands, face, hair, and clothes were filthy. She reeked of campfire smoke and body odor, and Susan had to breathe through her nose. Under the brim of her baseball cap, Jenna had dead-fish eyes and a hangdog expression that wasn't very attractive. If she cleaned herself up, and stood up straight and smiled, she might not be half bad. No, bad idea, Susan, thought with a glance at Gary. He couldn't be trusted around young women. Why was he grinning? What was he so cheerful about, today of all days?

"Any good campsites around here?" Susan asked, doing her best to make conversation.

"Sure, if you're willing to hike in. A little tough with a young one though," Jenna said.

Happy, good-natured Dorothea kicked and gurgled at her.

How could anyone resist an adorable baby? But Jenna didn't try to hold her or touch her. In her flat voice, the young woman said to Dorothea, "Aren't you a butterball? I could just eat you up."

"Whoa!" Gary exclaimed.

Ahead Jenna saw lines of vehicles inching toward a state police patrol car blocking both lanes. A cop stood in the middle of the road stopping vehicles. A checkpoint.

Susan made an audible intake of breath. "They must be doing a check of seatbelts or registration. Everyone make sure you're buckled in!" she said and laughed. But it was a forced laugh.

A road came up on the left, and Gary swerved onto it. "How about a scenic detour? That all right with you all?" he asked.

What was Jenna supposed to do? Protest? Make them stop and get out?

After an hour of winding through forest on a dirt road, they came to a paved road which led them back to Route 30.

Her mouth dry with fear, Susan reached for her soda in the cup holder and sucked on the straw. As she set it back down, she realized Jenna's eyes had followed her every move. "Oh, sorry. How rude of me. Care for one?"

"Sure," Jenna said eagerly.

Susan reached into the cooler on the floor at her feet and began to fish. "Diet or regular?"

"Regular."

"Susan is like a boy scout," Gary said. "Or a girl scout, as the case may be. She's always prepared. Drinks, snacks, first aid kit. Anything you need."

Susan pulled out a can of off-brand orange soda. As she started to pass it back, Jenna grabbed the can out of her hands, snapped it open with trembling fingers, and chugged. Two minutes later it was empty, and she handed it back to Susan. "Thanks," she said, her blank expression never changing.

Susan took the can, blinking with surprise, and shoved it in the plastic bag she used for trash. "Steve, can I offer you something to drink?"

Steve stared straight ahead, expressionless, giving no indication he heard or saw anything. She noticed his motionless lips were perfectly formed, like the statue of a Greek god.

"He doesn't drink soda," Jenna explained.

"Oh. Well, I have water?" Susan suggested, but she dropped the idea when the weirdo didn't respond.

"Whoa!" Gary exclaimed and pointed at a billboard along the road. "Look at that!" A hand-painted sign depicted an ice cream sundae and read, "Scoopy-doo 3 miles ahead."

"Who wants ice cream?" he called back.

"Honey…now?" Susan asked, her tone and gaze meaningful. "You want to stop now? Do you think that's a good idea?" She loved Gary's playfulness, but sometimes he had to be reined in.

"Oh come on, live a little, sweetheart. It'll be fine. My treat. I scream, you scream, we all scream for ice cream," he chanted. He chuckled at his own tired joke.

A moment later he pulled into the gravel parking lot of a mom-and-pop roadside stand. It was constructed entirely of rough-hewn logs and had an enormous ice cream cone in plaster mounted on its rusted tin roof. They were the only customers. Gary cut the engine and got out. Everyone else did, too, except for Steve, who sat in the back unmoving.

Not about to leave her daughter with him, Susan unbuckled Dorothea and picked her up, hoisting her onto one shoulder and the baby bag onto the other. It was probably time for a diaper change anyway. Gary was already in line with Kelsey and Jenna, flirting, no doubt. Just being social, he'd tell her later.

A sign with an arrow labeled "Ladies" pointed around back to a tiny addition. Expecting the worst, Susan opened the door tentatively. Inside, it was bigger than she expected, with a concrete floor, a vent fan that whirred away, and walls painted a vibrant, glossy yellow.

A community bulletin board papered with notices and flyers hung over a makeshift changing table. She surveyed it casually as she set to work getting Dorothea cleaned up. Posters for missing children leaped out at her. Dead center was a brand new one featuring a photo of Dorothea wearing her favorite pink duck outfit underneath the heading *Family Member Abduction.* If Dorothea hadn't been there, she might have cursed. Instead, she silently mouthed *sonofabitch.* In a sing-song voice to the little girl, she said, "What do they know? They don't know nothing!"

She took great satisfaction in ripping the poster down, wadding it in a ball, and flinging it into the wastebasket with the soiled diaper where it belonged. Then she finished changing Dorothea, put her in a different outfit, and stomped out with the baby and her bag, letting the door slam behind them.

Despite the fact that Jenna had inhaled her triple-decker rocky road, cherry jubilee, and butter rum with chocolate sprinkles and nuts before it melted, her face and hands felt sticky. It'd been weeks since she'd eaten any sweets, and the sugar buzzed in her blood like adrenaline. She felt dizzy and light-headed with it. She and Kelsey went in search of a restroom. At a place like this, she hoped it wasn't a porta-john.

She was elated to find a three-stall restroom with running water. *Hot* running water. The ease of it, the luxury of it was breathtaking. Vigorously, she scrubbed her face, hands, and neck. The water came away black. She washed until the water ran clear. Now she could play with Dorothea. Impulsively, she began to wash her hair. The sink filled with more black water. Disgusting. She must smell, too. Before she could stop herself, she'd peeled off her shirts and her tee and was giving herself a sponge bath.

Kelsey stumbled out of a stall, pulling down her short shorts and adjusting the straps of her skimpy tank top. Her eyes widened. "Take it easy on the water, girlfriend. You're going run their well dry at that rate. How long have you been homeless?"

"Homeless?" Jenna repeated, shocked. Then she laughed. "You think I'm homeless? I've been camping, living on the land, back to nature. As an experiment." She wrung out her hair, letting the excess drip into the sink.

"Unh-unh," Kelsey said, obviously not believing her.

"No, really. It's a research project at SUNY Adirondack." Jenna pulled a wad of paper towels from the dispenser and began drying herself.

"Yeah, right." Kelsey stepped up to the other sink and washed and dried her hands.

"It's the truth," Jenna said, studying the bulletin board absentmindedly.

When she discarded the towels, she noticed a crumpled-up poster lying in the trash can. Curious, she fished it out and smoothed it. On it was a photo of a baby wearing the same pink outfit as Dorothea. It said Dorothea's father had reported her missing from his home in Chestertown. Her mother, Susan Sheppard, was suspected of the kidnapping.

"Holy cow!" she exclaimed. "Kelsey, your parents are kidnappers?"

"Good photo of Dorothea," Kelsey commented, leaning over Jenna's shoulder to look at the poster. "But they're not my parents."

"What?"

"Wouldn't mind if they were. They're pretty nice. But they just picked me up a couple of hours ago."

"They kidnapped you, too?" Jenna asked, horrified.

"No," Kelsey giggled, and then returned to her normal sullen state.

"I'm running away from home. My stepmother is a psycho. I couldn't take it anymore. I'm hitching to Lake Placid, gonna get a job at one of the resort hotels."

Kelsey was tall and long limbed, but flat-chested, narrow-hipped, and gawky. She looked like she was thirteen. "How old are you?" Jenna asked suspiciously.

"Eighteen. Well, seventeen," Kelsey shot back. "But I turn eighteen in two months. That's plenty old enough to be on my own."

Doubtful, but her manner and voice did seem older than her appearance. Was it just a good act? Maybe. But Jenna had her own worries. "Well, good luck with that."

"Yeah, you too. I'm out of here. The police will be looking for those two. I'm getting my stuff out of the back and finding another ride."

"Wait," Jenna said, suddenly concerned for the girl's welfare. "Here. Take this." She pulled one of Steve's hundred-dollar bills out of her backpack and handed it to the girl.

"Wow. Thanks!" Kelsey said, her eyes bulging, and stuffed it in a pocket. "Tell Gary and Susan that I called my mom to come get me," she said and scurried out.

"Be careful!" Jenna called. "And don't accept rides from strangers!"

Jenna followed more slowly. If she stayed with Gary and Susan and they got caught, could she, Jenna, be charged as some kind of accessory? But if she bailed on them now like Kelsey, what would she do about Steve? The two of them would be stranded here waiting for another ride for who knew how long.

She went back to the van.

In the last row of seats, Steve was stretched out with the dog, side-by-side like lovers, with one arm over her furry shoulder, both snoring soundly. "Steve. Steve. Wake up." She shook him, hard, and when he didn't wake up, shook him even harder. Whatever he'd taken had left him dead to the world. Unless she deserted him, which she briefly considered, they weren't going anywhere soon.

From the bench of a wooden picnic table, Susan watched Jenna return to the van. The afternoon sun was just touching the mountain, like a fiery ball balanced on the tip of a pyramid. Already there was a chill in the air.

Gary handed Susan a baby sweater. "Starting to get chilly," he said. "Maybe she should put this on."

That's what Susan loved about him. He was so good with children and young people. She successfully wrestled her daughter into the sweater. "I don't like them," she said to him, taking care to keep her voice low. "They're both so weird. I wish we hadn't picked them up."

Gary was finishing the ice cream cone he'd bought for Steve even before he realized the guy was crashed in the back seat. It was a dripping mess. He had it all over his hands, his nose, his mouth, even a spot on his glasses. Just like a little kid.

She handed him more paper napkins.

He took them and held them in his fist instead of using them. "No, you got it all wrong. They're perfect cover. They're looking for me and you. No one's looking for a big, happy family." He popped the last of the cone into his mouth and crunched it with gusto. "It'll be fine. Trust me."

She wished he hadn't said that. It wasn't reassuring in the slightest. This plan had been his idea. Why she'd gone along with it she didn't know.

Back on the highway, Jenna heard the wail of the siren long before she saw it. They all did.

"Whoa," Gary exclaimed, his head swiveling, looking for its source.

Susan tensed, and clasped her pentacle, white-knuckled, her lips pressed into a thin line of anxiousness. She glanced at Gary. "Maybe it's just a fire truck or an ambulance," she suggested hopefully.

An instant later, a patrol car with flashing lights and wailing sirens appeared behind them and signaled them to pull over.

With a glance at Susan, Gary obeyed.

"Sweet Jesus," Susan moaned. "Don't stop. Go! Just drive, Gary."

"You mean flee the scene?" Gary asked, shocked. "He'd pursue us. Call for backup too. We'd be risking little Dorothea in a high-speed car chase. We might get her and the rest of us killed. No," he said. "It'll be all right, sweetheart." He slowed and pulled onto the shoulder.

The patrol car pulled in behind them, its lights playing over them. The officer took his time getting out of his car.

Jenna's heart was racing and she couldn't think clearly.

"All right?" Susan shrieked, her patience apparently completely gone. "How the hell is it going to be all right, Gary? They'll take you back to Ray Brook and add a couple of years to your sentence for busting out to help me get Dorothea. Meanwhile, I'll be doing time elsewhere." With a bitter smile, she added, "We can write each other from our cells. And what's going to happen to Dorothea? She'll be in the care of my ex, that monster!"

"You're an escaped convict from Ray Brook?" Jenna interrupted, gaping.

"I'm not dangerous. I never hurt anyone," Gary explained with his goofy grin. "It was check fraud. I got laid off. All I did was write a bunch of bad checks, in Vermont and New York. I'm not a menace to society."

The patrol car's door swung open. In a big hat and the tan uniform of a state trooper, the officer approached the driver's side, and leaned down, his gaze sweeping over the van's occupants. "How are you all this fine autumn day?" he greeted them.

His name badge read "Royston." He was fair and fresh-faced with striking blue eyes.

To Gary, Officer Royston said, "Please get out your license and registration, sir."

Sweat glistened on Gary's forehead. "Honey, could you oblige?" he said, and nodded toward the glove compartment.

Susan was trembling so much she could barely manage the latch. She rifled through papers while Gary took his time fishing his wallet out of his back pocket.

Jenna almost felt sorry for them.

"Is there some problem, officer?" Gary asked, his grin tentative. "I'm sure I was under the speed limit."

Steve woke and popped up from the seat like a jack in the box, sending Ripper sliding onto the floor. "What's going on?" he asked.

Officer Royston's gaze roved over Jenna to Steve. "Could you two show me some identification?"

"All I've got on me is my SUNY Adirondack student ID," Jenna said, apologetically. "I don't have a driver's license." Shc handed the plastic card over.

"What about you, sir?" the officer asked Steve.

"He's not carrying anything," Jenna answered for him.

Officer Royston bent lower, resting his forearm on the door, and peered more suspiciously at Steve. "Could you step out of the vehicle, sir?"

Obediently, Steve opened the door and climbed out.

Jenna rolled down the window and leaned out, watching.

"Sir, would you mind removing your eyewear?" Royston asked.

Steve pushed them up onto his head. His eyes were still red and bloodshot from all the pot he'd been smoking and whatever other drugs he'd been doing to "summon his muse" before he showed up at Jenna's campsite that morning.

Officer Royston stared intently. Jenna thought he was about to arrest Steve or at least search him for drugs. Instead, he asked, "Anyone ever told you look like…? Hey, aren't you…? The lead singer? From…?" In an instant, his expression went from authoritarian to worshipping.

"No," Steve said quietly.

"Aw, come on, stop pulling my leg." The state trooper's face and voice changed. He looked and sounded fifteen years younger—and much cooler and hipper. "You are. You absolutely are. I'd recognize you anywhere. I saw you in concert in Buffalo. You were great. Your lyrics are effing brilliant. When are you going to come out with another album?" Without giving Steve a chance to answer, he continued patting his own pockets, apparently looking for paper. "Sorry to bother you. I'd be so honored. My wife's your biggest fan. Would you sign an autograph for her? Our anniversary is coming up. It'd be the best gift ever."

Quietly, Jenna got out of the van with her pack. Though the officer glanced her way, he was apparently too intent on his quest for something, anything to write on. She pulled her field observation notebook out. She approached and offered it to him, turning, so that he was forced to face away from the van.

Gary took the hint and quietly pulled back onto Route 30.

Officer Royston didn't seem to notice. Gratefully, he took Jenna's notebook and ripped out a clean sheet. "Thanks."

"But really. He's not who you think he is," Jenna said in an effort to keep her promise to Steve not to reveal his identity to anyone. "Really."

Undeterred, Royston turned to Steve and held out pad and pen. "Would you mind? What are you doing out here, anyway? Vacationing in the Adirondacks? It's a bit off the beaten path for a rock star like you, isn't it?"

"I was seeking peace and spiritual enlightenment in the wilderness," Steve said in the quiet, melancholy voice that had always driven girls wild. "With my half-sister, Jenna. I needed to get away from it all. Get away from all that noise and people and, and, um, fame, so I could write new songs."

The cat was finally out of the bag. Jenna felt relieved.

Officer Royston nodded with apparent sympathy.

Steve looked down at the paper and pen in his hand with surprise, like he didn't know where they came from. "I can't write. My hand." He held up his bandaged wrist with a wince.

"What happened?" Officer Royston asked as if seeing the injury for the first time. "Have you been checked out? Do you need transport to a medical facility?"

"It's nothing. I tripped when we were hiking," Steve said.

Officer Royston suddenly realized the van was gone. "Oh hell," he said, but he didn't race to his own patrol car to give pursuit as Jenna expected.

An idea came to Jenna. "Steve's got to make an evening flight, or he's going to miss a sold-out concert in Boston."

"It's okay. Sign left-handed. My wife won't mind," Officer Royston said to Steve. To Jenna, he said, "You need a ride? Why didn't you say so? I can give the two of you a lift."

Devil Will Take Your Life

by Dennis Webster

John opened the door to nine-year-old Lilly's bedroom slowly, so the creak of the hinges wouldn't wake her from her slumber. A candlestick lit up the early morning darkness as he looked in on her before he left for the trip to the North Creek Railroad Station.

"Morning, Papa," whispered his daughter, who was already awake, waiting to see him before he left.

"Morning, Sweetie," replied John. He walked across the plank floor and set the candlestick on the nightstand. "You should be getting your rest." He sat on the foot of her bed and smiled.

"You heading off to the station?" asked Lilly.

"Yup. I got to leave early with the stagecoach so those rich New York City folk don't have to wait too long."

Lilly coughed. She slept with a hanky in her hand now because the disease assured deep sleep never visited. Her face turned apple red as she hacked into the cloth.

John's heart broke. He tried to avoid looking at the speckles of blood, stark against the starched, white linen, as he knew his daughter masked great shame in her affliction. He wanted to be strong. He could not let her see him crack. He had prayed to God many times, begging him to move the lung death from his little sweetie to himself, but, alas, it did not happen.

Lilly finally stopped coughing and looked up. She smiled, her teeth straight and white with bursting optimism, just like her mother's.

"Will you bring me something back?"

"I'll try." John stood and pulled the covers up to Lilly's neck, straightened her sleeping cap, pushed aside her wispy, blonde hair, and kissed her on the forehead. "I'll be back as soon as I can. Try to get some rest."

"I love you, Papa."

"I love you, too, my Lilly of the valley."

He stepped back into the hallway and blew out the flame, for the morning light was now coming through the windows and cracks in the clapboards. A single tear traversed his grizzled, sun-baked face. He wiped it slate clean with the back of his hand.

He heard a clink. Mary was in the kitchen, and the slight clatter of dishes told him she was making coffee and packing him a lunch. No need to be quiet now as he walked up behind his wife and tickled her in the ribs. She jumped off the plank floor.

"Stop that, John!" she said as she turned around with a big grin, slapping him across the shoulder.

His hound, Blue, who had been asleep on the floor, came alive and bayed his deep howl before John calmed him down with a gentle pat on the head. John stood back up, pulled Mary close, and gave her a kiss. "Thanks for getting up and making me coffee."

Mary smiled. "I'm hoping Lilly feels up to a trip to town and possibly the lake. It's going to be a hot August day, and I heard the other children in the area are gathering for a picnic."

"You think she should be around other children? They could catch her consumption."

"I know, John, but I just want her to have a childhood. Have you thought about asking for the money?"

"I will try, Mary."

"The Adirondack Sanitarium is her only chance to live, but it's not free. I've heard Doctor Trudeau is curing tuberculosis patients up there."

"If I do a good job today, perhaps Mr. Jones will be in an agreeable mood."

"You sit on that stagecoach every day in rain and snow and clouds of black flies. He's not given you a raise in years, and you're the best stage driver in the Adirondacks. Can you tell him about Lilly? That we need the money for her care?"

"I will try," replied John. He poured coffee in his cup and drank it hot and black, a few loose grains scraping his throat on the way down. They had a single goat, and they tried to save its milk for Lilly as it seemed to be the only thing that gave her strength.

John took up his sack lunch and kissed his wife goodbye. The last thing he did before he left their homestead was place his hand on the family bible that sat on the table by the front door. He closed his eyes and whispered a prayer, ending with "Give me strength."

The train was coming into the North Creek Railroad Station at high noon, and John was there a few hours early so he could water, feed, and brush the horses. Although they belonged to his employer, the stager, John treated them as if they were his own. He looked in his lunch sack for the crab apples Mary packed for him and grabbed a handful. He held out one apple on his palm for each of the horses, smiling as their warm, moist, rubbery lips tickled his calloused hands.

At the sound of the whistle, John walked up to the platform, where he straightened his sleeves and briefly took off his top hat to comb his thick black hair with his fingers. The sun was beating down as he put on his company wool jacket. Mr. Jones, the owner of the stagecoach, insisted on proper appearance; he would be unhappy that John had forgotten to shave.

When the train came to a stop, John met the workers to collect the mail and express packages he would load before taking on the passengers. As Mr. Jones always said, "staging optimizes profit." There was one large sack of mail and a dozen packages of all shapes and sizes. Next, the passengers would line up with their bags next to them. He looked over his shoulder and saw four well-dressed men and four elegantly adorned women. It would be a lucrative day, as the carriage fit eight passengers. He collected the fare from the group, exchanged pleasantries, and held the door open while the passengers ascended into the plush interior.

Mr. Jones had purchased the best Concord stagecoach on the market.

It was an older model, yet it looked almost brand new thanks to John's many hours of hard work. The passengers always remarked about the smoothness of the ride. John knew it was the forgiving leather strap braces underneath that delivered the silky journey. The stagecoach was large and heavy so he needed a six-horse hitch. They would be going through a rough patch towards Blue Mountain that was the most rugged terrain in the Adirondacks.

John loaded the luggage in the boot at the rear of the stagecoach and then went to the train to get his last passenger. It was the cash box that was under watch by two large, silent men with lengthy beards and longer shotguns. He nodded and tipped his hat to the grim guards, who neither acknowledged his presence nor assisted him in carrying the heavily padlocked, cast-iron strongbox. John didn't have a key and didn't need one; his only responsibility was to deliver it safely to Mr. Smith. It was heavy, but John was pleased he could carry it with ease. He wondered if he'd still have the muscle to lug it if he caught consumption from Lilly. He walked up to the stagecoach and slid it under the box where he sat. Many years ago he had a partner riding shotgun, but no more. Stagecoach robberies had been numerous out west but not in the Adirondacks. Besides, Mr. Jones didn't want to pay the price. John didn't even bring along a gun. He kept his firearm above his fireplace back at the homestead and only used it for hunting deer and other edible game.

John climbed up into the driver's seat and turned and spoke to his passengers. "Okay, ladies and gentlemen. It's a half-day ride to Blue Mountain Lake. I'm your whip, John. If you need anything, please don't hesitate to call out. The black flies are out but no worries, they won't get you while we're moving. There is a box back there with small towels soaked in basil oil. If the little vampires do get inside the carriage, just take one of the towels and wrap it around your neck. That will repel them." He snapped the reins and the horses pulled forward. They were off. John looked up to the blue sky and knew it was going to be a great journey.

The recent rains and sparse traffic had left some uneven roads, but they weren't the worst in the mountains. He knew the roughest part of the Adirondacks was a few hours away. That area tested the wheels and the horses' resolve. The mountains could be steep, and the pines leaned towards the road, letting just a crack of sunlight get through to the middle of the narrow track.

Several hours later he still hadn't seen a single soul or any bears or cougars. Not even a rabbit. The creaking of the carriage assured he couldn't hear the chatter of the passengers, which was fine with him.

John was coming around the large bend and steep hill they called "Jackbox," about five miles before Blue Mountain Lake, when two men wearing masks and brandishing guns burst out of the pine trees. He snapped the reins and yelled to the horses to run, but it was too late. The two men leveled their guns and fired into the two lead horses, causing them to groan in pain and slump to the ground.

The entire stagecoach came to such an abrupt stop that John was thrown from his seat; he bounced off one of the horses and slammed to the ground, hitting with such force that the wind was knocked out of his lungs. For a moment, all he saw was the boots of one of the robbers, who yelled out, "Stand and deliver or the devil will take your life!" Then he watched the other robber's boots as he walked to the side of the carriage and ordered the passengers to get out. The only other sound was the ladies screaming.

John could see that the robber closest to him was watching his partner and not him. He silently took the passenger fare money out of his front pocket and shoved it down his pants. Just seconds after he finished hiding the cash, he was kicked over and found himself looking down the barrel of a shotgun. "Don't you move," said the robber. John held out his hands as the man went through his pockets. "You ain't got nuttin," he snarled.

John was motionless on the ground for what seemed an eternity when the male passengers started running towards the woods, prompting a barrage of laughter and gunfire from the robbers. A loud cry let him know one of the fleeing men had been hit. One of the robbers then climbed up and took out the strongbox while the other tore open all the mail and packages, taking out any cash they contained.

"Any of you follow us and we'll shoot you dead as these horses," said the taller robber as they walked backwards into the woods on the opposite side of the road from where the cowardly men had fled.

John stood up and dusted the dirt off his clothes and picked up his crumpled hat. He didn't bother straightening it as he walked to the women. "Is everyone alright?"

The ladies nodded wordlessly. One pointed towards the woods where one of the passengers lay face down on the ground. The man had a hole in his back, and he was lying in a pool of blood. John knelt down, put his hand on the man's neck, and confirmed there was no pulse. The robbers had shot the man dead. One of the women—perhaps the man's wife—began shrieking, and it was John's sad duty to inform her that the man was dead. He took her by the arm and led her back to the stagecoach.

"Listen," he said, "they might come back, so we need to get the rest of the way to the hotel and get help. We will come back for him and the other men."

John unhooked the harnesses from the two dead horses, trying not to cry at the sight of the magnificent animals lying there in the Adirondack dirt. The other four horses—the swings and wheelers—would have to take the stagecoach the rest of the way.

He helped the ladies back into the passenger area and gathered up the opened mail and packages, quickly tossing it all back into the boot. Rubbing his throbbing ribs, he scanned the woods for any sign of the men who had run away. Seeing no one, he climbed up on his driver's seat, took up the reins, and steered what was left of the team around the bodies of the dead horses. He waved away a small cloud of black flies, leaving them behind as they gained speed.

The trip was slower moving with two less horses, but they eventually made it to Dunlap's Hotel, where there were a few people milling around when they pulled up. John jumped off before the coach came to a complete stop. Spotting the lad who always helped unload luggage for a few pennies, he shouted, "Get the sheriff, Samuel. We done been robbed."

When Samuel returned, John had him take the ladies and their bags into the hotel while he rode back out to the site of the stagecoach robbery with Sheriff Wilkins and the town undertaker, Ronald Tibbits. All three were armed; the sheriff had loaned spare weapons to the other men to form a makeshift posse. The sheriff and John were on horseback, riding as fast as the animals would go. John held his ribs as the ache from his fall grew and the bouncing on the galloping horse intensified the pain. The undertaker followed with his horse and the small wagon he used for carting bodies and coffins.

The sun blazed on the back of John's neck as they turned the bend where the dead horses lay upon the ground. The men who had fled were standing next to the dead man, looking down with their hats in their hands and blank looks upon their faces. As they stopped their horses and dismounted, the sheriff and John drew their weapons and scanned the area with darting eyes. Flies were already buzzing around the horses but not the dead man, as the living ones were using their hats to wave the tiny, black buzzards away.

"If you're looking for the robbers, they're long gone," said one of the men squinting at John and company.

They all stopped talking as the undertaker pulled up in his wagon and stepped off with a grim look on his face. John put his weapon away and held his ribs. No one said anything until the undertaker knelt down and officially declared that the man on the ground was dead.

"I need you men to tell me what these killers looked like," said the sheriff, "but first, we need to get this man back to the hotel so he can be properly taken care of. Then I'll interview you fellas."

The undertaker had a white linen sheet he used to wrap around the dead man. They lifted together and placed the body in the back of the wagon with two of the living cowards holding onto it while the third sat up in the front with the undertaker. They all stared at John and the sheriff with eyes as black and empty as gun bores.

"What happened out here, John?" asked the sheriff as he put his gun away.

John put his hand on his ribcage and replied, "They came out of nowhere. I tried not to stop, but they shot the horses and I was thrown. I managed to save the passenger money, but they took everything else including the strongbox that I'm sure had cash. I have no clue who they were. They had kerchiefs tied about their faces and their hats covered their hair. I didn't recognize their voices, so they have to be alien to these parts."

"Well, they knew enough that they hit you on the most remote part of the trek. And the way they slipped back into the woods, they must be guides or at least familiar with the area. I'll get back out here and find them. You know how I am."

"I sure do, Sheriff," said John as he winced and bent slightly over, grabbing at his side.

"You injured from the fall?"

"I might have a crack or two in my ribs. I'll live."

"Well, let's get back to the hotel and see if we can get more men and some hounds out here to track these murderers."

By the time they got back to Blue Mountain Lake, John's pain was much worse, and he felt clammy and queasy and was spitting up small amounts of blood. The undertaker made him lift his shirt, and already a large bruise had appeared on his left side. "You're going to need the doctor to look at you. You got some damage in there," said the undertaker.

"I hear what you're sayin'. I will see the doctor," replied John as he handed the gun back to the sheriff. "I'm sorry I won't be able to pursue the robbers," he told him. "I don't think I'm up to it."

"Of course, John," replied the sheriff as he placed his hand on John's shoulder. "Go home to your family."

John turned and took one step before a loud voice bellowed out.

"You won't go anywhere, John William Pepper!"

John shuddered as he turned around to face his boss.

"I'm sorry, Mr. Jones."

"That all you got to say for yourself?"

John's pain disappeared when he realized all the victims of the robbery, the sheriff, the undertaker, Samuel, and another dozen Blue Mountain Lake townsfolk had gathered around and were gawking at the display. John slowly reached into his pocket and took out the fare money he had concealed in his pants and held it out to the miserly stagecoach owner. "I was able to hide this from the robbers, Mr. Jones."

Jones swiped it hard from John's hands and shoved it in his vest pocket while narrowing his eyes in a look that seared John's soul. "Pittance compared to what was in that strongbox, Pepper."

"If I only had a man riding shotgun, Mr. Jones, this might not have happened," John said nervously, trying to explain himself to the stubborn, cheap man. As he bent over and coughed a little more blood on the ground, he thought of Lilly at home fighting for her life while he was here fighting for his job.

"So now it's my fault," said Mr. Jones. "You didn't even attempt to stop those land pirates. No need reporting to work tomorrow. You're fired."

"Please, Mr. Jones. My little girl..."

"Should've thought of that before you went and got my stagecoach robbed and an innocent passenger killed. You're lucky I don't charge you for the man's coffin and other considerations."

"Yes, sir," replied John. He held his side and started the walk home, leaving behind the company horse he was previously allowed to ride home and back. It belonged to Mr. Jones.

"Wait a minute, John," said the sheriff as he came over.

John stopped and turned. "Yes, Sheriff."

"Listen, I know that robbery couldn't have been stopped or prevented. I just want you to know that if Jones offers a reward, and my posse catches them, we'll pitch in for your family's maintenance."

John reached out and shook the sheriff's hand. "I appreciate that. I'd help you if I wasn't injured and if I had a horse."

The sheriff didn't reply, instead just shook his head and moved on to gather capable men to ride out in search of the killers. John waved away the black flies with his crumpled hat, thinking as he did that he was surprised Mr. Jones hadn't asked for it too, since he had bought it for him to wear on his job as a driver. He knew his ex-boss would not offer a reward—he was too cheap and would expect the sheriff to catch the robbers because it was his job as a paid lawman. The volunteers would go along for free with the motivation of assisting the manhunt.

The walk back to his homestead was a long and lonely one for John. He finally saw his house just as Blue ran down off the porch, wagging his tail in greeting. He paused to pet his good old hound before continuing towards his house. He winced as he walked up the front porch and through the door.

Mary stopped in the middle of her chores, and the look on her face crushed him. She knew he never came home this early, especially when he was making his stagecoach runs.

"What happened?" she asked as she took one step towards him while wiping her hands off on her apron.

"How's Lilly?"

"She's resting. I'm guessing you didn't get the raise." Mary walked over to the kitchen table, pulled out a chair, sat down, and looked up to her husband with her wide blue eyes.

John walked over and got down on one knee, gritting his teeth in pain as he looked up to her. "The stagecoach was robbed this morning. A man was killed by the robbers."

Mary placed her hand over her mouth as her eyes moistened. She had one strand of blonde hair that had fallen from her meticulous bun, and it fluttered as she sat silent. He placed his hand on her knee and said, "Don't worry. Everything is going to be fine."

The loud barking of Blue alerted John that people were approaching the house. He knew his hound's barks and could decipher friend from stranger. Blue even had different howls for animals. "I'll be right back," said John as he took his shotgun off the mantle and headed out onto the front porch. Blue kept howling as two men approached from the woods. He gave his dog the signal to calm down as he lowered his gun and went out to meet them. He knew who they were, and as he got close he saw they were carrying what he was waiting for.

"You got a posse coming after you so let's make this quick," said John.

The two men just nodded and set the strongbox on the ground. John waved them away and aimed his shotgun at the padlock, pulling the trigger and busting it off. The two robbers pulled the top up to reveal stacks of cash inside. The taller of the robbers counted the bills into three stacks; the robbers each took one, shoved them in their satchels, and left John, Blue, the broken strongbox, and the last pile of money. They had done all their talking with their expressions. John was upset at them for killing the passenger, but he wasn't going to give a sermon. He stood silently as the men walked into the woods and disappeared. John set his shotgun down and carried the strongbox into a thicket and threw it in. He returned to the blood money and whispered a prayer as he picked it up and walked towards the homestead, Blue running ahead and wagging his tail in glee.

John placed the shotgun back over the mantle of the fireplace before he went to the kitchen table and placed the money in front of Mary. She stared at it, and her expression told him she knew he was involved in the robbery.

"Why?" asked Mary.

"I did it for Lilly. She can go to the sanitarium. She will live."

A single tear streaked down Mary's cheek as she shook her head. "We cannot do this, John."

"Please, Mary. You must. Mr. Jones was never going to give me a raise. Without this money Lilly will not live through the upcoming winter. You can take her up to Saranac Lake and pay the full tuition. She can even be placed in the Little Red cottage for single patients."

"John. A man died."

"I didn't expect the men I entrusted to do that. It's my burden that I will carry. But God knows I had no other way. This blood money will save Lilly's life. She deserves to grow up. She deserves to fall in love."

John spent the night sitting in his rocking chair, smoking his pipe and reading his bible, taking the time to underline passages he thought would grant him peace, but nothing did. No book could supplant his thoughts, his guilt, or his shame. He was a thief and a murderer. He stayed up late into the night before he went into his bedroom with the candlestick lit to look at Mary sound asleep in their marriage bed. He blew out the flame and was able to see by the midnight moonlight that crept into the small window. The crickets were playing their serenade as he lay down next to his wife and spooned her, knowing this might be the last time he'd have the pleasure of her company.

In the morning John helped Lilly pack her things for the trip to Saranac Lake with Mary. She'd agreed to use the money to save their daughter. She knew what he was going to do, and she didn't try to talk him out of it.

"We'll need a horse and carriage to get you both to Dr. Trudeau. I will send one for you." John said. "I took out enough of the money to pay passage." He went into Lilly's bedroom. His heart stopped for a moment; for the first time in months she was standing there in regular clothes, wearing her yellow dress with the large, white bow, the one she used to wear to church when she was well enough to travel and be around others. It was baggy on her now, whereas at one time she'd filled it out with her healthy flesh. His heart crushed at the wasting away of his once vital daughter.

"Mother says you're not going with us?"

"You two will travel alone, and I'll be with you when I can," he said as he sat on the bed, reached out and took her hand. He looked up at her and smiled as he patted her hand.

"Will they cure me, Papa?"

"Of course. The next time you see me you'll be back to your old self."

"You mean I'll go back to school?"

"You bet." John stood up and hugged his daughter. "I'll be sending you a carriage. I have to go to town."

John took one last, quick glance at his little girl as she resumed packing her suitcase, and then walked out of the room, picked up his bible, and hugged Mary. She didn't say anything, but she had that look he knew so well. "I know," he said. "I love you too." He walked out of the house and had to shoo Blue back in. But first he leaned over to pet his loyal pooch. "They're going to take you on a trip, Blue."

The walk to town was the longest trek of John's life. He didn't even bother waving away the black flies; he took this plague as precursor to his punishment. When he reached town, he headed over to the stable to arrange a ride for his family. It wasn't the stagecoach company he had worked for but one that gave tourists rides to neighboring lakes and fun excursions. He had just enough for the fare and a sizeable tip as he paid the driver and asked him to go to his home immediately. He waited until the carriage and driver were gone out of sight before he walked over to

Dunlap's Hotel. As he got close he saw a commotion of people. There was loud talking and people milling about the front porch. The crowd cleared and there stood the sheriff, Mr. Jones, friends from the town, and the tourists that had been his passengers. The posse stepped to the side and there in chains were his two conspirators. Everyone stopping talking as John walked forward, gripping his bible tightly. Mr. Smith stepped forward and shouted, "You'll fry in the electric chair in Auburn for this, John William Pepper!"

John stopped short of the crowd. Holding the bible high over his head, he said, "*For I am conscious of nothing against myself, yet I am not by this acquitted but the one who examines me is the Lord.*"

Trickle-Down Death

by Larry Weill

January 15, 1962 – Shortly before midnight

The night of January 15, 1962, was cold and windy, with snowflakes streaking across the cockpit windshield from west to east. The flight hut and air strip on the air force base in Plattsburgh were close to deserted as the midnight hour approached. The howl of the wind was nearly drowned out by the high-pitched whine of the six jet engines affixed to the wings of the Air Force B-47, which sat awaiting final clearance for takeoff.

On board the plane sat three air force officers and a single enlisted man, ready to take flight into the frigid Adirondack night. Their official mission was to conduct a routine nighttime practice reconnaissance and bombing run. Their target was Watertown, New York, which was often used as a site for these exercises. The expressions on the faces of these men reflected very little that could be described as concern, or even interest. For them, it was simply another run from point A to point B, another chance to "wipe out the town" without hurting a soul. They had practiced this exercise to the point of boredom, and each crew member knew every waypoint of the voyage as well as he knew his own backyard. It was routine, and they were the best of the best, professionals in the highest sense of the word.

The clock now read 1:40 AM With less than fifteen minutes left until takeoff, two figures dressed in civilian clothes emerged from the flight hut and hustled across the tarmac. Between them they pushed a heavy handcart that was built for carrying small loads of cargo to waiting aircraft. Even through their heavy parkas and cold-weather gear, it was easy to determine that the two men were separated in age by a great many years. The older man moved slowly, and he used the wheeled cart as a source of stability over the frigid ground, while the younger figure appeared much more agile and limber, gliding along the with ease.

Loaded onto the main platform of the cart were a number of small, square boxes, heavily padded and labeled with numerous notations. Upon reaching the aircraft, the older of the two men handed a single piece of paper to the navigator, who in turn climbed into the cockpit and passed the document to the pilot. He then climbed stiffly though a lower hatch and began pulling the boxes up into a small cargo compartment. Then, after several minutes of stowing the crates, the younger man trotted quickly back into the flight hut, after seeing his partner safely onboard with his cargo.

After perusing the sheet of paper, the pilot's face clouded with anger. The plane was already overloaded with passengers. The normal flight crew on the B-47 consisted of three individuals. However, the addition of the observer they had taken on earlier plus this new passenger brought the total to five. On top of it all, the paper (which had been stamped "TOP SECRET") failed to provide the name of the new passenger or his reason for being onboard. And there was a new destination for the flight: Griffiss Air Force Base in Rome, New York. The orders also contained a highly unusual addendum that caught the pilot's attention. Handwritten on the bottom of the page was the declaration that "Deadly force is authorized in the protection of the cargo," which must be delivered to Colonel Gregory Simons immediately upon arrival at Griffiss.

The pilot didn't know whether this was an actual crisis, or just another training scenario concocted by his squadron. All he knew was that it smacked of the arrogance of his commander and his staff, who seemed to enjoy springing these little surprises in the middle of the night, especially in such inclement weather. With a grunt of aggravation, he folded the paper and stuffed it into his flight-suit pocket. He then instructed the new passenger on how to strap himself into the extra cavity in the crawl space, which would offer little comfort in the flight to Rome. There was precious little passenger space in a B-47, and this excursion was already overloaded beyond capacity.

As the co-pilot went through the preflight checklist and the revised flight plan, the pilot made a series of disconcerting observations. The newly boarded passenger, strapped into the space below the cockpit area, had positioned a large handgun across his lap. Every muscle in the man's face was taut with tension and concentration, his eyes focused on one of the boxes brought aboard the plane. Constructed of steel and reinforced with rubberized "bumpers" on all corners, it was adorned with a series of angular markings and notations across the exterior and a bright yellow label across one side. The newcomer was sweating profusely, despite the freezing temperatures outside the aircraft.

"You make sure to keep the safety lock 'on' on that popgun of yours," shouted the pilot, cupping his hands to overcome the roar of the engines. "You fire off a single round from that thing and we'll all end up as part of the landscape."

The gray-haired gentleman only glanced up, using two fingers to symbolize a brief salute to the lieutenant in charge of the mission. His gaze then quickly returned to the package secured in front of him, his eyes glued to the object as though it might explode.

The fact that the stranger looked like a civilian was, in fact, part of the ruse. Dr. Edgar Steinholtz was one part army officer, one part medical researcher, and three parts genius. A prestigious scientist and medical researcher at Johns Hopkins, he had pushed the limits on pathogen research and the science of deadly diseases, none of which escaped the attention of the Central Intelligence Agency and members of the Secret Service's task force on biological warfare. His work on genetic engineering was decades ahead of his time, and his clandestine activities were all kept classified to the highest levels. Much of his research would remain sequestered in locked vaults forever, known only to military scientists and intelligence organizations.

Dr. Steinholtz's family had a history of military duty on both sides of the ocean. His father, a senior officer in the German army during World

War II, was killed during the final year of fighting in the collapse around Berlin. His brother, who was two years his junior, was a U.S. marine sergeant, having immigrated into the U.S. with the rest of the family shortly after the war. Steinholtz himself had never counted on becoming a member of any uniformed service, and in fact very seldom dressed the part. His rank of major was almost more symbolic than anything, and he tended to dress in tweed sports coats, in recognition of his background in academia. No one on the aircraft that night would have guessed that he outranked every member of the crew, including the pilot.

Once the fuselage doors were bolted shut, the streamlined aircraft taxied out to the runway and pointed its nose into the wind. The pilot tested his radio, and then did one final check of his instrument panel. Finding everything in order and receiving final clearance from the air control tower, he gradually increased the engines' thrust until the plane reached takeoff speed and climbed rapidly off the runway. The cloud ceiling was very low that night, the wind intense and gusting from several directions. The pilot immediately felt the plane lurch from side to side as he quickly performed a series of deft maneuvers to bring the craft to a stable attitude. It was challenging, even for the highly experienced aviator, who immediately questioned the wisdom of conducting the exercise on such a night. This would be anything but a "routine training mission."

Once the plane crossed over fifteen hundred feet, all visibility was lost. "Pea soup" was how the pilot gruffly described the scene to his copilot, positioned directly behind his own seat. From then on, it would be a case of flying by the seat of their pants, using compass, altimeter, and air speed to plot their course across the total black void that was the Adirondack Park. He glanced at his watch and noticed that it was a little after two in the morning.

"Tower control, this is Flight 01BH89, flying on instruments at 4,700 feet, bound for destination as assigned," reported the pilot in a professional tone.

"Roger that, Flight 01BH89, we have you on radar. Proceed as assigned and report your progress after completing stage one of your mission. Over," came the official reply.

From the navigator's seat, the 1st Lt. pored over the new mission notes again and again. It didn't make sense, and it didn't fit protocol. They were to complete their mission—crossing the Adirondacks from Plattsburgh to the airfield in Rome, New York while making it appear as though they were conducting a routine round-trip training mission to Watertown, complete with low-level reconnaissance and simulated bombing—an impossible task on a night such as this, with zero visibility and ferocious crosswinds. Then, following a landing at Griffiss, they were to offload their mysterious passenger and his cargo, all without recording a single note of his presence on their passenger manifest document. None of it made sense.

The aircraft climbed higher, crossing over eight-thousand feet, all while being buffeted about by the severe winds of a midwinter storm. The pilot, also a 1st Lt., felt the aircraft being spun about like a crab in a wind tunnel. He couldn't hold his course steady for more than a few seconds at a time, and he quickly realized that his navigator would have the difficult task of tracking their location without the aid of visual guides. The level of tension was high, and the team quickly forgot about the presence of their passenger.

"I think we've got mountains below us," hollered the navigator, plotting their track as best he could. "You think we should play this one by our orders and start our low-level recon?"

The pilot thought long and hard over this one. It was a scenario from hell, and one in which he didn't want to tempt the fates.

"We'll drop down to five-thousand feet and do two passes," was the pilot's reply. "After that, the hell with the squadron's orders. If the Skipper wants a plane to bomb the Adirondacks, he can damn well come up here and do it himself."

"Roger that," called the navigator, acknowledging the pilot's sentiments. This was not a night to risk anything close to ground level. They all wanted to get out of the elements and set their wheels down on the tarmac as soon as possible.

Following recommendations from the navigator, the pilot made a series of maneuvers across the mountainous terrain, passing closer than he realized to the rocky summits of the High Peaks region. The wind had pushed them far off course from their expected location, into the unwelcoming arms of the MacIntyre Range. Had he realized that his first pass on their simulated run had almost swept the snow drifts aside on the summit of Algonquin, he would have abandoned the mission entirely and climbed to a safe altitude for the rest of the trip. However, none of this was comprehended in the absence of visual or radar display. The second pass, cutting a tighter arc, came from northeast to southwest, the aircraft flying at no more than 4,600 feet. Determined to complete all phases of the mission, the pilot kept his eyes glued to the front of the cockpit and his ears tuned to his navigator's reports.

"Maintain altitude for eighteen seconds, then come left to 350 degrees and climb to 7,000 feet" were the recommendations passed to the pilot.

"Maintaining altitude at 4,600 feet, commencing second simulated run at this time," replied the pilot, intensely focused on the control.

They would be the last words of his life.

As the second hand on the pilot's wristwatch crossed the number 12, signifying the time was now 2:14 AM, the B47 hit a small pocket of low pressure and dropped about seventy-five feet in altitude. The depression wouldn't have been critical in most missions, but tonight it was catastrophic. The craft had been flying on a southwesterly course at an air speed of about 350 knots, and was more than thirty miles off course. The resulting error placed them directly over Wright's Peak, an adjoining pinnacle of Algonquin, the second tallest mountain in the state of New York.

The irony in the story is that, despite all the mistakes and miscalculations, they still almost cleared it. The tip of Wright's Peak, which appeared out of nowhere, was barely a wingtip below their fuselage when first sighted. If the plane had been maintaining a level flight profile, the summit rocks would have passed safely below her belly. But unfortunately, this was not the case, and the descending aircraft clipped the very tip of the storied peak, which tore into the fuel tanks and fabric of the streaking war machine. The impact spun the plane into a frenzied series of gyrations and explosive somersaults, with pieces of the craft being thrown off into the darkness like a centrifuge spitting off shrapnel. A few of the larger, sturdier pieces survived, including the engine turbines and some of the other more solid components. All else was ground and burned into tiny shards of unrecognizable debris, which showered down the mountainside in an apocalyptic cascade of destruction. The billowing fireball and ensuing thunderclap were all swallowed quickly and completely by the elements. Then, all was silent.

Had the calendar been turned to the summer months, with warmer weather and enthusiastic hikers camped in the scenic mountain lean-tos, they might have observed the horrific crash, accompanied as it was by the blinding explosion and combustion of the nearly full fuel tanks. However, given the conditions, with extreme cold and wind-driven snow, the woods were empty, with nary a soul to bear witness to the spectacle from up on high. The entire crew died instantly in the fiery calamity, incinerated with most of the aircraft and its cargo. Only the wreckage remained on the rocky buttresses of the lofty peak, dispersed across the seemingly endless expanse of desolate wilderness.

January 18, 1962 – Fifty-two hours after the crash

It was late in the day, and Army Captain Michael Forchey sat in his laboratory in Fort Detrick, Maryland, reading the report of the accident. He had spent the past three years studying under the tutelage of his mentor, Dr. Steinholtz, and had modeled his own young career after the respected scientist's ambitions. He, too, was an expert on deadly viruses and pathogens, although he was far more involved in the military side of army life than his mentor. Forchey had originally been trained as an infantry officer, and he was recruited into the medical sciences field because of his academic prowess and work as a research assistant during his college years. However, his fascination with artillery and weapons was still quite active. In fact, he was highly interested in shooting and was a nationally ranked sharpshooter with a variety of long and short weapons. He still enjoyed spending a day at the range when time permitted, teaching the new recruits the fine points of marksmanship.

Tonight, target practice was the furthest thing from Forchey's mind.

His hands shook as he scanned the details of the Adirondack incident. "Entire plane destroyed at high altitude. Consumed by explosion and flames. All hands lost in arctic conditions." It was more than he could fathom, and he leaned back in his swivel chair, eyes closed in thought. How could this be possible? Less than three days ago, he had accompanied the senior scientist to the airfield on the east side of the Adirondacks and helped him prepare the top secret cargo for transport to a classified location. They had shared a hotel room, a meal, and some laughs over a beer at a favorite local pub. And now this—so sudden, abrupt, and final.

And potentially deadly.

The young scientist ran through all the possibilities, considering the consequences of each scenario. Surely most of the cargo containers brought onboard by Dr. Steinholtz should have been destroyed under normal circumstances. Yet given the highly engineered construction of these parcels, which were designed to withstand extreme abuse for extended periods of time without rupturing, he couldn't be sure.

In fact, Lieutenant Forchey could be certain of only one thing. If, by any chance, the one "protected cargo" box of the six loaded onto the aircraft had fractured without being completely destroyed by the heat and flames of the fire, the consequences could be astronomical. Forchey himself had been involved with the research and development of the new virus, which was developed for possible use in the Bay of Pigs invasion of 1961. The virus, known as H7IIQN, was a hybrid that combined the worst elements of small pox and influenza, and it could be passed between infected individuals as an airborne pathogen, although this particular strain was much more easily contracted by ingestion. Its release into the public water supply could spell the end of entire civilizations. Its catastrophic potential led the military to quickly cease development on the strain, although it did decide to maintain a culture of the virus in its top-secret, deep-freeze storage facility. Even the thought of its potential release into the public was a nightmare of the worst magnitude. Forchey's stomach churned as he considered the possibilities.

Although he regretted the inevitable consequences, he realized that he had to notify the proper authorities within his own army command. He knew with grim certainty that "the authorities" would already be starting their own emergency search detail, so this was more of a formality than anything. His fingers still trembling, he managed to feed a sheet of typing paper into the carriage of the typewriter and start his brief but vaguely coded message to his superior officer.

"Colonel Redman, I'm sure you have heard the reports, which have now been confirmed. Flight with Dr. Steinholtz and cargo were lost in mountainous region of Adirondack airspace. Destruction of parcel with quarantined cargo cannot be confirmed. I am departing tonight to assist with the search and implementation of protective measures. I expect both army and air force personnel to be involved in the recovery operation. I will call from search site when time permits. Very respectfully, Lieutenant Forchey."

The young officer walked quickly down the polished-tile hallway and dropped the sealed letter into the colonel's mailbox. He was the only person left in the highly guarded building that night, although his feeling of loneliness and foreboding was not due to his physical surroundings. Without wasting an additional moment, he headed out the door and into his car for the drive to Frederick Municipal Airport. From there, he would catch a small, army-personnel plane for the flight to Plattsburgh. Life was about to get very interesting.

January 22, 1962 – Six days after the crash

Mike DeWitte, a senior official of the New York State Conservation Department, sat in his temporary office in Lake Placid. It was nothing more than a mobile trailer that had been towed into the Heart Lake hiking region parking lot. On most days, he was a man in charge of his elements, a tough, hard-nosed manager who was able to cut through bureaucratic red tape with a swift slash of his authoritarian sword. DeWitte had been an employee of the conservation department for close to forty years, rising through the ranks of conservation officer to district supervisor and finally to his current role as regional manager. Not one given to formalities, he respected ability and competence more than he did rank or pay grade. He wasn't known for beating around the bush.

Much to DeWitt's dismay, he found that he wasn't able to control his own territory in this crisis. The woods were literally swarming with people in winter uniforms, none of whom seemed the least bit interested in what should have been DeWitt's role as the state's focal point for the operation. Only one man, Air Force Major Pete Gilleland, had even bothered to stop into the trailer, and that was to introduce himself and request that DeWitte keep his search parties out of the area around the crash site. It was an awkward and tense meeting, with the major offering very little in the way of information.

"Mr. DeWitte, I appreciate your concern and your obvious desire to help in the search for any survivors," said Gilleland, his short red hair and pale complexion glistening under the lighting in the low ceiling. "But there are a few things that you need to know. The first is that there are no survivors. Our initial search party already established that within forty-eight hours of the crash."

"I'm sorry to hear that," replied DeWitte, who already realized that the chance of anyone surviving such a crash would have been nil.

"Secondly, there are factors involving this accident that are classified well above what I am authorized to disclose to you. It's a matter of national security that cannot be divulged or allowed to become public knowledge."

DeWitte tried to preserve a calm appearance, even though he could feel the hackles on his neck abruptly rising.

"Are you inferring that there is a danger to people in this vicinity, and we're not allowed to learn about it?"

"I'm only saying, sir, that we need you to close off the area surrounding the crash site until we can account for all the cargo on the aircraft and safely transport it back to our own facilities," replied Gilleland, his voice revealing an unmistaken shade of impatience. This audience had already lasted longer than he desired.

"I'll do what I can, Major, and I'll keep my own people out of the area, since you obviously know much more about this region than any of us," said DeWitte, his words dripping with sarcasm. "But I cannot control the hikers who enter the area from dozens of different trails, and are sometimes bushwhacking without trails or climbing the slides up the sides of these peaks. They're there, and there's very little you or I can do to keep them away."

The officer nodded silently in agreement, his eyes cast downward in thought. He stood suddenly to leave, zipping his parka closed while still considering his host's last remarks.

"You're probably right, Mr. DeWitte. And all I can say is, God bless their souls." Then, without further comment, he turned away and exited the mobile office.

The next two weeks of activity brought hundreds of additional troops into the area surrounding the High Peaks. Lieutenant Forchey arrived in the early phases of the search to work with both Major Gilleland and Mr. DeWitte. One of the main goals of everyone involved was to remain out of sight as much as possible so that the public was unaware of the massive hunt. The army troops were seeking the remains of a series of small, padded boxes containing securely wrapped contents. They were instructed to avoid contact with the parcels, but to mark their locations with radio beacon equipment and then immediately use their radios to call for help.

As for Forchey, he served as a liaison between army and air force brass and the conservation department's senior officials. He pleaded with the state to have the entire area sealed off, only to receive a partial agreement to advise climbers to remain clear of the crash site and the adjoining rock slides. It was an agreement that didn't provide much comfort to the scientist, and he feared the worst in terms of the eventual consequences.

Working in severe weather, with wind-driven snow and sub-zero temperatures, the army troops were able to find four of the six cargo parcels, which had been scattered down a half mile of mountainous slope. They were located amongst the other debris from the crash and exhibited varied degrees of burns and damage. However, they had been so well constructed that none of them had been totally breached, and all still held their original cargo intact.

This was good news for Lieutenant Forchey, as it meant that there was probably no immediate danger to the public from leaking pathogens. However, the truly scary news was that one of the still-missing containers held the very lethal strain of H7IIQN, and two hundred men searching for fourteen days had failed to find it. The very fact that the first four containers had held up so well meant that the other two had probably also survived intact. But if they had become buried in the snowpack, or worse, bounced into an exposed cleft in the rock, they might never turn up.

The military's ultimate decision was to scale down the hunt, but to keep four men in the area as a permanent search team throughout the spring and into the snowmelt of early summer. Forchey remained with them, and he became intimately familiar with the routes and rocks that formed the southwest side of Wright Peak. He felt as though he had scrambled over every boulder on each of the slides that scarred the steep side of the mountain. He even established a semi-permanent camp, located well over a mile off the trail, where he erected a small hut in which he stayed for weeks at a time. Still the consummate sharpshooter, he kept his high-powered rifle in the woods with him, even though he never used it for anything other than to sight in on imaginary targets in the clearing around his rickety camp.

By the time Forchey was ordered back to Fort Detrick, the last of the air force searchers had been detached, and Forchey had given up hopes of finding the lethal cargo. Over the seven months they worked together, he had even become friends with Mike DeWitte, who had moved back into his Albany office but still visited from time to time. They called their visits "The Mike and Mike Show," having spent so much time together on the case. Together, they retraced the path of the aircraft in its final moments and the path of destruction it left behind as it came to rest in its final location.

The details of their last conversation were more revealing than DeWitte cared to admit. It would be the final time the two men would see each other face-to-face, and Forchey decided to let it all hang out.

"Mike, if this virus is ever allowed to come into contact with humans, the results could be catastrophic," said Forchey, his forehead covered with sweat from the summer heat.

"You've alluded to that before," nodded DeWitte, the concern showing in his eyes. "What did you say it was called? The code name?"

"That doesn't matter, and I really don't want that to become known beyond you and me," said the army officer. "What's important is that someone must keep track of any unusual sicknesses in the area, anything with symptoms resembling smallpox in any way."

"Smallpox!" DeWitte. "You mean to tell me that we've got a ticking time bomb up here containing the smallpox disease?"

Forchey fell silent, thinking of a diplomatic way to answer the question. There was no easy way to explain it, because he knew that the truth was even worse than it sounded.

"Mike, this virus, if it ever escaped, has the destructive capability of smallpox, but with a slightly different method of infection. It was engineered to survive well in a water supply, which would have wreaked havoc on a small nation such as Cuba which has very little fresh water. If the containment system failed, it could infect the groundwater in the area until nature eventually purged it out of the system."

"And just how long would that container hold up? How long could it sit outside in the elements without rupturing, or rusting, or whatever it would take to create a leak?"

"The book answer is about fifty years, or half a century," replied Forchey. "It was designed to hold samples for very long periods, even in extreme conditions."

"But what if it was damaged?" asked DeWitte.

"That is indeed a wild card," sighed Forchey, acknowledging the possibility. "That could shorten the containment period to a matter of a few years, or even less."

"And how long, my friend, could this virus survive on its own, if left to broil and freeze in the Adirondack wilderness? Is it possible that the weather itself could kill off the contents before it ever became a risk to the public?"

The question put Forchey notably on edge, and another period of silence ensued. DeWitte waited patiently for the officer's response.

"No, I'm afraid not. This is something that I'm going to tell you because you should know, but you must not pass along, because it is classified as top secret. This virus is special for a number of reasons. One of them is that it is particularly long-lived in a way that we have never observed in any other virus. Over the course of a few decades, it may lose only a fraction of its potency. This is one of the reasons why the military was so interested in Dr. Steinholtz's research. He engineered viruses decades before the process was known to the scientific world, and he created this as a military Armageddon to be used against a hostile force. This virus will not be destroyed by a few years of heat and cold. It will remain a terror for decades, possibly even for centuries."

The answer hit DeWitte with the effect of a punch in the gut, and he stood, rooted in place, considering the consequences.

"No wonder all your searchers had gas masks and space suits," murmured DeWitte when his voice finally returned. "With that kind of risk, anyone would be crazy to expose themselves to the smallest trace of the stuff."

Forchey simply nodded in agreement.

"So what do we do now?" asked the forester, suppressing the lump in his throat.

"We sit and wait," replied Forchey. "We go about our jobs, and our lives, and we wait. And we hope and pray that we never hear a word about it, and that no one ever gets sick, and this whole thing just goes away by itself."

The two men ended the conversation with a handshake, and then headed their own separate ways. They both said a silent prayer that nature would serve to clean up the problem on its own, as it so often does. However, they both harbored doubts, and anticipated the day when Armageddon would escape its weatherproof container and announce itself to the world.

Had Captain Forchey realized just how close he'd come to the object of his search, he would have been mightily shocked. The first of the two missing crates, the one with the nonlethal payload, never left the plane. The impact of the collision had rammed it into the front corner of the fuselage in such a way that the frame of the cockpit had literally wrapped itself around the corners of the square container. It had no chance of remaining intact, and part of the casing literally fused with the structural members of the aircraft body. Even if it had been discovered, it bore little or no resemblance to the original package, and would have been ignored or discarded. Regardless, it contained little more than samples of attenuated biowaste that were bound for the same army storage facility.

Not more than another two-hundred yards further down the slide rested a huge rock monolith that resembled a squared-off egg, resting on its wider end. It made a great stop for anyone climbing the slide, as it was surrounded by a few smaller boulders that could serve as either seats or small tables. A steady trickle of ground water flowed down the slide under the rocks, accumulating in a small pool that was ice cool and crystal clear. Hikers found it inviting, and many of them drank from it rather than draining the precious supply in their canteens.

Off to one side of the boulder was a short drop-off, with large chunks of anorthosite stacked erratically like giant blocks of Legos tossed in a heap. Wide gaps appeared between the rocks, some of them spacious enough to conceal a small object. Although Forchey and others from the search party had examined this geological jumble, none of them realized that the gaps between the rocks were interconnected in a labyrinth of maze-like tunnels. In an incredible, one-in-a-million chance, the intact crate had been jettisoned down the slope and into the crevasse, where it had pinballed its way into an impossibly concealed tomb. Had the high winds not blasted the snow from the ledge earlier that evening, the parcel would have wedged itself into the snowpack and been sighted immediately. However, coincidences do happen, both good and bad.

This one, unfortunately, was deadly.

October 10, 2012

Seismology is a rather inexact science. So it was no great surprise that experts from the United States and Canada measured the quake differently. The Canadians calculated the tremor at 4.5 on the Richter scale, whereas the Americans announced a reading of 3.9. In either case, the low magnitude of the quake would hardly set off a tsunami on the Great Lakes, if that were even possible. However, houses across the Montreal region felt the ground shaking, as did the residents of the mountainous northern Adirondacks. No structural damage resulted from the event, but ground was definitely shifted, and precariously stacked items were seen to settle.

For people climbing in the Adirondack High Peaks region, the noticeable effects would have been negligible. Most of the hikers on the trail that morning were probably unaware of the earthquake that struck the area northwest of Montreal slightly after midnight that night. However, the action was enough to send loose rock and debris tumbling down some of the steeper Adirondack slides, shifting the position of some larger boulders if even by a few scant millimeters. One of these massive stones had received just enough pressure to slip downward by about four inches, its lower ridge ramming into the greatly weakened case that had been concealed for over half a century. The impact tore a great hole through the outer casing of the metal box and shattered many of the vials that were still arranged neatly inside. In an unstoppable, deadly chain of events, the water seepage from farther up the mountain flowed through the small gully and directly over the cargo crate, filling the inside until it overflowed and gushed back out the ruptured hole. Unseen death, carried in the form of life's smallest organism, cascaded from pool to pool underneath the rock until finally coming to rest in the tiny collecting pond on the flat landing.

Had the weather been as hostile as it was on the day of the crash, the consequences would have been delayed, or perhaps even eliminated. No one in the scientific world would have bet on the survival of the pathogens once released into the open environment for any length of time. However, this strain of virus, securely packaged in the test tube containers, could remain viable for periods that were unimagined by civilian pathologists. Once exposed to the elements, it was anyone's guess.

The first "anyone" happened to appear on the scene within a matter of twelve hours. Wright Peak is a popular and scenic mountain, and it receives hundreds of visitors every day. Most climbers tend to take the more routine trail up from Heart Lake. However, a significant number of enthusiasts enjoy climbing the less conventional slides, and this was a popular time of year to be making the trek. Even though the leaves were past peak, the temperature was still moderate, and significant colors still remained in the lower valleys. At least a half dozen climbing parties passed by the shimmering pool of water that day, and that pattern was repeated for most of the next week. Each of the visitors gawked wide-eyed at the view from this perch near the summit, all the while unaware of the perils that lay within inches of their feet.

October 22, 2012

This was one for the books. Dr. Janet DuPres had been practicing medicine in the Philadelphia area for over thirty years and was widely respected by her patients both young and old. A general practitioner, she prided herself on keeping abreast of the latest developments in medical research and treatment. Known as "Doctor J" to her patients, she was warm and cheerful in her bedside manner, and she was one of the few physicians in the city who was not above making house calls when the situation warranted.

Early in the evening, Dr. DuPres stopped in to visit a new patient who was experiencing severe flu-like symptoms. Ron Staffen was a carpenter by trade, although he had fallen on some hard times and had moved back into his parent's house for temporary lodging. He was in great physical condition, and he enjoyed hiking and camping with his friends when time permitted.

The moment that Dr. DuPres completed her initial examination of the patient, she knew that something was seriously wrong. The twenty-seven-year-old man had a soaring fever, hacking cough, blood-red eyes, and a temperature of 105.5 degrees. Instinctively, the doctor—already in rubber gloves—pulled on a surgical mask and a disposable gown. She sat by the side of the bed and interviewed her patient, all the while making notes of the symptoms. Even before she began the examination of his eyes, ears, nose, and throat, she noticed something that made her blood freeze. On the lower part of Staffen's face was a series of slightly raised oval bumps, each one tinted a pinkish-red hue.

The physician rose and turned on a bedside light to further illuminate the patient's skin. In the brightened room she could see that the profusion of bumps was not confined to the man's face. They had spread across his entire upper torso and arms, with some being more pronounced than others. As she stood, rooted in place, with her eyes fixed on the pustules, the patient coughed again. A bit of blood-stained saliva escaped his lips and stuck on the side of his chin.

Dr. DuPres made some small talk with her patient, and then backed quietly out of the room, saying "I'll return shortly, as soon as I speak with your parents for a few minutes, OK?"

Just outside the door she encountered Mrs. Staffen. She had been observing the exam from outside the room, and her face was white as a ghost. "Is he very ill, Doctor?" she asked, her voice strained.

Dr. DuPres said nothing. Instead, she peeled off her disposable gloves and mask, placing them into a medical waste bag. Her paper gown quickly followed suit. Then, taking Laura Staffen by the arm, she guided her down a long hallway and into the kitchen, where her husband, George, sat reading a newspaper. She sat down across from them and removed her glasses as the couple regarded her anxiously.

"Mr. and Mrs. Staffen, I'd like to have a few tests performed on your son. I believe he has a very serious disease, and I want to make sure that the two of you don't catch it from him. I'd like to have a specially equipped ambulance come to transport him to the hospital."

Laura's eyes quickly misted over, her lower lip quivering with emotion. "Oh my God, is he going to be all right? He...he...he's not going to die, is he?" she whispered, the tears beginning to fall down her cheeks.

"No, no, please don't even consider that," said the doctor. "But this is very serious, and if it is what I suspect, it is also very contagious. I'd like to ask you to stay out of Ron's room, and do not have contact with any of his belongings."

"What do you think it is?" asked the father.

"I've never seen a live case of smallpox, since it's been wiped out in this country for over one hundred years, but your son has all the classic symptoms of the disease," replied DuPres. "It's a virus that's been eliminated by vaccine, but sometimes these things can come back."

After speaking with the parents about her suspicions, Dr. DuPres stepped outside and placed a call to the Center for Disease Control (CDC) in Atlanta, Georgia. Then, after providing a full description of her patient's symptoms, she recommended a course of action that included a full quarantine at the CDC facility in the city of Philadelphia. She also advised that the parents be quarantined as well, knowing the virus could have been passed between members of the household. Finally, she used an antiseptic lotion to clean her own hands, wiping the solution liberally up her arms to reduce her own chances of contracting the disease until she could take a full decontamination shower.

As Dr. DuPres drove home through the Philadelphia traffic, she sensed a strong feeling of foreboding over the case. The CDC would need to know where her patient had contracted the disease, and how many others may have been exposed to the same pathogen. Nothing about this case looked good.

If Ron Staffen had been an isolated case, it might have been chalked up to a single, bizarre occurrence. A virus could have been transported into the United States from a foreign source and somehow found its way to an isolated Pennsylvania carpenter. Stranger things have happened. However, within two days, additional cases with identical symptoms were reported in several New York cities, including Buffalo, Jamestown, and Utica, as well as a case in downtown Toronto. The source was a mystery, although it was commonly accepted that the simultaneous appearance of the sickness in five different locations was not a coincidence. Somehow there was a link, a common connection that must tie the afflicted individuals together.

Within twenty-four hours, the CDC was mobilized and fully engaged in the case. They sent medical teams into each of the communities where the stricken individuals resided, interviewing family members, employers, and other potential sources of the disease. All the while, new cases of what appeared to be a strain of smallpox were reported on a slow but steady basis, and one victim died. Throughout the crisis, health care professionals were doing everything they could to prevent the spread of the virus. It was a nerve-wracking and tense period of time, and within days the military as well as the FBI's anti-terrorism group were called into play.

It didn't take long for the investigators to find a common thread among the individuals smitten with the virus. All of them had, within the past month, visited the Adirondack Park, and each had climbed unorthodox routes into the upper reaches of the McIntyre Range. The meaning of this was a mystery to almost everyone involved. Mike DeWitte had been dead for over fifteen years, having passed away with the top secret information locked inside him. Major Gilleland, the Air Force search team leader, was now in the latter throes of Alzheimer's disease, and resided in a Florida nursing home, confined to a bed.

In fact, the entire institutional knowledge of the Air Force tragedy of 1962 had, by now, been erased by the ever-creeping hands of time. The only vestigial information about the event lay in yellowing reports that were confined to the classified vaults of the army's biological-weaponry facility. It was as though the crash of the B-47 had never happened, and the sleeping giant never batted so much as an eyelid.

November 3, 2012

The weather in the Adirondack High Peaks was warmer than on most November days, with clear skies and temperatures in the forties. With very few days left in the regular hiking season, the trails were dotted with peak-bagging enthusiasts out on weekend excursions. As usual, most of the climbers stuck to the mountains' trails and well-established routes, while a smaller number tested their mountaineering skills on the less traditional routes.

One of the more experienced groups on the mountain slides that morning was a local trio from Saranac Lake. Ryan Seely, a handsome twenty-six-year-old computer programmer, was climbing with his girlfriend, Natasha Fields, who was also twenty-six. Climbing with them was their mutual friend, Devon O'Malley, who had accompanied his two friends on numerous expeditions throughout the High Peaks region over the past five years. But today his mission was different. Today, Ryan had asked his friend to come along to act as photographer when he proposed to Natasha on the summit of Wright Peak. In his pocket, Ryan carried the one-carat diamond ring he would give to his soon-to-be-fiancée when he popped the question.

Rather than climb the trail from Heart Lake or Lake Colden, the three friends decided to try one of the slides that creased the rocky southwest side of the peak. Once they found their route, they set about the arduous task of picking their way over the jumble of rocks and stumps that constituted the steep chute up the side of the mountain. The going was slow, but they were determined, and they made steady progress throughout the morning hours and into the early afternoon.

About a half mile below them, Ray Madden and Jerry Ferris, a pair of conservation officers with the New York Department of Environmental Conservation (DEC) started their ascent via the same route. Both seasoned professionals, Madden and Ferris were men on a mission, having attended a briefing on the appearance of the smallpox-like virus amongst Adirondack climbers. They didn't know what their target would be, but they were determined to seek out anything that didn't resemble the rest of the terrain and then bring it to the attention of the authorities.

As the local trio climbed the slide, they stopped occasionally to enjoy the view and take some pictures. Natasha noticed that her boyfriend was taking more breaks that usual, as he normally went from point A to point B with very few stops. Today he seemed preoccupied with the scenery and having Devon take photos of the two of them posed in different picturesque spots. "It'll look nice on a project I'm making," explained Ryan, his mind set on a completely different photo album.

Meanwhile, the two conservation officers were closing the gap between themselves and the group ahead of them, moving steadily up the incline until they were a mere two hundred yards behind the young climbers. Madden watched as they crossed over a shallow landing in the slide and took off their packs. Ryan leaned his against a tall, uplifted bolder that sat on the narrow plateau. A pool of sparkling clear water lay at their feet, and Devon looked at it in delight.

"How about you get out your camera and take a couple shots of me and Natasha here, sitting side-by-side on these rocks?" asked Ryan.

"Sure, we can do that" replied Devon, who was about to soak his bandana in the pool. "Then, I say we grab a quick drink here before we head for the summit."

"Sounds like a plan," nodded Ryan, and he and Natasha settled into position for the photographs. Ryan took extra satisfaction knowing that his girlfriend was still clueless about his plans for the celebration to come.

By coincidence, the two conservation officers picked the same time to take a break, with both men sitting down to a granola bar and a sip from their canteens. Each knew the surrounding country so well that neither was interested in the scenery. It was all part of the job, and they both kept their eyes peeled with the hope that they might see something worth reporting. This search had been assigned the highest level of priority by their supervisor.

Officer Ferris glanced up the hill between bites of his snack. In the distance, he saw one of the male hikers bend over with a plastic drinking cup and fill it with water from the ground. He then placed the cup on a rock and stepped over to his pack.

Meanwhile, Madden was focusing his attention down the slide, his mind taking in the sheer magnitude of the drop-off in altitude. Suddenly, he stopped, his hand frozen in place with a piece of granola bar suspended just inches away from his open mouth. What he saw was impossible, a horror so real and so imminent as to be surreal. Was he imagining things? Was his mind playing games with him? He felt his heart suddenly jump into his throat as he watched the apparition below.

About one hundred yards further down the slope, Officer Madden saw a man kneeling behind a desk-sized rock. The man's skin was well-worn, creased with age, and his pure gray hair was swept back over his head, covering his ears and collar. But what Madden noticed most was the high-powered rifle with the telescopic lens that was poised and focused up the hill at the three hikers. The shooter's concentration appeared to be complete, his rock-steady hands and body locked in on at least one member of the climbing party. But why?

Up above, Ryan heard a commotion from down the mountain. It was the sound of a man, frantically screaming at the top of his lungs. "Put it down! This is Officer Madden, New York State Police. PUT DOWN

YOUR WEAPON!" However, to Ryan, the words were incomprehensible, the voice attenuated by the distance and wind. He figured it was probably a hiker calling to a friend farther down the mountain. He quickly decided to ignore it. He stood up again and moved towards the glass of water.

"I'm ordering you for the last time, PUT DOWN YOUR WEAPON!" called Madden, his hand releasing the holster strap from his own weapon and drawing it into a firing position.

No response.

Ryan's hand extended outward towards the cup, his fingers reaching to grasp the upper lip of the vessel.

Abruptly, all hell broke loose. The entire side of the mountain seemed to erupt in a unified volley of gunfire. The cup that Ryan was about to lift to his lips suddenly vanished. An unseen force had snatched it from Ryan's impending grasp and thrown it out of sight down the slope. One moment it was there, the next it was gone.

In a separate action, Officer Madden's gun discharged, creating a flash and roar of its own. The force of the recoil hammered home the point to Madden that he had never before fired his gun in the line of duty. He stared anxiously down the mountain, intent on seeing whether he had prevented the shooter from discharging his own weapon.

At first, Madden saw nothing, just an opening in the rocks where he had spotted the rifleman just moments earlier. Then Ferris chimed in from behind. "There he is, on the ground to the left of the big rock."

He was indeed on the ground. On the ground and not moving, his head turned upward from his body at an awkward angle.

The two officers took off at a trot, jogging down the mountainside as fast as their feet would permit. Madden was in the lead, his eyes still alert to the possibility of the shooter squeezing off another round. But for now this looked impossible, as he appeared to be either wounded, dazed, or both. Even though Madden considered the elderly gunman to be armed and dangerous, he prayed that he had not killed the man. The thought ran through his mind in endless waves as they descended to the lifeless body below.

Up above, Ryan, Natasha, and Devon observed the carnage, and they also took off on a sprint for the wounded man, leaving their packs behind. They hadn't been able to observe the initial position or intent of the shooter. They only knew that gunshots were heard, and then they saw a pair of uniformed law enforcement officers running to help a downed man.

It took Officers Madden and Ferris less than two minutes to reach the prone body of the old man, who was now face down in the rocky debris. As Madden arrived, slightly ahead of his partner, he observed a minute bit of movement from the figure. A hollow groan escaped the concealed lips of the man as he rocked ever so slightly on the ground. Madden instantly saw the bloody hole that had been ripped through the back of his azure-colored fleece jacket. The red stain just below the shoulder seemed to grow by the second.

Madden first checked to make sure that the gunman was no longer holding his rifle. Seeing the weapon thrown six feet in front of the body, Madden dropped to his knees to inspect the wound.

"Are you OK?" asked Madden, all the while knowing that the gunshot from his service revolver could prove to be fatal.

The man on the ground lifted his head and looked up the rocky incline towards the summit. His eyes were open wide, with an expectant expression on his aged face. "Did I get it?" he asked, as though he'd never heard the officer's question or didn't care about his own condition.

"Did you get it?" repeated Officer Madden, baffled by the question. "Get what? What are you talking about, and why were you shooting at those hikers?"

The man continued to squint at the trio up the hill, who were rapidly approaching down the slide.

"The cup. The drinking cup. Did you see it?" asked the downed shooter. "Did I hit the cup before he took a drink from it?"

The question was so absurd that Madden took it to be the ranting of a lunatic. Either that, or the wounded man who lay on the ground before him had lost so much blood that he was starting to hallucinate. As he stood there pondering his next action, the three hikers from above arrived on the scene.

"I thought I hit it," the man continued, his voice fading in the wind. "I swear, I thought I hit it. My God, I hope they didn't drink out of it."

Ryan reached the officers first, and he gasped when he saw the bloodied man stretched out across the rubble.

"I had to hit it. I had to hit that damn cup. It should have been so easy; it was just sitting there on a rock. Oh my God, what's wrong with me?"

Ryan looked down and asked the same question Officer Madden had posed a moment ago. "What cup, sir? If you're talking about my drinking cup, and you were shooting at it, believe me you hit it. I don't even know where the thing landed. But why did you do that? You could have killed one of us. Was that some kind of a joke?"

"Thank God, son, thank God. That cup could have killed you."

This statement from the man, who seemed to be starting to lose consciousness, startled the two conservation officers, who instantly launched into interrogation mode.

"What is your name, and why are you here with a high-powered rifle in an area where weapons are not allowed?" asked Ferris.

The wait for a response lasted a full thirty seconds as the dying man coughed up blood and then cleared his throat. "My name is Mike Forchey, and I'm a retired air force colonel who was involved in the search following the crash on Wright Peak in 1962."

Even the exertion of making the short statement cost the man dearly, and he spent the next minute regaining his wind for the next sentence.

"That was over fifty years ago," gasped Madden. "Why are you back on the mountain shooting at hikers? Have you lost your mind?"

"This is important; you must follow my instructions," wheezed Forchey, his glazed eyes staring at the officers without fully focusing. "The plane carried a deadly cargo, a strain of smallpox virus that survived in a cargo case since the time of the crash. I found that box early this morning. It is under a rock pile near the big, upright boulder, just up the slide."

"Oh my God, that's where we just stopped for a break," cried Natasha, grabbing Ryan's arm.

"I know. I saw you though my scope, and I saw you about to take a drink from that pool," said Forchey, he eyes fluttering as he spoke. "I'm sorry I shot at you, but I had to knock that cup away before you took a sip. It would have been your last."

"Have the authorities been notified?" asked Officer Ferris, anxiously stealing glances back up the slide toward the source of the deadly pathogen. Meanwhile, Madden stepped aside and placed an emergency call for a medical evacuation helicopter to attempt a rescue, hoping that Forchey could hold on until it arrived.

"No. I only discovered the location of the case this morning. I've been out here for three days, ever since I heard about the hikers who became ill." There was another pause as the old man stopped to catch his breath. He didn't have much time left. "I knew it had to be nearby, but I didn't find it until this morning, and by then my phone had died. It's been here all along, all along. It's under the rock pile just to the right of the upright boulder near the pool. Drop down the gulley to the right and look up, into the space between the bottom two large stones. You can see the corner of the case from there."

"But how did you know?" asked Ferris, sensing that time was growing short. "How did you know that the virus came from the crash, and from that site? I've worked here for over twenty years, and I've never even heard a rumor of this story."

"In 1961, I worked with the government and a scientist named Dr. Edgar Steinholtz to develop a series of viruses that could be used against hostile countries," replied Forchey, his voice barely more than a whisper. "The strain in that crate was the worst of the worst. We knew we had to get rid of it. The plane crashed in route to its final disposal site."

"Can the virus be killed off now, or will the High Peaks be contaminated forever?" asked Madden, who had completed his call for the rescue bird.

"No, now that it's been found, the right people will take the case away and decontaminate the area. We know how to do that now. Finding it was everything. Thank God I found it."

"If it's any consolation to you, they've halted the spread of the virus in the cities and have successfully quarantined the few individuals who contracted the disease," offered Ferris. "At least it didn't escape into the general population."

The old man nodded weakly, his chest heaving with every breath.

"I'm so sorry I had to shoot," said Madden, dropping to his knees next to the dying man. "If only you'd said something, or waved, or given me some sign…" His voice wavered as it dropped off.

"It's OK, son," said Forchey, reaching up to pat Madden's shoulder with his good arm. "I would have done the same thing if I was in your shoes." As he spoke, he closed his eyes, appearing to rest. "How ironic, though," he continued weakly. "Fifty years ago, I would have given my life to ensure that no one died because of my research. Now, today, I have closed the circle, and I will die knowing that I have been granted my wish." As he finished speaking, his head tilted off to one side and he exhaled his last breath.

Considering the lethality of the cargo and the amount of seepage, the clean-up operation was surprisingly quick and completely successful. The possibility of a trickle-down death was averted, and the top secret file was finally closed and sealed shut.

Retired Air Force Colonel Michael Forchey had been the last man alive who knew the story of the deadly cargo and understood how close it came to creating a doomsday scenario. He died with a smile on his face, knowing that he had saved the world from a disaster—and that his shooting hand still hadn't lost its touch.

Author Biographies

John Briant

John Briant is the author of the *Adirondack Detective* series. "Ghosts of Santa Clara" was the last story he wrote before his passing.

Tico Brown

Tico Brown was born and raised in Upstate New York and enjoys vacationing in the Adirondacks. "Beyond the Blue" is his latest addition to the Adirondack Mysteries series; he also has stories in volumes 1 and 2. He can be reached at tico.brown@gmail.com.

Cheryl Ann Costa

Cheryl Ann Costa is a New York native and currently lives in Syracuse. She has a degree in entertainment writing from SUNY Empire State College. Cheryl works as a newspaper columnist.

Marie Hannan-Mandel

Marie Hannan-Mandel lives in Elmira Heights, New York, and is an assistant professor at Corning Community College. Her story "The Perfect Pitch" was selected to appear in *Malice Domestic Anthology 11: Murder Most Conventional* (Wildside Press 2016). She was short listed for the 2013 Debut Dagger award. She also received an honorable mention in the 2014 Writers Digest Popular Fiction Awards competition, and she was long listed in the RTE Guide/Penguin Ireland short story competition in 2014.

G. Miki Hayden

G. Miki Hayden won an Edgar award for one of her mystery stories and has had several novels in print, the latest of which is a science-fiction fantasy, *Question Woman & Howling Sky*. Miki has also published a writing style guide, *The Naked Writer*, and teaches writing online at Writer's Digest University.

Jordan Elizabeth Mierek

Jordan Elizabeth Mierek is the author of *Escape from Witchwood Hollow*, *Cogling*, *Treasure Darkly*, and *Born of Treasure*. She has contributed to and compiled multiple anthologies. Check out her website, JordanElizabethMierek.com, for contests and bonus short stories.

Jenny Milchman

Jenny Milchman is the award-winning and *USA Today* bestselling author of three critically acclaimed thrillers set in the fictional Adirondack town of Wedeskyull. The founder of Take Your Child to a Bookstore Day, an annual holiday celebrated in all fifty states and on five continents, Jenny serves on the Board of International Thriller Writers. She visits the Adirondack Mountains any chance she gets.

W.K. Pomeroy

W.K. Pomeroy is a third-generation writer who has published more than seventy short stories, poems, and articles. In addition to Damir's Adirondack mysteries, he has written steampunk stories in *Gears of Brass* and *Under a Brass Moon*, a different kind of ghost story in *Ghosts Have No Shadows*, and even a story about a girl who only speaks by dancing in *Welcome to the Dance*. He has published in genres as diverse as horror and romance. He was president of the Utica Writers Club for six terms and also served as the group's treasurer, vice president, and webmaster. Whether as an author, editor, contest judge, or promoter, he always supports the art of writing.

Woody Sins

Woody Sins is an engineer who lives in New Hartford, but he grew up in the wilds of Tug Hill. He dedicates his story, "The Rebel," to the memory of Otto Van Schoonhoven, who tragically passed away in a word processor accident.

Gigi Vernon

Gigi Vernon writes historical mysteries and thrillers. Her short fiction has been published in the *Alfred Hitchcock Mystery Magazine* and elsewhere. Her short story "Show Stopper," about killer Soviet fashion, in the anthology *Ice Cold: Tales of Intrigue from the Cold War*, was nominated for an award by the International Thriller Writers in 2015. Gigi's website is www.gigivernon.com.

Dennis Webster

Dennis Webster is a ghost hunter and paranormal investigator with the Ghost Seekers of Central New York. He's the published author of books on insane asylums, haunted houses, and gruesome true crimes. He can be reached at denniswbstr@gmail.com.

Larry Weill

Larry Weill is a writer and author who spent three years living in a tent as a wilderness park ranger in the Adirondack Park. He has authored four books on his experiences in the woods (*Excuse Me, Sir... Your Socks Are on Fire*, *Pardon Me, Sir... There's a Moose in Your Tent*, *Forgive Me, Ma'am... Bears Don't Wear Blue,* and *Thanks Anyway, Sir... But I'll Sleep in the Tree*) and two novels (*Adirondack Trail of Gold* and *In Marcy's Shadow*). He frequently speaks on the topics of writing and the Adirondacks. Now a retired naval officer, he lives with his family in Rochester, New York.